"Laura V. Hilton continues to impress me with her fresh, original, and creative narratives, weaving the lives of her characters together with substance and sensitivity. *The Amish Firefighter* introduces family dynamics, betrayal, and misunderstanding, while revealing haunting secrets from the past that could influence the future. Forgiveness and redemption are imparted through unexpected circumstances. This book will leave you weak in the knees!"

—*Nancee Marchinowski*
PerspectivesbyNancee.blogspot.com

"I seldom attain the depth of compassion for a book character as felt for Laura V. Hilton's Abby in *The Amish Firefighter*. Fast page-turning only fans the flames of family deceit, arson investigations, and community secrecy; but this book is also doused liberally with romance and the struggles of living a godly lifestyle."

—*Alan Daugherty*
Weekly columnist, *Bluffton (IN) News-Banner*

"This book is on fire, *wow*! While it is about a firefighter and acts of arson are part of the story, the fire is in the romance between the main characters. Laura Hilton never disappoints with her complex stories that weave in and out of the character's lives. Abigail and Sammy's story make *The Amish Firefighter* come to life. You will be vested in this story by the end—truly a must-read for 2016."

—*Cindy Loven*
Co-author, *Dianna's Wings*, *The Parables of Trevor Turtle*,
and *Swept Away* (Quilts of Love series)

"*The Amish Firefighter* is a beautifully written, can't-put-it-down page turner with a perfectly woven mix of romance, mystery, humor, and inspiration. Laura V. Hilton has once again written a lovely story that will not only tug at your heartstrings, but will also have you doing some reflecting and discovering of your own."

—*Dali Castillo*
This and That/Esto y Aquello blog

"Laura Hilton's latest is heart-pumping, intense Amish fiction that will surely captivate you until the very end."

—*Cheryl Baranski*
Cherylbbookblog.wordpress.com

"This latest novel from award-winning author Laura V. Hilton ignites on the first page and burns bright to a smoldering end."

—*Angela Arndt*
Angelaarndt.com

"Of all the books I've read by Author Laura V. Hilton, The Amish Firefighter is my favorite. It is filled with misunderstandings and secrets but woven throughout, like a beautiful Amish quilt, with the emphasis on God's love and forgiveness. A definite five-star read!"

—*Linda McFarland*
Goodreads reviewer

"It is good to have Laura V. Hilton back among the Amish genre authors. She has outdone herself with *The Amish Firefighter*. It is easy flowing with very detailed storyline that keeps your attention to the very end."

—*Tina Watson*
Amish genre researcher

"*The Amish Firefighter* is one of the best Amish novels I've read! Laura Hilton has created a community with well-developed, easy-to-love characters, a strong plot, and enough twists and turns to keep the reader involved until the very end. Laura has written a perfect Amish story of faith, love, family, commitment. If you enjoy reading Amish fiction, you're going to love *The Amish Firefighter!*"

—Donna Mynatt
Author, *You Can Write 50,000 Words in 30 Days*
Donna's Bookshelf blog

THE AMISH FIREFIGHTER

LAURA V. HILTON

WHITAKER
HOUSE

All Scripture quotations are taken from the King James Version of the Holy Bible.

THE AMISH FIREFIGHTER

Laura V. Hilton
http://lighthouse-academy.blogspot.com

ISBN: 978-1-62911-685-3
eBook ISBN: 978-1-62911-686-0
Printed in the United States of America
© 2016 by Laura V. Hilton

Whitaker House
1030 Hunt Valley Circle
New Kensington, PA 15068
www.whitakerhouse.com

Library of Congress Cataloging-in-Publication Data (Pending)

1 2 3 4 5 6 7 8 9 10 ⨄ 22 21 20 19 18 17 16

Dedication

For the One who saved me:
Jesus, who died, and is now glorified, King of all kings.

Acknowledgments

Special thanks to…

Candee Fick and Nancee Marchinowski, for reading through the entire manuscript and sharing their thoughts. I appreciate your gift of time.

My daughter Jenna, for reading over my shoulder as I wrote and catching typos as I made them.

My husband, Steve, for looking the manuscript over, as well, and giving me his thoughts.

My critique partners in Scribes 230 and 202.

Dr. Ronda Wells and Dr. Harry Kraus, for offering their expertise on knee injuries.

My son Michael, for his expertise as an EMT, first responder, and criminal justice major.

Josh Poole, Billy Edwards, and Michael's college instructor Sean Buttry, for assistance with the firefighting scenes.

The prayer warriors who always lift me and my writing up in their prayers. I couldn't do it without God's help.

Michael and Jenna, again, for brainstorming with me to decide who was behind the fires, and why.

My agent, Tamela Hancock Murray, for all she does.

Whitaker House, for taking a chance on me.

Glossary of Amish Terms and Phrases

ach:	oh
aent/aenti:	aunt/auntie
"ain't so?":	a phrase commonly used at the end of a sentence to invite agreement
Ausbund:	Amish hymnal used in the worship services, containing lyrics only
boppli:	baby/babies
bu:	boy
buwe:	boys
daed:	dad
"Danki":	"Thank you"
der Herr:	the Lord
Gott:	God
großeltern:	grandparents
dochter:	daughter
ehemann:	husband
Englisch:	non-Amish
Englischer:	a non-Amish person
frau:	wife
gelassenheit:	self-surrender
großeltern:	grandparents
grossdaedi:	grandfather
grossmammi:	grandmother
gut:	good

haus:	house
"Ich liebe dich":	"I love you"
jah:	yes
kapp:	prayer covering or cap
kinner:	children
koffee:	coffee
kum:	come
liebling:	a term of endearment meaning "darling" or "little love"
maidal:	young woman
mamm:	mom
maud:	maid/spinster
morgen:	morning
nacht:	night
nein:	no
onkel:	uncle
Ordnung:	the rules by with an Amish community lives
rumschpringe:	"running around time"; a period of freedom and experimentation during the late adolescence of Amish youth
ser gut:	very good
schatz:	sweetheart
schnuckelchen:	beautiful girl
sohn:	son
to-nacht:	tonight
verboden:	forbidden
"Was ist letz?":	"What's the matter?"
welkum:	welcome

Chapter 1

"And there she goes." The man's voice was a hushed, hoarse whisper.

The strong odor of gasoline filled the air.

Gasoline?

Abigail slowed as a black cat wove its way around her ankles. Her new friend, Miranda, continued toward a lantern-lit room in the back of the barn. She'd said they were meeting her boyfriend and a couple of his friends at the small engine repair shop. That probably explained the odor.

The cat purred as it wrapped itself around Abigail's ankles again. She picked it up and cuddled it close to her chest, then hurried past the dark shadows of a buggy, in the direction Miranda had gone. She'd been eager to make friends here in Jamesport, even if they were Englisch, like Miranda. It was nice to be wanted instead of thrown out. Rejected. Abandoned at the bus station.

Pain knifed her. She firmed her shoulders and forced a smile.

She'd almost reached the room where Miranda disappeared when several silhouettes darted past, heading out the big barn doors. Miranda snickered, then turned to chase after them. "Come on, Abby. Hurry!"

"Where are we going?"

Miranda didn't answer. She just giggled again, more faintly this time, as she disappeared from sight.

"*Wait!*" Abigail didn't want to be stranded in a dark, unfamiliar barn. She turned and started to follow Miranda and the others, scrunching her nose as the stench of gasoline burned her nostrils. She tightened her grip on the cat. She wasn't sure whose barn this was, since she'd been in the area only a week.

Something crackled behind her. Abigail stopped and glanced over her shoulder. A dim light flickered in the small engine shop. Had a lantern been left burning? That'd be dangerous. It wouldn't take long to put it out. The last thing she wanted was for some poor farmer to lose his barn to a fire. Especially if she could prevent it.

She turned around and retraced her steps, stopping to peek in the room. The lantern was flickering on the table where it sat, but a separate fire flamed from some rectangular hay bales stacked alongside the opposite wall.

Abigail caught her breath, her heart pounding. Her fists curled into the cat's fur. *Ach, nein.* Had Miranda's friends done this? The glow burned brighter. A pail—she needed a pail. And water. She'd seen a pump earlier.

She whirled around. A fire would be a devastating loss for an Amish farmer. For anyone. She cringed. She should've listened to the inner voice that had warned her to stay home to-nacht. But, *nein,* she'd *had* to go along. And now…now….

Behind her, the barn wall whooshed into flame. A horse screamed. In the distance, a dog barked loudly, warning the family sleeping inside the haus.

The black cat clawed its way to Abigail's shoulder and jumped, disappearing into the darkness.

Abigail raced toward the barn doors. Maybe there was a pail on the pump behind the haus she could use to start fighting the fire. Or should she begin by releasing the animals?

Nein, the first step would be to ring the emergency bell to summon help.

She tripped over something in the darkness and went sprawling.

⌒

Sam Miller's car made a chugging sound as he drove down the dark road toward home. The vehicle shuddered, too, as if it were having seizures. Tomorrow, he'd try to find some time to tinker under the hood and figure out what was wrong. The fuel filter might need to be replaced.

The schoolhaus came into view. It was dark, as on every Friday nacht. Nobody would be there over the weekend, and he considered taking his car there to work on, away from his brothers lurking around. But that would mean having to haul his tools across the road. And if a deacon or the bishop happened by....

Nein. He'd have to work on the car in the buggy shed, as much as it would bother Daed.

Sam activated his turn indicator out of habit, even though the dark road behind him was abandoned.

Park at the school.

Sam braked to a stop. Why would he park at the school instead of behind the barn? He could just as easily move the car in the morgen, and it'd save him a scolding from Daed for working on his "fancy" car at the schoolyard.

Not that the car was really fancy. But that was beside the point.

He pressed the gas pedal and turned the steering wheel to the right, preparing to drive past the barn so he could park behind it. Per usual.

Park at the school.

The command seemed more urgent this time.

His friends and new brother-in-law, David, often talked about the importance of surrendering to the leading of der Herr. But why would He care where Sam parked his car?

Still, it was the first time Sam had ever received what seemed to be a direct instruction.

He flipped the left turn signal on and stopped in front of the school.

Once he'd parked and turned off the car, he locked his textbooks and Tablet in the trunk before starting across the road.

The family dog, Jute, started barking. Sam wasn't sure how his little sister Mary had kum up with the name, but it sounded more like "Chute" when pronounced in their Deutsch dialect.

Jute continued to bark. Only this wasn't the normal "Welkum home, Sam" bark. It sounded urgent. Angry.

Then Sam noticed smoke. A red glow.

Nein, not again. He broke into a run.

⌒

Abigail pushed herself to her feet, ignoring the ache in her right leg. Nein time to waste. She would ring the emergency bell first. Then start releasing the animals.

Before she could move a step, an iron grip clamped her upper arm. Shock waves raced through her, radiating from the point of contact with the hand grasping her.

"How dare you?" growled a male voice.

She tried to wriggle her arm free. "Nein, I...."

The viselike grip tightened—probably enough to leave a bruise—and her captor dragged her toward the dark farmhaus. She tripped over her own feet in an effort to keep up. When they reached the porch, he grabbed the cord of the emergency bell and yanked, causing a loud clang that made her ears ring.

A lot more would be hurt than her hearing.

She hadn't started the fire. She was just in the wrong place at the wrong time. Guilty by association. And she was the only one who'd gotten caught.

Four tugs and four clangs. Five. Six.

"I didn't do it," Abigail squeaked.

He turned to her, his eyes teeming with scorn and disgust. "Don't lie," he spat. Then he opened the door to the haus. "Go in and wait." He released her arm with a slight shove, then pivoted and sprinted toward the burning barn.

"Go in and wait." Right. She remained on the porch and shut the door.

Where was Miranda? She needed to show up. Whoever had started the fire needed to turn themselves in. To clear Abigail's name.

It's going to be okay. Maybe the man who'd found her would forget. She could leave when the fire was out, and it would all be over. The chances of his identifying her were as good as those of her identifying him. Zero.

She scanned the yard. Would it be wrong to sneak away and blend in with all the people coming to help fight the fire?

On the other hand, if she was caught, she'd be sent home to Mamm and Mamm's new ehemann, Leo. Even if they didn't want her. At least then she could be with her boyfriend, Mark.

But she would be returning in shame. For burning a barn. And her stepdaed and Mark were farmers. Jah, that'd win them over, for sure and for certain. Her upper lip curled.

She wanted to go home. But not like this.

She spun around and surveyed the porch. There—a pail. Upsidedown, almost hidden by the shadows.

Steps thundered just inside the haus. Seconds later, the door burst open. An older Amish man ran out, hoisting the straps of his suspenders as he did. He was illuminated by the headlights of a vehicle turning into the drive.

"Nice of you to ring the bell, young lady," he said as he dashed past Abigail.

She'd intended to ring the bell. Did that count?

An Englisch man climbed out of the pickup. "I called the fire department," he said to the older man.

The older man nodded. "Danki, Viktor."

Both men ran toward the barn.

Abigail was long past the point of escape. Already, there were two who would be able to identify her, if—no, *when* the first man accused her. Tears filled her eyes.

Someone shouted, and a shower of sparks lit the interior of the barn.

This would be a terrible loss for the family. And with the real culprits long gone, they'd blame her.

Her hands shook. She needed to try to make this right.

She hurried to retrieve the bucket as two teen buwe raced past toward the fire. One of them hopped along on one foot, yanking his shoes on as he went.

Abigail's adrenaline surged as she snatched the bucket and ran to the outside pump. Another pail hung there, so she dropped hers beneath it and started pumping. It seemed to take an eternity for the water to start to flow.

She heard another vehicle arrive. Then shouting, as the men released the animals from the barn. Soon, an older woman carrying three buckets joined her at the pump. She replaced the full bucket with an empty one as someone else grabbed the full bucket and ran off.

"How'd you kum to be here, kin?" the woman asked Abigail. "Did Sammy bring you home with him? I thought I heard his car right before the emergency bell clanged."

Who was Sammy?

The woman's shoulders slumped. "They were having a party in the barn, ain't so? Smoking cigarettes?"

Someone had been smoking—Abigail had seen the glow of his cigarette as he'd raced past—but none of Miranda's friends was called Sammy, as far as she knew. The fire probably wasn't from cigarettes, though. Just…gasoline. Maybe. She didn't know for sure. It might've been a party. She wasn't certain about that, either.

Abigail opened her mouth, ready to tell the woman she didn't know whether Sammy was there or not. That she didn't know what they were doing.

"I'm sorry. So sorry." Words she hadn't intended to say came out in a rush. Abigail kept pumping water.

The woman blinked as she handed the pail off to someone else. "Well then, I forgive you."

Forgiveness. For a crime she didn't commit. Why did this woman assume that she needed forgiving? Well, maybe she did. She hadn't tried to stop Miranda and her friends as they raced past. Hadn't tried to put out the fire by beating it with her apron. Instead, she'd stood there like a dummchen, dismayed and horrified by the unexpected turn of events. Shocked into a stupor.

Buckets disappeared and reappeared faster than Abigail could get them filled.

In the distance, a fire truck's siren screeched, gradually growing louder. Anyone who'd managed to sleep through the deafening peal of the emergency bell was surely awake by now.

Abigail filled another bucket, and the woman replaced it with an empty one. Seconds later, several fire trucks tore into the gravel driveway, sirens wailing, as flames shot from the barn's roof.

Hopefully, all the animals had gotten out. All the men, too, for that matter.

The barn would surely be a total loss by the time the firefighters extinguished the flames. Any remaining feed would be saturated with water. All the hay they'd put up for the winter…gone. And in midwinter. This was beyond bad.

Abigail swiped at a tear and finished filling a pail. Before she could reach for an empty one, someone slid one toward her. As she accepted the pail, she looked up into the face of a handsome, clean-shaven Amish man. When their gazes caught, her heart tripped. *Odd.* She offered a tentative smile, not sure what else to do.

He glowered. "Go inside afterward." Then he grabbed the pail she'd just filled, and left.

Ach, lovely. Between the bright flames of the fire and the blinding beams of the Englisch vehicles, the man who'd found her in the barn had gotten a clear view of her.

Now there was nein chance he would forget what she looked like.

Chapter 2

S am shoved the pail of sloshing water at his younger brother Eli, then raced for the fire truck that had just arrived, and began unfurling the fire hose. He fell into his role as a volunteer firefighter as naturally as if he'd jumped into his car and raced to the station in time to catch a ride on the first engine.

This time, instead of arriving on the scene with the squad, he'd just arrived home and caught the arsonist in the act. Well, post-act, still standing in the barn. Gut thing he had parked his car at the schoolhaus. The part of his life that was locked in the trunk would be safe from the flames. *Danki, Lord.*

Perplexing that the arsonist was a woman. An Amish woman, at that. Seemed she, of all people, should know better. He glared in her direction.

Not that she noticed. She still worked the pump, keeping the water flowing.

At least she tried to help put out the fire. The fire she'd started. Did she think she'd get off easy for that?

A slow burn started in his gut.

Arsonists often stuck around to witness the destruction. A sign of probable guilt, for sure. Was she trying to divert attention away from herself by lending a hand? Had she acted alone, or did she have accomplices? Was she waiting on a getaway buggy?

Sam aimed another glare in her direction. She'd get a piece of his mind when this was over. He'd have to make sure she didn't slip away during the heat of the action.

Right now, though, he needed to focus on keeping the fire from spreading to the haus.

His throat clogged with bile. His eyes burned. Blame it on the thick smoke. Nein way would he cry over this loss, however devastating.

Even though....

Even though the part of his life that had been safe from the haus fire earlier that year had undoubtedly gone up in flames with this latest barn fire.

Ach, Lord. Nein.

His stomach clenched. *Focus.* He closed his fists around the hose and hustled toward the barn with the rest of his squad.

He couldn't think about it now.

But this fire had gone way beyond a random, bored Englisch kids' "prank" to something that almost seemed...personal. Especially since his family had lost nearly everything to a fire once already. Why would Gott make sure to save the part of himself locked in the trunk of his car, but allow the books on small-engine repair he'd saved from the haus fire to go up in flames? Not to mention the machines he'd actually been using to practice on?

Jah, the girl would pay. One way or another.

⌒

Abigail watched the lone Amish fireman—her accuser—race toward the barn, dragging the hose. He was surrounded by a team of Englischers who appeared to accept his presence without question, even though he wore the simple homemade pants, shirt, and suspenders of the Plain people. His straw hat blew off, landing in the dirt. Upside-down and forgotten.

She brushed the kapp strings back from her face, along with several strands of hair, and stepped away from the pump. Nothing more she could do here.

Time to make her escape.

"Danki for your help." The older woman touched her arm. "Kum on in. My dochters should have set out drinks and cookies by now. You can have some. Gut thing we baked today, ain't so?"

So, the woman was a member of the family whose barn was burning. How did she manage to have a sense of humor at a time like this?

Abigail looked around, still wondering where Miranda and her friends had disappeared to. Were they hiding in the cornfield, watching the action? Or had they run off, abandoning her to face the fallout? They weren't in the crowd fighting the fire, for certain.

"Kum, now." The older woman started for the haus. "You are from another district, jah? You don't look familiar."

"Jah, another district." Her onkel and aenti—the ones she'd learned about just prior to being banished from home and sent to live with them—occupied a nearby farm. Abigail had thought she saw Onkel Darius going into the barn earlier, but she hadn't spotted him in the throng since then. Hopefully, her onkel was okay. The rest of the men, too.

Abigail retrieved the Amish firefighter's straw hat and followed the woman into the haus. Two young girls were at work steeping tea in boiling water and brewing koffee. The older woman smiled at the girls, then looked back at Abigail.

"Meet Jenny, eight, and Mary, twelve. I have another dochter, Rachel, recently married. And four sohns…." She rattled off a list of names, but the only one Abigail caught was Sammy. "Help yourself to some cookies. What's your name, again?"

"Abigail." She immediately grimaced. So much for being an anonymous bystander. Instead, she was an identified suspect for the crime. One who'd virtually confessed when she apologized. She would be sent home in disgrace—after Onkel Darius berated her for bringing shame on him and his family in his own community.

The woman smiled. "And I'm Elsie. Preacher Samuel's frau. I'm so happy to meet you. I thought sure Sammy dated some Englisch girl. So glad it's one of our own." She turned to a cabinet and got out some paper plates.

Most mamms wanted their sohns to court within the faith. Except Abigail had nein idea who Sammy courted—or even who Sammy might be. Was he the Amish firefighter? The one who'd grabbed her? She touched her upper arm. Still sore.

Wait. Did Elsie think Sammy courted *her*?

She opened her mouth to correct Elsie, but the door opened and more women came inside, carrying tins of undisclosed goodies. A couple of them lugged large plastic beverage dispensers, probably full of tea, water, or lemonade. Plastic cups were stacked beside them, and napkins were laid out.

There was nothing else to do.

Except go.

Abigail didn't want any cookies. They'd probably turn to sawdust in her mouth.

Her stomach churned, nein doubt due to the awkwardness of standing in a strange kitchen, doing nothing, except waiting for him to kum in and yell at her.

She turned and headed for the door, hoping nobody would miss her. She hated herself for sneaking out, but she'd make it up to this family somehow.

She opened the screen door and stepped outside, glancing over her shoulder to see if the friendly Elsie noticed her departure.

Nobody seemed to pay her any mind.

A serious relief, at this point.

The stenches of smoke and burnt wood was strong. She tried to smother a cough as she silently shut the door and turned around.

Right into a pair of strong arms that closed around her like a snare.

Her stomach flipped. She was going to be sick. She planted her hands against the man's solid chest and pushed.

"Going somewhere, feuerzeug?"

Fire-lighter?

Sam hadn't intended to wrap his arms around the culprit and hug her close. He'd meant to grab her shoulders, stopping her. But she was nearer than he'd thought. Her softness pressed against him. He relaxed his grip a little. Not enough for her to get away, but now they weren't touching inappropriately.

She pushed against him again, then jerked back, struggling to get free. He released her, then gripped her by the arm and spun her around. She yelped, so he adjusted his grasp and then marched her inside, to his parents' bustling kitchen. He hooked the bottom of a chair with his booted foot, slid it away from the table, and sat her down. Gently. He didn't intend to get yelled at for manhandling a woman. Mamm scolded him often enough for his ways.

He crouched in front of her, staring up into her pretty—nein, beautiful—face. Her hazel eyes, filled with unidentifiable emotions, met his. Then she lowered her gaze to her lap, where she alternately clenched her blistered hands into fists and splayed her fingers. A few strands of golden-brown hair had fallen free from her kapp. The curls brushed against her reddened cheeks.

Sam felt an inexplicable urge to tuck the strands back into place. He ignored it.

"I brought your hat in." Her voice was small.

"Danki." The word slipped out before he could stop himself. The angry avalanche of words he wanted to unleash hovered on the edge of his tongue, barely held in place. But the accusations would wait until Daed came in. Until the other firefighters and the community members had left. He'd make sure she didn't escape.

"He that is without sin among you, let him first cast a stone at her."

Sam cringed when the poignant verse from John's gospel came to mind. He'd committed enough sins to acknowledge he was far from blameless.

Okay, maybe he wouldn't be shouting accusations at this girl. He looked away.

Mamm was smiling her pleased smile, and his young sisters were clearly trying to hide their giggles. He knew what they were thinking.

A tear trailed to the end of the young woman's nose. She reached up with a callused fingertip and wiped it away.

His heart twisted. Hopefully, Mamm wasn't paying close enough attention to notice that he was the one who had made her cry. It was bad enough he'd given Mamm reason to be so pleased. She believed he courted an Amish girl.

He didn't. But as long as Mamm was under that impression, she wouldn't give him the woeful look she usually did. Not for a few hours, at least. Nein need to break the spell by setting her straight.

Of course, if someone asked, he wouldn't lie. He dated an Englisch girl. Much to his parents' chagrin.

He reached up and tapped the top of the girl's—woman's—fisted hands. "Who are you?" he whispered.

She didn't pull away from his touch.

Her gaze shot back up to his. Tears still glittered on her lashes.

This time, the emotion was obvious.

Fear.

Plain, unadulterated fear.

Chapter 3

Abigail swallowed the lump in her throat. Why couldn't this gorgeous Amish man be interested in her for a reason other than that she was the prime suspect for having set the fire? Not that she wanted him to desire her, with her boyfriend, Mark, waiting back home. But interest would be preferable to suspicion. Better than being blamed for a crime she didn't commit, with nein witnesses to vouch for her innocence.

Ach, well. As Mamm always said, "If ifs and ands were pots and pans, there'd be no work for tinkers' hands."

"I didn't do it," Abigail whispered with fierce insistence. "Really."

His eyes narrowed, the blue orbs becoming mere slits. "Not what I asked."

Abigail's throat hurt. And not from the unshed tears she held back. Must be due to the smoke still heavy in the air. She scanned the room full of women, all of them bustling around, and sending the occasional knowing look in her direction. A couple of the younger girls glanced over and giggled. Nein doubt they thought the two of them were courting. How to correct their misconception?

If the Amish firefighter weren't keeping her trapped in the chair, his hand on hers effectively pinning her in place with a deceptively gentle touch, considering his apparent rage, she'd leave. Quickly. Her stomach fluttered and her nerves tingled. She *had* to get away from him.

As if Gott Himself were against her, the door opened, and men started tromping in—Amish and Englisch alike—talking about the fire, speculating how it might've started, and making plans to have a barn raising.

Onkel Darius was among them. When his glance lit on her, he raised his eyebrows, then looked down at her hand, still being held by what's-his-name.

Abigail hastily pulled her hand free.

Onkel Darius smiled as he lifted his gaze. *Smiled!* "What are you doing here, Abigail? Kum to make sure everything was fine? Didn't your aenti tell you to stay home?"

The man who'd been crouching before her smirked and rose to his feet. He'd gotten all the information he'd asked her for...and more.

Abigail closed her eyes. How long before the local bishop or some preachers appeared on Onkel Darius's doorstep? Wait. Elsie had mentioned she was married to a preacher. Things had gone from bad to worse. How long before Onkel Darius wrote his sister—Abigail's mamm—and informed her of her dochter's supposed misdeeds? Demanded she return home for discipline?

Again, that might be a gut thing. Mark was at home. She could explain everything, and he would understand. He loved her.

Well, he used to, anyway.

He'd believe her.

But burning a barn....

Abigail shook her head. She'd talk her way out of the false allegations and find another way—a more positive one—to get sent home again. To Mark.

If he would have her.

Worry clawed at her stomach. She *couldn't* take the blame for this.

She opened her eyes and stood. "Okay, then. What's *your* name?"

Of course, the din of conversation lulled the second she asked that too-revealing question. Several of the women gasped dramatically.

He set his lips in a line and aimed a harsh glare at her. "Feuerzeug, you're going to know a lot more than my name by the time I finish with you."

Now the room went completely silent. All eyes were on them. On Abigail.

She should've known he would again get the upper hand. Calling her "fire-lighter" in front of the whole community...why hadn't she considered that possibility before she opened her mouth?

She made another attempt to swallow that stubborn lump in her throat. She blinked back the still-threatening tears, squared her shoulders, anddid what she should've done in the first place.

She ran.

⌒

Sam didn't have to look at Mamm to know that the light in her eyes had been snuffed out, replaced by disappointment, shame, and embarrassment. He hadn't meant to put her through those emotions—not on top of the pain of losing the barn. He'd apologize later. Nothing new there. Apologizing was something he had to do almost daily.

He ignored the startled gazes, as well as the deafening silence, and dashed out the door after the runaway. *Abigail.* Such a sweet name for such a handful of a girl. Nein, woman.

She zigzagged across the yard, apparently never having learned that the shortest distance between two points was a straight line.

All the better for him. He didn't intend to let her get away.

But what to do when he caught up to her? Tag her, as in a game of touch football? As if that would be enough to stop her from running. No, he'd have to tackle her. She might get hurt, but he didn't see another option. Unless he simply pulled her into his arms.

Suddenly, his heart raced faster. Probably because he was sprinting.

Best to stick with tackling and let his anger stifle his inappropriate thoughts. Except that tackling also involved full body contact, followed by lying sprawled together on the ground....

He swallowed. Hard.

Better yet, maybe Gott would intervene.

Lord Gott, a little help?

Ahead of him, Abigail tripped. She cried out as she pitched forward and fell to the ground. He hadn't considered the possibility of that happening.

Guilt flared within him. Maybe he shouldn't have chased her. It wasn't necessary, now that he knew where she lived.

He crouched beside her. "You okay?"

She rolled over and sat up. "What do you care?" Tears clogged her voice.

His guilt burned hotter.

The beam from a flashlight lantern bounced as someone stepped off the porch and walked toward them. "What's going on out here?"

Daed.

Sam got to his feet and extended his hands to Abigail.

She ignored him. Or didn't notice. In the light of the lantern, she studied the bits of gravel imbedded in her palms. Her pale green dress was torn. Wet. And dirty.

"Sam?" Daed neared. He held the lantern aloft as he gazed down at Abigail. "Ach, it's you. Danki again for sounding the emergency bell."

"I didn't." She caught her breath and looked up at Daed. Then she shifted her gaze, her eyes locking with Sam's. "You're Sammy?"

Sam swallowed.

"He's Sammy, jah," Daed said as he offered a hand to Abigail. "Why did you call her a feuerzeug, Sohn?"

She ignored his attempt to help, as well, and winced as she stood on her own.

Sam glared at her, then turned to Daed. "She started the fire. I caught her outside the barn."

Daed's gaze darted to her.

"Nein, not so," she insisted. "I was just...there."

Sam couldn't quite describe what her tone conveyed. Maybe defiance. He stiffened. Or maybe brokenness, as if her fight was gone.

Opposite extremes. He studied her, confused. And for the first time that evening, his sense of certainty shifted.

Nah, you're right. She started it.

He wouldn't give up or give in. Not yet.

"Explain yourself," he growled.

Daed cleared his throat, a silent warning to remind him to be courteous.

Abigail lowered her head, avoiding both their gazes. A sure sign of guilt. "I was with friends—a friend. At least, I thought she was a friend. But I didn't know what the group was doing until...until it was too late." Her voice broke, and she looked up. "I'm sorry."

Daed tugged his beard and sighed heavily. Then he nodded toward the haus. "Best go have those hands cared for. Don't want you getting an infection."

Abigail shook her head. "All those people.... I made enough of a spectacle of myself, ain't so?" She started to step backward.

Sam had contributed to the spectacle, too. Touching her hand. Letting the community think they were a couple, just for the few short minutes of happiness it afforded Mamm.

Not that he'd meant to deceive her. It was just that when he saw her smile of joy, he wanted to keep it in place, despite...well, despite the terrible situation.

Sam glanced across the road. "I'll get her cleaned up at the schoolhaus, Daed. I have an emergency first-aid kit in my car. Then I'll drive her home."

Abigail bristled. "I can take care of myself."

"I'm going to see that you do," Sam retorted. "It's not like I want a glimpse of your knee." He gestured to her tattered hemline.

Except the idea of seeing her knees somehow set his heart to racing again.

Abigail's eyes widened. Color flooded her cheeks. She bit down on her bottom lip.

"Darius is inside," Daed said over his shoulder. "He'll see her home and handle this."

"I'll do it, Daed." Sam balled his hands into fists. He had plenty more to say to her.

Daed cleared his throat. "Nein more accusations, Sohn. Whether she did, or whether she didn't, *'Vengeance is mine; I will repay, saith the Lord.'*"

Sam eyed Abigail, his attention caught by her soft-looking pink lips. Something in his stomach pulled and tightened. He forced himself to look away. Too bad such a pretty face was wasted on a criminal.

Vengeance may belong to der Herr, but He might need a little help from Sam.

Especially since all his treasures had been burned in a barn fire.

Anger ignited anew.

"Ach, I wouldn't dream of it, Daed." Sam tried to keep his voice calm.

But he was right. She was a feuerzeug. If not literally, then verbally. Emotionally.

The tug and fight of his response threatened to fan the flames.

Very dangerous, indeed.

He pulled in a shaky breath. Looked at her. "The schoolhaus, then?"

~

Abigail limped across the dirt road to the school, the too-cute and much-too-aggressive Amish man striding silently by her side. Too bad his manners didn't match his looks. At least he wasn't hurling insults and accusations in her direction at the moment.

Gut thing, because any more, and it'd be all she could do to keep from breaking down in tears. And then he'd probably accuse her of crying as a ploy to convince him of her innocence.

She wouldn't resort to that. She tried to mentally prepare herself for more to kum.

"School's unlocked. Bathroom's in the back. Go in and get cleaned up." Sam's voice was curt, barely veiling his rage. He unclenched one fist, reached inside his pocket, and pulled out a miniature flashlight, which he handed to her. Then he waited while she climbed the stairs, opened the schoolhaus door, and stepped inside.

The room smelled of books and pine-scented cleaner. Abigail shut the door and turned the dead bolt to the locked position, then pivoted to survey the unfamiliar space. There were many rows of student desks arranged in neat lines. Two doors stood open on the far side of the room behind the teacher's desk.

It was strange being in a schoolhaus after dark, and she found herself shuddering as she tiptoed across the creaky wood floor toward one of the open doors, the tiny flashlight clutched tightly in her hand. In the bathroom, there was a small sink mounted to the wall just inside the door. Nein washcloths in sight; just a roll of paper towels. And a bar of lye soap.

That would sting. Abigail grimaced.

Leaving the bathroom door open, she set the flashlight on the back of the commode, closed the lid, and propped her leg on the edge. Then she carefully lifted the hem of her torn dress to examine her sore knee. There was a bloody gash on it.

She filled the sink with hot water and lathered up her hands. Sure enough, the strong lye soap stung. Tears sprang to her eyes. She hurriedly rinsed off, then grabbed a sheet of paper towel, dampened it, and attempted to clean her wound. She gritted her teeth at the burning sensation caused by the soapy water on the wet towel.

The floor creaked behind her. Someone tapped on the open bathroom door.

"Nice knee." Sammy smirked as he stepped past her. "Here, I have a better light." He lowered a lantern-style flashlight to the window ledge. In his other hand was a first-aid kit and real towel.

Heat rose in Abigail's cheeks. She straightened her posture and yanked her dress down as she turned toward the sink. "What are you doing, following me into the bathroom? Didn't your mamm teach you better?"

"I told you I'd make sure you took care of yourself. I have some alcohol wipes in here." He opened the kit and took out a few small packets.

"Danki, but soap and water work fine." Abigail gingerly submerged both hands in the hot, soapy water once more, wincing again from the pain.

"Jah, well, just to be on the safe side, you should follow up with these." Sammy set the wipes next to the lantern and came up behind Abigail with the towel. His chest brushed against her left shoulder as he moved around beside her.

Her breath caught. A delayed reaction to the stinging soap, maybe.

Sammy reached around in front of her, gently lifted her left hand from the water, and patted it dry.

Abigail had to remind herself to breathe. Her pulse pounded like the hooves of a runaway horse. "I thought…I thought I'd locked the door."

He chuckled. "You did. But I have the key."

This whole situation was out of control. She had to find some way to lighten the tension.

She cupped her right hand, filled it with warm soap bubbles, and flung them over her shoulder at Sammy.

The bubbles hit him full in the face, and he sputtered. Stilled.

Too late, she remembered the way Mark had responded the one time she'd done that very thing to him. He'd pulled her close and kissed her.

Until his daed—her new stepdaed—interrupted them. Resulting in her being sent away.

Pain knifed through her.

The next moment, she found herself being grabbed by the upper arms and spun around. Sammy's eyes bored into hers. "What was that for?"

Chapter 4

S am was still blinking his eyes from the stinging, soapy water as he stared down at the trembling, wincing woman in his arms, her body too close to his. The towel was clenched in his fisted hand, pressed against the hollow of her back.

He brought the towel around and mopped his face. He still held her with his other hand. Close. Too close.

"What are you doing?" She sounded breathless. Her hands wedged their way between herself and him and pushed against his chest.

She was dangerous, for sure.

He released her as quickly as if she'd branded him, and stepped back until his spine pressed against the opposite wall.

Her magnetism terrified him. Why was he constantly pulling her near? He'd probably had more physical contact with her tonacht than he'd had with his girlfriend the entire time they'd dated. Okay, maybe that was an exaggeration. Still, he wasn't supposed to feel this…whatever it was…for a complete stranger he'd caught in a compromising position near a burning barn, with flames licking at the rafters.

She'd been in another compromising position mere moments ago, with flames of a different type licking at—

Nein!

If Daed or one of the other preachers had kum into the schoolhaus at that moment and caught them, Sam and Abigail would have found themselves wed even before he bowed for believer's baptism.

Of course, he hadn't quite made up his mind on that subject yet. Gott was one thing; subjecting himself to the Ordnung, quite another.

He shoved the towel at Abigail, gathered the rest of the medical supplies, and hightailed it out of the bathroom. "Bring the light, if you please, feuerzeug."

"Will you stop calling me that? I *didn't* start the fire." She punctuated her complaint with a stomp of her foot on the wood floor.

Actually, she had started the fire. Trouble was, he didn't know how to put out this particular blaze. Probably a side effect of his pent-up anger. He dropped the first-aid kit on the teacher's desk with a thump. "Bring the light, please," he grumbled.

She huffed.

Hey, he'd asked nicely. Somewhat.

Okay. Maybe he could've been nicer.

Sam's arms hurt—actually ached—to hold her again. What was wrong with him?

He started tugging the window shades down, one by one.

Just in case.

⌒

Abigail held the flashlight lantern low, hoping Sammy wouldn't notice the renegade tears tracking down her cheeks. Nein part of today had gone as planned, and now she would end the day not only mourning the loss of Mark but also worrying about her fate now that she'd been accused of starting a fire. Of committing a crime, even though Sammy's kind family downplayed it. Even said she was forgiven.

The light pooled around Sammy's feet as he stood at a window and gave the shade a downward tug. Then he turned and approached the teacher's desk. "Sit, jah?"

She almost asked him—again—what he was doing. But it went without saying. If anybody looked inside and saw him bent over her hands in the light of the lantern, the gossip would rage for weeks to kum. Especially on the heels of the earlier scene in his family's kitchen.

Thankfully, nobody saw him holding her the way he had in the bathroom.

Her heart raced—again.

What would she have done if he'd kissed her, as Mark had?

Her gaze drifted south, to his firm-looking lips.

Her heart lurched.

Would his kiss be hard and demanding, as Mark's had been, right before his daed caught them? Or gentle, as the first time Mark kissed her?

A shiver worked down her spine.

Ach, her thoughts....

Sammy cleared his throat, and she looked up. Their gazes met. His blue eyes held her captive.

"Let's see your hands." His voice was husky. As if maybe she was getting under his skin, just as he was getting under hers.

Impossible.

More likely, the huskiness was a result of smoke inhalation.

Abigail swallowed. Held out her right hand. One of his large hands engulfed it, holding it steady, while his other hand tenderly swabbed the alcohol wipe over her palm. She focused on the stinging sensation, welcoming the distraction.

She didn't want to get to him.

Didn't want him getting to her.

Her heart belonged to Mark.

At least, it had until his daed—Mamm's new ehemann—decided to put an end to what he deemed a "sibling romance" and sent her off to Jamesport. Not fair, considering Mark had courted her longer than Daed had been dead.

Sam started slathering some sort of ointment over her hand. He cleared his throat. "So, you're living with your aenti and onkel. Where's your family?"

She would have said that he'd read her mind, but that would mean he already knew the answer to his question.

"Ohio." The word came out as a whisper.

"How long are you here? Just for a visit?"

"A visit." She swallowed. "Hopefully. Not sure how long...."

He looked up and raised an eyebrow.

"My beau...." She swallowed.

Ex-beau. Past tense.

Unless she could somehow get home and change her stepdaed's mind.

"Ach, you have a beau." Relief filled his eyes. As if he'd been worried she would chase after him.

Not likely.

"I'm dating a girl." His mouth stretched into a smile that didn't quite reach his eyes. "PJ."

"Odd name."

He chuckled. "She's Englisch. PJ is short for something, but she won't tell me what. I tease her and say that it probably stands for Prune Juice." He bandaged her hand.

"Your mamm thought I was the one you were courting."

Sammy reached for her left hand. "Jah, I know. I probably fueled that belief a bit. It's rare that I make Mamm happy, so when it happens, I like to enjoy it. Guess I'm somewhat of a troublemaker."

She gasped, feigning shock. "Nein."

He lowered his gaze and got to work on her left hand, giving it the same treatment as he'd given her right one.

Maybe he could be nice, after all. Maybe he would forget his foolish notion about her being a feuerzeug, and they could form a friendship.

She needed friends. Nice Amish friends.

He looked up with a slight smirk as he released her hand. "Now, how about that knee?" With his callused finger, he snagged the hem of her dress.

Abigail's breath caught. She planted her hands firmly on the fabric, ignoring the sudden pain. "Nein."

Sammy grinned. "Just teasing. You can bandage it when you get home, ain't so? Now, what'd you do to your arms?"

Abigail blinked. "My arms?"

"You grimaced when I grabbed you above the elbows."

"Ach. I…um…one of them's bruised, I think."

"How'd you do that?" His voice had turned insistent.

How could she tell him the truth, after he'd spent time taking care of her wounds?

Sam frowned. "I never took your onkel Darius as being abusive. Or did your daed do it?"

Her face warmed. She shook her head.

"Who hurt you?" he demanded.

She winced. "You did, when you grabbed me…in the barn."

His eyes widened. "Ach. So sorry. I didn't mean to…." He pulled in a breath and started over. "I didn't mean to hurt you. I'm sorry for that."

"I forgive you." The phrase was rote, but it needed to be said. In exchange, maybe he'd forgive her for failing to put out the fire.

He returned the medical supplies to the first-aid kit, then leaned against the desk, his hands propped on either side of her hips. "Tomorrow, feuerzeug, I'll kum by your onkel's haus, and we'll go for a walk. Or a ride, if your knee hurts too much to walk. And we'll talk about the fire." His voice had hardened.

So much for him forgiving and forgetting.

She scooted back a little. "I didn't do it."

He leaned closer. "So you say. But someone did. And you were there." His gaze sharpened. Speared. "You should know, the fire chief and the sheriff will be conducting an investigation. And right now, feuerzeug, all fingers are pointed straight at you."

⌒

Sam hated himself for scaring her. He studied her, looking for a sign of guilt. But all he saw was her sudden pallor. The tears welling in her eyes.

But a barn fire, so close on the heels of a haus fire, and with so many other barns going up in flames recently…. Seemed the influx of fires had started around the Fourth of July last summer.

Okay, so maybe Abigail wasn't the feuerzeug. Admittedly, most of the fires had happened before her arrival. But maybe she knew something about who was behind them.

And he'd surely get further with honey than vinegar. Daed was always saying that. But when Sam's family was under attack—from any direction—his first instinct was to fight back.

Not an appropriate reaction for an Amish man. They were non-confrontational. Or were supposed to be. Kind of hypocritical to talk the talk but not walk the walk.

Granted, he hadn't joined the church yet. So, in his case, maybe he was walking the walk but not talking the talk.

His head throbbed. Maybe it was neither. He'd figure it out later. After he figured out what to do with Abigail.

As if he had a dead body to dispose of.

She'd scooted as far away from him as possible and now sat there, frozen, staring at him with wide eyes.

Sam blew out a puff of air. Nobody had died. At least, not this time.

He needed to fight his fears that *she* might make him forget PJ. Go figure, he'd felt a nudge from Gott to break up with PJ today. He'd selfishly decided to wait, not having anyone else he was attracted to.

That had changed.

He should've broken things off.

He scooped up the first-aid kit and the smaller, dimmer flash-light, then started toward the door. "If you won't let me tend to your knee, should we get going? I'll drive you to your onkel's."

"Danki." She sounded uncertain. Or fearful. Or both.

Of course, he'd deliberately threatened her. Before thinking it through. Shame filled him.

He swallowed. "Sorry, feuerzeug. I…."

She made a sound—kind of halfway between a growl and a whimper—and he shut his eyes. Should he tell her that he knew she couldn't be behind all the recent fires? Or would it be better to let her think she was the sole suspect, and hope she'd name names?

Well, she *was* the sole suspect for this particular fire. He'd been truthful there.

But someone else had to have been behind it. That was just as certain as his name was Samuel Elijah Miller, Junior. Sammy to the womenfolk, Sam to the men.

He shook his head and continued to the door without finishing his apology. How could he, when he didn't know what to say?

As he stepped outside, he shivered at the chill in the air. Funny, he hadn't noticed it before. But then, his adrenaline had been pumping....

He put the emergency kit in the trunk. Slammed the lid.

Abigail made her way down the steps, slowly. Favoring her right leg.

Maybe he should've insisted on taking a look at her knee. But she'd done a thorough job washing her scraped palms. He'd leave her with some extra supplies, just in case Darius's Ruth didn't have them on hand.

He opened the front passenger door with a flourish. "Your chariot awaits, my lady."

Abigail eyed the rusty, dented vehicle doubtfully. But unless she could make a buggy appear from the ashes of the buggy shed—which had burned with the barn—there wasn't any other mode of transportation available.

Well, he supposed she could ride home with Darius. Sam glanced across the street toward the haus but couldn't tell whether her onkel was still there. Many of the helpers had left already.

"Danki for the ride." She still sounded wary. As if she suspected him of having ulterior motives.

And maybe he did. Some protective urge made Sam determined to see her safely home. "Safely" being the key word.

Once she'd pulled her tattered skirts out of the way, he shut the passenger door, then thumped the top of the car with his hand. Hopefully, it wouldn't break down on the way.

He would voice nein more accusations to-nacht. For now, he was her knight in shining armor upon his trusty steed....

Or in his ancient Dodge sedan.

He crossed in front of the car, climbed into the driver's seat, and twisted the key already in the ignition. The engine coughed to life. He shifted into reverse, and the vehicle shuddered violently in response.

Abigail gave him a dubious look.

"She needs some work, but hopefully she'll get you there in one piece." He'd planned on attempting some repairs tomorrow, but his tools had been in the barn. Maybe an Englisch friend would let him tinker with it in his garage. Or he could go to his cousin Greta's ehemann, Viktor Petersheim, for help.

Sam backed the vehicle into the road, then shifted into drive. "I need to take PJ into town Sunday afternoon after church. She's supposed to meet her ride to Kansas City, where she goes to university."

He'd break up with her then.

Abigail looked at him. "She trusts this car?"

"Buckle up. It's the law." He pressed on the gas, and the vehicle jerked, then settled into a somewhat normal motion. "And, jah, she trusts this car. Either that, or she trusts me to take care of her."

Abigail's seat belt clicked as they passed the first farm.

"Besides, I'm hoping to have it fixed by then."

Or not. He still needed to figure out the problem and buy the necessary parts.

Sam rubbed his chin as they passed the second farm. There were times when a horse and buggy definitely trumped a car.

This was one of those times.

He sighed and glanced over at the woman beside him. She rubbed her right knee, as if it ached. It probably did.

He pulled into Darius Zook's drive and cut the engine. "I'll see you in. I'd like to make sure Ruthie has the supplies she'll need to treat your injuries."

"Ach, I'm sure she does," Abigail said dismissively. "Besides, she's probably gone to bed."

Sam stepped out of the car. As if to spite Abigail, the door to the haus opened, and Ruthie stepped out, holding a lantern. "Sammy Miller. What are you doing here? Is the fire out?"

"Jah, the fire's out. I'm seeing Abigail home. She fell and hurt herself. Hasn't Darius returned yet? I'm sure he'll be here soon." Sam came around the vehicle and opened the passenger door for Abigail.

Her right leg buckled as she stood. She grabbed the car door for support.

Sam reached for her. "You okay?"

"Jah." She nodded quickly. "Just a little...um...." She brushed past him and hobbled toward the haus.

Sam went to the trunk, opened it, and retrieved his first-aid kit. Maybe he would take a look at her knee. With Ruthie as a chaperone, it'd be above board.

Her leg shouldn't have buckled from a mere scrape. Had she injured it worse than she was letting on?

Chapter 5

Abigail carefully made her way up the porch stairs, her movements surely making her look like Mark's feeble great-grossmammi. Her right knee throbbed almost as badly as it had the previous summer, when she'd torn a ligament playing volleyball. She'd kept her leg wrapped and iced for weeks, a regimen she didn't care to repeat.

It couldn't be that she'd sustained the same injury, or it would've started aching right away. Unless she simply hadn't noticed the pain due to the adrenaline rush.

Nein. She wouldn't consider the implications of that.

As she entered the haus, Sam stayed close behind her, as if prepared to reach out and support her. Sweet of him, but unnerving. Her emotions were off-kilter. The thought of his hands on her again… *nein!* She wouldn't think of that, either.

She couldn't figure him out. He started off curt, angry, and quick to condemn—though, given the situation, she really couldn't blame him. Then, all of a sudden, he was kind, caring, and compassionate. Add to that a heaping dose of flirtatiousness…intriguing.

He trailed her into the kitchen, then stepped around her and pulled out a chair from the table. "Sit."

She recoiled. "Nein. Absolutely not." She tried to steady her shaky voice. "You're *not* touching my knee." The throbbing worsened at the thought.

"Actually, I *am*. Ruthie will chaperone us, ain't so?" He glanced from Abigail to Aenti Ruth. Aenti Ruth patted Abigail's shoulder.

"Sammy needs to take care of your knee, for sure. He's almost a doctor."

Sammy scoffed. "Hardly. But I am working toward my paramedic license. And I'm an EMT."

Abigail was surprised not to detect even a lick of pride in his voice. Those were simply statements of fact.

But an Amish EMT? An Amish paramedic? An Amish firefighter? Was it possible? The Ordnung in this district must really be liberal. Either that, or he'd strayed way outside the lines.

A car, she could understand. Those were normal for buwe in their rumschpringe.

Abigail rubbed her forehead and studied the mysterious man standing in front of her.

Sammy sighed. "Sit, please, Abby." He set the first-aid kit on the table and opened it.

"Abigail," she corrected him. "Aenti Ruth can do it, ain't so?" She glanced at the older woman.

"Ach, I'm nein doctor." Aenti Ruth moved to the stove, grabbed the kettle, and started filling it with water. "I'll make some hot chocolate. It's late, so you don't mind if I use a mix, do you? It won't take as long." She opened a cupboard and pulled out a box of Swiss Miss packets. "It's getting so cold outside. I heard something about freezing rain coming in tomorrow nacht."

"Jah, but then it's supposed to turn to just rain, with temperatures in the high forties, I think," Sammy said. "Ice shouldn't last long." He returned his attention to Abigail. His gaze caught hers. "Please, sit. I'm a professional."

A professional flirt, maybe, judging by some of his schoolhaus ministrations. But Aenti Ruth was in the room. Never mind that she didn't seem to pay them any attention. Abigail sat in the chair and gingerly lifted her dress enough to reveal her injured knee. The warmth of a blush nearly scalded her cheeks.

Sammy's lips flatlined as he studied her leg. "Bruising. Swelling. Not gut."

His muttered words, spoken mostly to himself, sent worry skittering through her every nerve ending. *Nein. Not again.*

Sammy reached for something in the kit, then knelt in front of her. "Abby, I'm going to clean this up, but I'm going to need to see if you fractured your kneecap or tore something. It may hurt."

It already hurt. Not only that, but she burned with embarrassment. She gulped. "My name is Abigail. And it's probably just a sprain." She hoped.

Mark called her Abby. Nobody else had the right.

"Probably," Sammy cheerfully agreed. "Either that or a bad bruise, but we'll check to be sure. Neither a bruise nor a sprain should cause your leg to buckle."

He was muttering again—to her, a bad sign.

Abigail forced her attention to Aenti Ruth, arranging four mugs on the counter, and tried to ignore Sammy as he ripped open another packet containing an alcohol wipe. His touch was one of professional detachment as he cleaned and bandaged the cut, the whole time explaining in murmured tones what he was doing and why. He set the bandage wrapper on the table and looked up at her. "Tell me if anything hurts." He slid his hand over her knee, poking and prodding.

"It doesn't hurt any worse now than before." That should be a gut sign, right? When she'd torn a ligament, even the gentlest touch of one part of her knee had almost made her cry out.

"Nein sharp pain in any particular spot?" Sammy asked.

Abigail shook her head. "Nein. That's gut, jah?"

"Jah. That *is* gut." Sammy scooted to the side. "Extend your leg as straight as you can, then bend the knee."

She did as he asked. It wasn't a straight kick, and her speed was slow. At least the leg extended the way she thought it should.

"Hurt?"

"Nein." Not any worse than before, anyway.

Sammy stood. "Okay. If your knee starts swelling more, makes a loud popping sound, or gets to be so painful that you can't walk, you'll need to see a doctor." His gaze shot to Aenti Ruth. "A real doctor. I'm tentatively diagnosing it as a bad bruise or a sprain."

Aenti Ruth set two mugs of hot chocolate on the table. "Danki for taking care of her. She hurt her leg real bad last summer and was laid up for several weeks."

The door opened, and Onkel Darius entered, ushering in a blast of cold air. He hung his hat and coat on a hook and toed off his shoes. "You made hot chocolate, Ruthie. Sounds gut. Danki for bringing Abigail home, Sam. I looked around for her and figured you'd wanted to see her here." He winked.

Abigail couldn't believe her onkel was among those who believed the two of them were courting. Seemed he should know better, considering she'd been here only a week and hadn't yet gone to church.

Sammy cleared his throat. "Actually, we met just to-nacht. But, with your permission, I'd like to kum by around noon tomorrow and take her out for lunch. I need to pick up some parts for my car, anyway, and there are…some things I'd like to talk over with her."

"I *am* right here," Abigail muttered.

Sammy sent her a smirk.

Onkel Darius grinned. "Jah, that's fine." He slapped Sammy good-naturedly on the shoulder, then sat at his place at the table. Aenti Ruth set a mug in front of him. "It's late, but we all need to unwind, I'm thinking. Have a seat, Sam, and stay a bit."

"I will, but just for a moment. I need to get home." Sammy sat next to Abigail and sipped his hot chocolate. "Danki, Ruthie. It's ser gut."

"So, Sam." Onkel Darius leaned forward.

Aenti Ruth frowned. Seemed to tense. *Strange.*

Sammy hitched an eyebrow, leaned back, and flashed Abigail another smirk. "So, Darius."

Onkel Darius glanced at Aenti Ruth, then looked back at Sammy. "You need help with that car?"

Aenti Ruth moved her fists to her hips and shook her head at her ehemann. There'd likely be a whispered conversation about this later.

"That'd be great. I lost all my tools in the—" Sammy swallowed, his throat muscles visibly constricting. "The fire. I figured I might head over to Viktor Petersheim's."

"You can work here," Onkel Darius offered. "I have all the tools you'll need. Between the two of us, we might be able to fix it up. I used to know a thing or two about cars, back in the day."

Aenti Ruth muttered something under her breath, then stood and retrieved the cookie jar.

Sammy grinned. "Ach, jah? I'd appreciate your help, for sure. I'm learning the ins and outs of cars the hard way. By trial and error." He drained his hot chocolate and pushed himself to his feet. "I hate to turn down cookies, Ruthie, but it's getting late, and chores start early, as you know." His expression darkened. "Not that there'll be as many chores to do now. But when I'm finished, I'll kum by."

Onkel Darius beamed.

Sammy moved toward the door. "See you tomorrow, Abby."

"Abigail."

He glanced over his shoulder and winked. "Abigail." Her name was drawn out as a caress.

Her stomach twisted. Knotted. Then settled in a lump.

Maybe "Abby" would've been better. That hadn't sounded like an endearment.

The door shut behind him.

⟜

At a quarter to twelve, Sam drove to the Zooks' in the truck he'd borrowed from Viktor. Parts of his rusty Dodge were scattered all over the floor of the Zooks' barn. But Sam had some general idea about what might be wrong with his car. At least he knew where to start.

Darius opened the passenger door of the truck. "I'll tell Abigail you're ready to go. Just let me know when you get the parts, and I'll help more, if I can."

"I'll do that. Danki." The simple word of thanks didn't begin to cover Sam's gratitude. He hadn't realized Darius had worked as a mechanic for a while. He still didn't know where he'd gotten his training. Maybe, like Sam, he'd taken classes during his rumschpringe.

Sam sat in the truck a moment after Darius had left, then slid out. Maybe he'd better check on Abigail's knee and see if she was capable of going along with him. If she wasn't, it'd make it tricky to talk to her, but he'd figure something out. He didn't want to wait until the fire chief started the investigation. He wanted Abigail to tell him who was behind the arson. She was there. She *had* to know.

When Sammy opened the door, he found Ruthie bustling about in the kitchen. His stomach roared in response to the aroma.

"Hallo, Sammy. Abigail went to her room to get her bonnet and coat." Ruthie nodded toward the stairs. "I know you mentioned wanting to get lunch out, but would you rather eat here with us? I made smothered pork chops with mushroom gravy. There's plenty."

Sam grinned. "Jah, that sounds gut. Danki. Is her knee any better today?"

Ruthie lifted a shoulder. "She's hobbling a bit but keeping it wrapped, and when she sits, she uses ice. But otherwise, it hasn't slowed her down much. I can't imagine how her mamm is managing all those new stepkinner without Abigail there to help. I don't know how I ever got on without her, and it's just Darius and me now." Sadness colored her voice.

Sam only nodded. A year ago, their three teenage dochters had been killed in a tragic buggy accident, leaving them childless. But Sam didn't have any words of comfort. Really. They'd all been said already. He bent to take his tennis shoes off, then hung his coat and hat on a hook.

"You're dressed in Englisch clothes today," Ruthie noted.

Sam laughed. "Easier to work on an Englisch car this way. Plus, I'm going to town."

"Your mamm must be wearing her knees out, praying for you." Ruthie's voice was dry.

"Probably so." His gaze moved to the doorway as Abigail stepped into the room. She looked beautiful in a pale purple color Mamm would've called mauve. His mouth went dry. She was so pretty. He smiled. "Change of plans. We're eating here. How's the knee?"

She looked down at the offending injury. "Fine. It still hurts, but I think the swelling has gone down, and it isn't popping. It's still bruised." She hung her coat and bonnet next to Sam's and went to wash her hands. She did limp a little. Not too bad, considering. "Does the change of plans mean I don't have to go shopping for car parts with you?" She smiled hopefully.

"Ach, you're going." He followed her to the sink. "I still need to talk to you."

She reached for a towel and moved out of his way. "What if I don't want to talk to you?"

Sam chuckled. "You wound me." He took the towel she offered him. "I'll make it worth your while."

"Humph." She turned, shuffled over to the cabinet, and pulled out four plates.

Abigail proceeded to set the table, her skirts swaying enticingly. Sam forced himself to look away, to Ruthie, as she heaped buttery mashed potatoes into a serving bowl, then set it aside and spooned green beans into another bowl.

"Um…anything I can do to help?"

Ruthie smiled at him. "Nein, danki. We'll eat as soon as Darius gets back." She carried the bowls of food to the table.

The clink of glass tumblers drew Sam's attention back to Abigail. He studied the short tendrils of wavy golden-brown hair brushing against her neck.

"You'll want koffee, jah?" Ruthie asked, a note of humor in her voice.

Sam jerked his gaze away again. "Huh? Ach, nein, danki. I…uh, water's fine."

The opening strains of the song "You're the One That I Want" broke the silence. It was the custom ringtone PJ had assigned herself in his cell phone. His face heated as both Ruthie and Abigail stopped what they were doing and stared at him. "Uh, better take this." He slid the phone out of his pocket and stepped outside. "Hey, PJ. What's up?"

"I hate to ask, but could you take me to Walmart? My ride for tomorrow called, and he needs to pick me up way earlier than we'd planned, so I need the items tonight. Mom was called into work, so she needs the car. You won't need to take me in the morning anymore. Mom can drop me off when she goes to work."

"Sure," Sam agreed. "I was going into Chillicothe today, anyway." *With Abigail.* "I need to buy some parts for my car."

"You need to sell that hunk of junk and get a new one."

A long-standing complaint. His car wasn't classy enough. It embarrassed her.

He should've broken things off yesterday.

Shouldn't have gotten involved with her in the first place.

What was the saying about hindsight being 20/20?

Sam rubbed his forehead. "I'm borrowing a friend's pickup. And I'll have someone else with me. If it's okay with you, I'll drop you off at Walmart so you can shop while I go get my car parts."

PJ liked to shop. Sam should have plenty of time to go to an auto supply store and also have a talk with Abigail.

And having PJ along would provide a buffer from whatever it was that had flared between him and Abigail.

He hoped.

The door opened as PJ said something else. He turned, meeting Abigail's eyes.

She silently motioned him inside the haus.

Sam cleared his throat again. "Time to eat. I'll be by in a bit." He disconnected the call and tucked his phone back into his pocket. Then he followed Abigail inside, fighting to keep his focus off the sway of her skirts.

Abigail climbed inside the extended-cab pickup and settled herself in the passenger seat. Sammy was kind enough to wait until she'd adjusted her skirts before he shut the door. A few seconds later, he climbed into the driver's seat. He started the engine and drove out to the road. The engine's growl was much louder than Sammy's car, but this vehicle felt safer, somehow.

"I need to pick up PJ," he told her. "She has some shopping to do."

Abigail would rather not have the "talk" Sammy insisted on in front of a stranger. But she was curious to see what kind of girl Sammy was attracted to. "She can't do her shopping tomorrow?"

He shrugged. "She said her ride needs to meet her much earlier than planned. Don't worry, I told her I'd leave her at Walmart while I ran my errands."

"Did you mention me?" Or would she be facing a jealous girlfriend who wondered why Sammy had brought an Amish girl along to shop for car parts?

That still seemed strange. And if he knew he'd have his girlfriend with him, why did he still want Abigail along? When would they talk?

"I told her I'd have a friend along." He shrugged, as if unsure why it mattered.

"Ach." So, Abigail *would* be facing a jealous girlfriend. She swallowed. "I wasn't aware that we were friends."

"We're not." Sammy's shoulders lifted again. "I might not have used the word 'friend.' I don't remember what I said, exactly." He paused at an intersection and checked for oncoming traffic, then turned right. "Besides, it doesn't matter. You and I already had plans. She's the one who invited herself along. She'll understand. She's a great gal." The volume and certainty in his voice had tapered significantly, which Abigail found odd.

He drove into Jamesport and pulled to the side of the road in front of a small yellow haus. A girl with short black hair ran out the door and started jogging toward the truck. She wore blue jeans and a bright red V-neck shirt. When she reached the vehicle, she threw open the front passenger door. "Nice ride." She hesitated, her gaze sweeping over Abigail. "Who's this?"

Abigail shifted. "I'll move to the backseat so you can sit next to him." She climbed awkwardly over the console, her arm brushing against Sammy's shoulder as she did.

PJ got in, buckled her seat belt, and looked at Sammy with arched eyebrows.

In the rearview mirror, Sammy met Abigail's gaze for a second. "She's the, uh, the friend I said I'd have with me."

"I thought you said you needed parts for your car." PJ twisted in her seat to look at Abigail. "Are you a mechanic? Do you know how to fix cars?"

Abigail blinked. "Um, no."

"Never said she did, PJ." Sammy drove back out into the road. "She and I need to talk about some things. Our barn burned last night." He looked at Abigail in the rearview mirror again. "Abby, this is PJ. PJ, Abby."

PJ sighed heavily. "I hate it when Mom gets called into work while I'm home for a visit. We had plans. We were going to shop, rent a chick flick, get carry-out pizza, and just spend the evening vegging on the couch."

Abigail glanced at Sammy, surprised that his girlfriend hadn't acknowledged his comment about the fire—or the introductions. And Abigail didn't understand some of the terms PJ had used. *Chick flick? Vegging?*

Sammy frowned.

"Maybe you could come over. We could still get carry-out pizza and watch a movie. It wouldn't have to be a chick flick, but something with a romantic plot would be nice." There was a suggestive tone to PJ's voice, reminding Abigail of the sparks that flew in the cramped schoolhaus bathroom.

"Sorry, PJ, but I'm busy tonight." Red crept up Sammy's neck. He glanced in the rearview mirror, his gaze meeting Abigail's again.

She bit her lip and looked away. She shouldn't be here with them.

"But we spent only a few hours together yesterday, and…."

Abigail glanced at Sammy. How would he respond to PJ's pouty tone?

"You had plans with your mom. I made my plans after I heard about yours. Besides, we're together now." He adjusted his grip on the steering wheel.

PJ glanced over her shoulder. The look she gave Abigail could've curdled fresh milk. Nein wonder Sammy joked that her initials stood for Prune Juice.

"Yeah, but *she's* with us now." PJ jerked her thumb toward the backseat. "I bet your evening plans are with *her*, huh?"

Chapter 6

Sam growled deep in his throat at PJ's comment, but PJ either didn't hear or chose to ignore him. She was gut at both.

Although he didn't actually have any concrete plans for that evening, he refused to give in to her now. He would find something to do. And if that activity happened to involve Abigail, what was it to PJ? They were dating, sure, but they weren't exclusive. *Her* decision, not his. He was gut enough when she was home with nothing better to do. But when he'd attended a fire training in Kansas City and had looked her up, she'd treated him like he was something disgusting she'd found stuck to the bottom of her shoe. And then she'd told him never to visit her there again.

That hurt. And it had pretty well guaranteed she wasn't the one he'd want to settle down with. She'd be just like her mamm, running off with the latest guy to catch her fancy. Nothing like Sam's mamm, who believed marriage was based on a sacred vow to be honored and kept.

So, Sam had broken up with PJ.

But when PJ came home for winter break a few months later, she'd called and apologized. And because he'd since experienced the power of second chances, he'd given her one. He forgave her and took her back.

It gave him something to do. Besides, PJ could kiss.

He cringed. He really shouldn't allow his hormones to rule his decisions.

He bet Abigail could kiss, too. And, judging by the lightning bolt that'd about knocked him senseless when he'd simply touched her....

His gaze wandered to the rearview mirror, and he took in the reflection of the intriguing girl in the backseat. She stared out the window now, watching the heavy traffic that increased the closer they came to the large town. "City," some of the Amish called it.

Compared to Kansas City, it was nothing.

Lord Gott, should I break up with PJ again? Permanently? I need a sign.

As if he hadn't been given several signs already. But now wasn't a gut time to break up with PJ. Not with Abigail there to witness it.

A church sign caught his attention. "Consider This a Sign from God."

Sam grinned at the obvious coincidence. It still wasn't a gut time.

He drove up to the entrance of Walmart and idled by the crosswalk. PJ gathered her purse, shot another baleful glance at Abigail, and got out of the truck. "I'll call you when I'm finished," she told Sam.

"Take your time."

He winced as she slammed the truck door, then walked—nein, strutted—into the store. He glanced back at Abigail. "You want to move up front again?"

"I'm gut." She sounded nervous.

"I don't bite. Promise." He meant to reassure her, but she stiffened and shook her head.

Sam waited for the latest two-way parade of shoppers—some entering the store, others leaving, laden with bags or pushing carts—to finish before he drove out of the parking lot.

A few minutes later, he parked outside a nearby auto supply shop. "Want to kum in with me?"

"Ach, not really." Abigail eyed the store dubiously.

"Kum on. I might be a while."

That wasn't exactly true. Darius had given him a short list of the supplies he'd need. All he had to do was hand it to a sales associate and trail that person around the store. Still, he didn't want to leave Abigail alone in the truck.

"I'll be fine," she insisted. "I brought something to do. Aenti Ruth is forcing me to write home."

"Forcing you?"

"Would you want to write to someone who abandoned you at the bus station?" Pain edged her voice.

"Ouch." He grimaced. "Well, if you kum with me, you can postpone the agony."

"That's okay. I'll just write a quick note and drop it in that mailbox down there." She pointed to a big metal mailbox at the edge of the parking lot, near the road.

"Suit yourself. But stay in the truck. I'll drive you to the mailbox." He got out and clicked the lock button on the key remote as he walked away.

Abandoned at the bus station? Really? She seemed like such a sweet girl. What had she done to warrant being sent away in such a manner?

⌒

Abigail pulled out the stamped, addressed envelope and tri-folded sheet of lined stationery Aenti Ruth had handed her that morgen. This letter wouldn't take long to write. Mamm didn't deserve a long, newsy missive. Not after throwing Abigail over the way she had.

Abigail refused to dwell on that, though. It had already claimed too many of her thoughts. She turned her attention to searching for a pen. She found one, pulled it out, and clicked it open.

Then she stared at the blank sheet of paper. How should she begin? She clicked the pen closed, open, closed, open. A red truck rumbled into an adjacent parking spot. A beat-up car, in worse shape than Sam's, pulled in on the other side.

It'd be easier to write if she had a hard surface. She climbed into the front seat again and used the dashboard as a writing desk.

Dear Mamm....

And then she thought some more.

Arrived safely in Jamesport.

Nein news. I'll write again sometime.

When Aenti Ruth made her.

Abigail

She refolded the paper, slid it inside the envelope, and licked the seal. Task accomplished. She tucked the letter back into her purse.

Sammy came out of the store, lugging a box. He put it in the truck bed, covered it with a tarp, and got into the cab next to her. "Think I bought all I need. You want something to drink? We could stop at McDonald's."

"A Coke sounds gut. Danki." For some reason, soda tasted so much better from a fountain than in a can or bottle. "I wrote the letter." She pulled it out of her purse.

Sammy nodded. As they left the parking lot, he slowed beside the mailbox and lowered Abigail's window. She slid the letter into the slot. Then he drove to McDonald's, parked, and followed her inside.

She spotted the display case of toys that kids could pick for their Happy Meals. Plush conversation hearts bearing various words and phrases. Ach, Valentine's Day. It was only a week away. "How cute!"

Sammy gave the display a cursory glance. "Jah. Cute. Whatever." *Men.*

"Find us a table," he told her. "Secluded, so we can talk."

Abigail looked around. One side of the restaurant was almost empty. She headed for a vacant table.

A few minutes later, Sammy strode over, carrying two large drinks and a bag. He unloaded the items on the table and lowered himself into the chair across from her.

Her gaze lit on the bag. "You bought food?" They'd eaten less than forty-five minutes earlier. He couldn't possibly be hungry again already.

He shrugged. "Hot apple pies. One for you, one for me."

"Ach. That sounds gut." Abigail reached for the bag. Anything to stall the private conversation Sammy had planned.

"There's something else in there for you."

Abigail reached in and grasped a plastic bag containing one of the plush conversation hearts. She stared up at Sammy.

"You said they were cute." He raked his hand through his hair.

"They are. Danki. They just gave you one? You didn't buy a Happy Meal, did you?"

Sammy grinned. "I asked for one. The cashier knows me. I took care of her grossdaedi after he suffered a heart attack. She figures she owes me. So, what's that one say? Whatever it is, it's true." He winked.

She glanced at the peach-colored heart, then turned it around so he could read it. *#LOVE*. "Why did they put a pound sign in front of the word?"

Sammy's lips twitched. "PJ calls it a hashtag. Don't ask me what it means, though. I have nein idea."

She reached into the bag again for the apple pies but picked out another toy, instead. "Ach, you got one for PJ." She glanced at it. *I Luv You*. Someday, she'd like for a man to give her a conversation heart—or anything, really—that carried that message. *Ich liebe dich*.

Sammy frowned at the plush heart. "I didn't ask for two. And I wouldn't give her that one, anyway. She'd want a box of chocolates for Valentine's Day. And a bouquet of flowers with a note signed 'Secretly yours.' That way, she'd get lots of attention when the delivery was made." He shrugged then muttered, "I won't be getting her anything this year, though. You can keep both toys."

Abigail didn't quite get Sam's relationship with PJ. He didn't treat her with any sort of caring. But then, PJ didn't treat him as if she cared, either. Maybe it was all due to Abigail's presence, though.

She reached inside the bag once more and lifted out the pies. "Danki for the hearts. And for the dessert." She set her pie on the table. "You probably should've told PJ you'd have a female with you before you picked her up. She's clearly upset with you. Jealous."

Sammy blew out a breath. "Jah. I realized that too late. Sorry for putting you in an awkward position. I didn't mean to embarrass you, or to upset her." He slid one of the cups and a straw toward her, then reached for his pie. "Why did your parents abandon you at the bus station?"

Abigail cringed. Mamm hadn't put up a fight, and she hadn't kum along to the bus station. She'd "needed" to stay home to watch her new stepkinner. She'd acted as if Abigail were going on a quick shopping trip instead of being kicked out. Her failure to even say gut-bye had been the ultimate rejection. It was Abigail's stepdaed, and Mark, who'd actually abandoned her. And Mark had refused to talk to her, other than to whisper, "Trust me, it's better this way." He wouldn't look her in the eye. *Traitor.* Probably due to his daed's presence.

"My stepdaed wanted me and Mark to break up."

Sammy studied her with a quizzical expression. "Why's that?"

"Mark's his sohn. Technically, he's my half brother now."

"Ah. Tricky." Sammy took a bite of pie. Chewed and swallowed. Then he frowned at the flat-screen TV mounted on a nearby wall. On the screen was a weather report, with pink splotches coloring the Midwest. "Looks like the ice is coming in sooner than they originally thought." He returned his attention to her. "We need to talk. If you didn't start the fire, who did?"

◠

Nothing like bluntness. Considering how Abigail winced and looked away, Sam probably should've planned a more gradual lead-in. He glanced at the TV again, eyeing the digitized models of the approaching storm. Then he looked out the window beside their table at the gray sky overhead. The rain had already started. Or was it freezing rain? Panic coursed through him. He had nein experience driving a vehicle on ice.

Better get this conversation over with. Then call PJ and tell her they needed to head back. She wouldn't be happy about being rushed, but with ice in the forecast, Walmart would be a madhaus.

Abigail sucked Coke through her straw as if trying to draw in courage. Her hands shook. A sign of guilt?

"Who did it?" he asked again.

"I don't know."

Sam choked. Coughed. "You don't know." Did she hear the derision in his voice?

"I. Don't. Know." She spoke more firmly this time. "I've been here only one week. I met one person, an Englischer. She invited me to a party with some of her friends. I wish I would've said nein, but I wanted to meet people, and she called it a party. That's the Englisch equivalent of a frolic, ain't so? I didn't know where we were...whose barn it was. I didn't even meet her friends. All I know is, we walked into a barn. I picked up a cat while she continued to some room in back, and then she immediately ran out with four or five other people. Laughing. I saw a light flickering in the back room and went to extinguish the lantern, and that's when I saw the fire. I went to ring the bell and tripped on my way out of the barn. Which is when you found me."

He saw the truthfulness in her eyes. "Who is she—the Englischer?"

Abigail bit her lip and looked down. She twisted the straw wrapper around her finger. "I don't want to be a snitch."

Sam nodded. "Commendable. But, based on what you've told me, she didn't do it, either. It wouldn't be too hard to find out who she is." He waited a beat. Two. Three. Then he frowned. "I told you before, you're the only suspect right now. It'll go easier on you if we know where to look for answers."

With a grimace, Abigail shoved her untouched apple pie away. "Miranda. I don't know her last name. She lives next door to my onkel."

"Danki." Sam knew Miranda. And the people she ran around with. Trouble, all of them. Fresh anger worked through him, destroying his dreams. His hopes. And everything he'd kept stashed in the dark, hidden corners of the upper loft. He would pass along this information to the fire chief and leave him to tell the investigator.

"Please…don't tell her I told." Abigail sent him a pleading gaze.

"I won't even talk to her." Sam met her eyes, trying to keep his rage under control so he wouldn't scare her. "Promise."

He was relieved to know for certain Abigail hadn't started the fire. She didn't seem like the type. And he was glad she'd ignored his blunder in boldly stating that whatever the plush conversation heart said was true. He'd figured it would be something generic, like "Cutie Pie." Which she was. Or maybe "Dream Big" or "You Rock." Whatever that meant.

They could salvage their relationship from its rocky beginning and become friends, ain't so?

There was a ping as something struck the window. Sam glanced outside. The ice had started.

He shot to his feet. "We've got to go."

Chapter 7

Abigail stuffed the unopened apple pie and the two plush conversation heart toys into the bag while Sammy gathered their drinks and the discarded wrappers. After dumping the garbage in the trash can, he held the door for her. Abigail bent her head against the sleet and wind as she stepped outside. The ice pellets bounced around her feet as she hurried toward the truck, her sore knee causing her to hobble.

"I should've told you to wait inside and I'd pick you up." Sammy ran ahead of her and opened the front passenger door of the truck.

Abigail hesitated and glanced up at him, squinting through the icy rain. "PJ should be in front, ain't so? We're picking her up next."

Sammy started to protest, but Abigail opened the back door and climbed in. Sammy handed her her soda, then shut the door and jogged around to the front. As he slid inside, he pulled his cell phone out of his pocket. Then he pushed a button and held the phone to his ear.

"Hey, PJ. It's sleeting. I need to get Abby home before it gets worse. Are you ready to go?"

He clicked his seat belt as PJ answered him, loud enough that Abigail could hear her voice, though she couldn't understand what was being said. Abigail reached for her seat belt as Sammy inserted the key into the ignition. "I can't wait, Peej. I borrowed this truck, and I need to return it soon. Check out now. Whatever you didn't get on your list, you'll just have to pick up in Kansas City."

As the engine roared to life, Sammy twisted around in his seat and grinned at Abigail. His gaze lowered to the belt stretching across her upper body before he turned to face front again. "Whatever, PJ. Fifteen minutes. We're on our way to pick you up." He pressed a button on the phone, then dropped the device into the console and started the windshield wipers. "Stubborn woman. Always has to have the last word." He sighed. "Danki for obeying when I said kum."

A touch of irritation washed through Abigail. His comment made her think of her stepdaed—except he didn't bother expressing gratitude when she obeyed. "You make it sound like I'm a well-trained dog."

Sammy's neck turned red. "I didn't mean it that way. I meant... uh...."

"I don't want to be stranded any more than you do."

Sammy turned onto the main road. He pursed his lips as he peered through the windshield. The wipers could hardly clear the ice quickly enough.

Abigail clutched the seat belt. At least the bad weather removed the urge to rub her knee. Sammy would notice, and insist on her getting medical attention. Hopefully, she hadn't done further damage by climbing over the seats. "Is it hard driving in this stuff?"

He shrugged. "It's not too bad yet. Hoping to get home before the worst of it." He pulled into the Walmart parking lot and joined the line of idling vehicles. PJ scurried down the sidewalk carrying two bulging bags by the handles. She opened the front passenger door, then climbed in and glared at Sammy.

He ignored her.

PJ tucked both her bags into the space at her feet and slammed the door shut.

Sammy glanced over at her. "Easy, there."

"I'm really *not* happy. That was so hateful of you, calling and telling me I had fifteen minutes to finish shopping. How dare you treat me like that? I'm not some submissive little...." PJ launched into a tirade.

Sammy didn't respond as he navigated his way out of the parking lot. Of course, if he'd said something, it would've been lost in the avalanche of shrewish statements filling the air. Abigail felt sorry for Sammy. He may be a bit rough around the edges, but he didn't deserve the emotional beatdown PJ was subjecting him to.

Sammy pulled off the road into a different parking lot, shifted into park, and stared at PJ. "Look. In case you haven't noticed, there's a winter storm starting. Ice is collecting on the windshield. The road conditions are getting dangerous. I'm driving a borrowed vehicle, and you aren't the only passenger. Excuse me for wanting to safeguard the people and things entrusted to my care. I'll take you back to Walmart, if you want, but I'm going home."

"Just shut up."

His hands clenched the steering wheel so tightly, his knuckles turned white. "Walmart or home, Penelope June."

"That's not my name." PJ crossed her arms and looked at him with the flicker of a smile. "Home."

"Okay then, Patti Jo."

"Not it, either." The grin widened. "You'll never guess."

"Sure I will, Petunia Jane. But not right now." He drove back onto the road. "Not another word, okay?"

But PJ clearly didn't understand the meaning of "not another word." She kept talking. At least the tirade seemed to be over.

Traffic became sparser as they entered Jamesport. When the truck skidded around a corner, Abigail gasped. *Gott, get us back safely.*

A few moments later, Sammy eased the vehicle to the side of the road in front of PJ's haus. "Here you go."

PJ gave him a flirty grin. "You were pretty rotten, but you can make it up to me, you know. Drop *her* off and come back. Mom won't be home till late." She winked and slid out of the truck.

Sammy got out, too, and followed her up the steps to the covered front porch, his shoulders hunched against the stinging ice pellets. PJ opened the door and set her bags inside, then stood in the entryway as Sammy said something to her. A moment later, PJ stomped her foot, glared at him, and shot a baleful look toward the truck. Then she threw her arms around Sammy's neck and kissed him.

A knot of emotion that felt a lot like envy rose in Abigail's chest. She looked away.

⌒

Sam disentangled himself from PJ's arms and stepped back. He wished he could just tell her it was over and walk away. But he couldn't. He didn't want Abigail to witness the drama that was sure to follow.

So, he delayed the inevitable. "See ya later, Priscilla Joy."

She giggled.

At least the guessing game was enough to tease her out of her foul mood. They parted on a gut note. A rare occurrence.

It was time to break things off. Past time, really. Kum May, Sam would graduate college with his coveted degree, and move on to the next phase of his life—which wouldn't include a fickle, two-timing, unwilling-to-commit, demeaning, selfish, unreasonable Englisch girl. He wanted someone sweet. Someone he could count on.

Abigail's face flashed in his mind. He blocked it out. He didn't know who his future would include, but if Abigail had a beau, Sam wouldn't be the one to break them up. Though, from what she'd said, it sounded as if they'd already ended things, or were about to. And since Sam had never heard of a courting couple having to separate because of the reason she'd given, not even in districts that followed a stricter Ordnung, he suspected something deeper and darker was in play. But what?

PJ's fingers trailed up his chest, tantalizingly. "See you later, lover."

Sam swallowed the bile that rose in his throat. Leaned forward and pecked her cheek—the expected gesture, and a necessary one to maintain the momentary peace. Then he turned and walked—skated, more accurately—back to the truck. The concrete sidewalk was slick. The roads were probably getting bad, too. Providing the perfect excuse for why he couldn't kum back to see PJ that evening. He'd text her later to let her know.

Chicken. It was pathetic, he knew, to rely on technology to communicate what he couldn't tell her to her face. But it was easier to turn off a phone than to get her to shut up when she was ranting in an effort to manipulate a situation.

He opened the truck door and climbed in beside the pretty, curvy, fascinating girl who'd moved to the front seat. Maneuvering as easily as she did, she definitely hadn't torn a ligament in her knee.

He put the truck into gear and merged onto the road. Abigail remained blessedly silent, allowing him to wrestle with his thoughts. Feelings. Decisions.

He knew he ought to break up with PJ sooner rather than later. Doing it over the phone seemed wrong. Cowardly. But risking a borrowed truck and his life to drive back out here this evening would be stupid. Their relationship wouldn't reach its end to-nacht, for sure.

He turned onto the circular drive in front of Darius's haus and parked as close to the porch steps as he could. "I'll see you inside."

Abigail shook her head. "Nein need. I'm sure you're anxious to get back to PJ's."

He shut the driver's door on her objection and hastened around the front of the truck. She had already gotten out and was retrieving the McDonald's bag and her drink from the console.

"Danki, again." She held up the bag.

"Welkum. But I'm *not* going back to PJ's." He moved aside as she climbed the porch steps.

Darius came outside and held the door open for Abigail. He greeted his niece before shutting the door behind her. "You got the parts?" he asked Sam.

"Jah. I'll leave them in the barn, then take the truck back to Viktor's."

Darius glanced up at the sky. "Best hurry. You can spend the nacht with us, if you'd like, since Viktor's haus is in the opposite direction from yours, and you'd pass by here on your way home."

That would save Sam a couple of miles' walking in this weather. He shivered as some ice pellets trickled between his shirt and back. Of all the days to leave his coat at home. "Danki."

Darius nodded. "Just be sure to call the phone shanty and let your daed know. I'll go inform my frau."

Sam unloaded the box of auto parts from the bed of the truck, then returned the vehicle to his cousin's haus before starting the trek back to Darius's. The sleet showed no mercy as it bit his face. At least he didn't have to walk an extra mile on this skating rink. On the way, he called the phone shanty near his parents' and left a message.

When the Zooks' haus came into view, Sam saw Darius standing in the open barn doorway.

"Glad you're back," Darius said as Sam neared the barn. "I need you to hold the flashlight." The older man wiped his grease-stained hands on a rag and glanced at the sky. "I think this storm is going to be worse than predicted."

Sam nodded. "Roads are bad. My cousin offered to let me stay at his place, but…." Sam shrugged and glanced toward the haus. Abigail was here, not at the Petersheims'.

Darius chuckled. "Jah. I know."

"Didn't want you to worry—" Sam's phone buzzed then. He was thankful for the interruption, though he would have preferred the text to be from someone other than PJ. He read her message as he entered the dim interior of the barn, following Darius toward his broken-down car.

Where r u?

He tapped "Reply." **Not coming 2nite.**

Her response came immediately: **Then we're thru.**

She'd done that before. Her way or the highway.

At first, he'd thought it was just an Englisch thing. And he'd resigned himself to getting used to it, since he'd been planning to jump the fence. He'd figured it was worth it. After all, PJ was verboden and exciting, and….

And, well, she could kiss.

Stupid reason to stay with a girl.

Besides, not all Englischers were rude.

Sam didn't want to break up with PJ via text message. It just seemed wrong. But there really wasn't any point in trying to smooth things over now, just to break up with her later. He shouldn't put off what needed to be done.

K. We're thru. Bye.

He still hated doing it this way. But PJ had technically initiated the breakup, by expecting him to endanger himself to get to her haus. Demanding he accept her decree. Bend to her whim.

Jerk.

Sam did feel like a world-class jerk, and not only because he'd ended the relationship by text message instead of in person. It was just another addition to a lifetime of poor choices, right after deciding to get back together with a heartless girl because she could kiss.

He would try not to be such a jerk in the future.

Sam deleted PJ from his contacts list, then turned off his phone and tucked it into his pocket. He wasn't on call with the fire station, Daed had been notified of his whereabouts, and he had the whole evening ahead of him—an evening to spend with another exciting girl.

One who could probably kiss. But that would be a discovery for another day.

And nein interruptions. Not to-nacht.

⌒

Abigail took her shoes and outerwear upstairs to her room, then retrieved some fresh sheets and towels from the linen closet to make up the spare room for Sammy. He would be sleeping right next door to her, and she wasn't sure how she felt about that. There was a flutter of something—excitement?—when she envisioned his head on the pillow just on the other side of the thin wall separating them. Would she be able to hear him snoring? Would he notice every time her bed creaked?

If only the other extra room—the one down the hall—had a bed. Abigail peeked inside. Aenti Ruth's foot-pedal sewing machine sat against the wall under one window. On the long table in the middle of the room was a pattern for some new dresses for Abigail. The one she'd worn here wasn't quite the right length for the local Ordnung, the color not the right shade. Her kapp was the wrong style, too. Not that she minded an excuse to have a new wardrobe made. She would've needed clothes, anyway, since she'd been put on the bus with nothing. Her stepdaed had said her dresses would be needed for her stepsisters. And Aenti Ruth had let her pick out the fabric, since the only clothes she had to wear were strangers' hand-me-downs.

Under the other window sat Onkel Darius's rolltop desk with his ledgers, checks, and bookkeeping records for the dairy farm. His reading glasses lay beside his black pen.

An old recliner was situated between the desk and the sewing machine. Sammy could sleep there, but Aenti Ruth would overrule that idea, since there was a bed available in the other spare room.

Abigail frowned. There was nein hope for it: She and Sammy would be sleeping about a foot apart. That would've thrilled her beyond measure if Mark's room had been next to hers.

Maybe she could move the bed. She went back down the hall and into the spare room. Jah, she would rearrange the furniture in short order.

She set the stack of fresh linens on a chair, then eyed the old-fashioned bed with the high wooden headboard and footboard and the big, heavy antique mattress covered in a Glacier Star quilt of red, white, and black. She gave the bed a shove.

It didn't budge. Not even half a centimeter.

She moved to the foot of the bed and yanked. Her injured knee threatened to give.

But not the bed.

Was it bolted to the floor? If so, she didn't want to consider the possible reasons why. Her face heated.

Nothing to do but make up the bed.

As soon as she finished, she went back downstairs and found Aenti Ruth searching the pantry.

"What do you think about pizza? Buwe like pizza, don't they?" Aenti Ruth selected a jar of pizza sauce, a can of mushrooms, and a tin of anchovies.

Ewww. Abigail shuddered. She could pick those things off her slices. "Sounds gut."

"Then that's settled." Aenti Ruth nodded. "I have pepperoni and ground venison, too. After we make the pizza, I'll get the checkerboard out, and you and Sammy can play."

It was as if her aenti thought Sammy was coming courting.

An involuntary thrill worked through Abigail at the prospect.

"Or maybe Scrabble. Then Darius and I can play, too." Aenti Ruth glanced out the window and scowled. "That is, if we can get those two out of the shed. As soon as Sammy left to return that big ole truck, Darius headed out there to work on Sammy's car. *Men.* Like there's nothing else to do around here."

That explained why it was so quiet in the haus.

Abigail was relieved that Sammy hadn't gone back to PJ's. Was it solely because of the weather? She hoped not. Considering the way PJ treated him, it seemed something was terribly wrong with their relationship.

Not Abigail's business.

Besides, who was she to judge? It wasn't like her relationship with Mark was wunderbaar.

Abigail dared to relax. As long as Sammy was engaged in repairing his vehicle, he wouldn't be pestering her, teasing her, and wreaking havoc on her emotions.

He'd be fine-tuning his engine, not messing with her heart. Flirting with her affections.

Whatever. For now, she could breathe without worry.

She took the cans Aenti Ruth handed her and headed into the kitchen. Seconds later, the door opened, and Onkel Darius came inside carrying an armful of logs for the wood-burning stove.

Sammy entered after him and winked at Abigail. "I'm all yours."

Her stomach flipped. She struggled for a nonchalant response. Or, even better, something snarky. But what came out was, "We need to move the bed."

Chapter 8

Darius tossed in a piece of wood into the stove, causing the fire to hiss with a volley of flying sparks. "Move what bed? Where? And why?" He stepped back and grabbed the poker to prod the split log into place.

Ruthie dropped the iron skillet on the woodstove with a thud. "Abigail?"

Abigail's cheeks turned an alarming shade of red. "I...I wanted to rearrange the room." She bunched the fabric of her apron in her hands. "The beds are, um, too close together," she whispered.

"Beds? What beds?" Darius shut the stove door with a bang. "There's only one in that room."

Ruthie laughed. "There'll be a wall between you." She patted Abigail on the shoulder. "Don't worry so much. You'll be fine."

Sam's imagination sprang to life at the realization of the proximity he'd have with Abigail. Excitement filled him. And Abigail must have felt some of the same thrill, to become so red in the face as she brought it up.

"But...but...." She freed her fingers from her apron and motioned to Sam, as if he were the sole cause of her distress. "Never mind." She let her hands drop, along with her gaze.

Wait. Distress instead of temptation? Sam felt a twinge of disappointment. What had he done to make her so wary of him?

"I'm going down to the root cellar for some vegetables," Ruthie said to Abigail. "If you'll get the venison browning, I'll be right back."

Darius shook his head and strode out of the room, muttering something about women, beds, and courting boards. Sam didn't catch exactly what he said, but it didn't matter.

What did matter was Abigail's apparent fear. Sam reached out to lift her chin with his finger, and she shied away from him like a spooked horse.

Since she'd witnessed PJ's seductive come-ons and insinuations, Sam could guess at Abigail's concerns. She probably thought he wrestled with raging male hormones. Okay, so maybe he did. But, two separate rooms with chaperones? "Don't worry," he assured her. "It'll be fine."

Her eyes flashed with unvoiced thoughts he couldn't decipher.

He swallowed. Glanced out the window at the darkening sky. Ice pellets still pinged against the glass. He looked back at Abigail. "Would it make you more comfortable if I left?"

He saw the affirmation in her expression, but she firmed her shoulders and shook her head. "It'll be fine, just like you said."

"I'll go." He stepped back. "I don't want to cause you discomfort."

Ruthie came back upstairs. "Don't be silly, Abigail. Sammy's a gut bu. You'll be perfectly safe. Sammy, you've already called your daed, and there's quite an accumulation of ice. You're staying put for the nacht. Besides, I'm looking forward to beating you at Scrabble."

Sam laughed. "You probably will. Daed told me you won all the spelling bees when the two of you were in school together."

"And you, with your fancy GED and college education," Ruthie teased.

Abigail edged toward the stove during the exchange, probably preparing to brown the venison. But then she continued into the other room. A stair creaked.

"She'll adjust," Ruthie said.

Sam sighed. "She shouldn't have to."

Ruthie laughed. "You probably flirted with her too much, ain't so? Made her a wee bit uncomfortable? I don't see how that's a problem, being that her mamm wants her to find someone new. You're a gut choice. And it'd ease your mamm's worries about you dating an Englisch girl."

Sam shifted. "Jah, it would. PJ and I just broke up, in fact."

If he ever ran into PJ again, she'd probably call the whole thing a big misunderstanding and want to get back together. But he was through with her. Done. Finished. Mamm didn't have to worry anymore.

"Why did Abigail's mamm and stepdaed want to separate her and her beau?"

Ruthie shook her head. "There are stories. Rumors, mind you. But I'm not one to gossip." She turned away.

Jah, right. But that meant the conversation was over, and Sam wouldn't hear the reasons from Ruthie. He would probably never know, since Abigail herself didn't even seem to have an explanation.

"Get out of my kitchen and go sit with Darius." Ruthie made a shooing motion with her hand. "Oh, before you go—do you sauté the onions and peppers before you put them on the pizza? How do you make pizza crust, anyway? I guess with biscuit dough. Or is it more like a pie?"

Sam paused on his way out of the room. "You're asking me? What's 'sauté,' anyway?"

Ruthie huffed. "You go tell Abigail that if she wants you to have pizza, she'd best get down here and help. I'll brown the meat. I know to do that much."

"Uh...sure." Sam veered toward the staircase and headed up. He peeked in the open door of the first bedroom.

Abigail was flopped across the bed, her face buried in a pillow.

Sam stopped in the doorway, and his gaze traveled the length of her body. He focused on the curve of her neck. The strands of golden-brown hair that'd escaped from her kapp. He wanted to get to know her. What was she really like? What were her interests? Her past?

She sniffled.

What had happened today to put out her fire? Was it the encounter with PJ? Talking to him about the barn burning? Being forced to write her mamm? The stress of all those things combined?

He didn't like it.

He needed to ignite a spark of another sort.

Sam leaned against the doorframe. "Hey, feuerzeug."

◦◦◦

Abigail rolled over and sat up. "Stop calling me that. Please. What are you doing up here?" She wiped her eyes and shot to her feet, her cheeks burning.

"Ruthie said to tell you if you want pizza, you need to kum down and help. Something about salting the onions and peppers."

Abigail blinked. "What?"

"Ask her." Sammy shrugged one shoulder. "So, what's wrong with the bed? It looks fine to me."

She glanced down. "It's okay. It's just that…well, my pillow is here. And your pillow is right on the other side of the wall. And…."

He chuckled. "Afraid I'll hear you snoring, Abby?"

She stiffened. "Nein. Afraid I'll hear you."

Sammy pushed away from the doorframe and lowered his gaze to her lips for a second, then met her eyes. "Or is it something more?"

Her heart rate increased. "Like what? I don't have any idea what you're talking about." She tried to look away. Tried. She couldn't tear her focus from his broad shoulders.

"Really, Abigail?" He drew her name out in a caress and made a tiny move, as if he wanted to step closer. But he didn't. There was a hint of mischief in his eyes. "Because I'm thinking that maybe—"

"Maybe you shouldn't think." Abigail pushed past him and started down the stairs. She tried to will her pulse back under control, but it wouldn't cooperate. This—being alone with Sammy—it wouldn't work.

But, ach, she wanted it to.

His chuckle sounded behind her. Too close.

"PJ and I broke up."

Her breath caught, and she missed a step. Started to pitch forward.

Sammy's strong arms wrapped around her waist and yanked her against his firm chest. His breath tickled her neck. "Easy there, Abigail." Her name was still a caress.

How *did* he do that?

He chuckled again. "I knew it was only a matter of time before you ended up in my arms."

Suddenly aware of where Sammy's arms were grasping her, she felt her cheeks burn with embarrassment. "Put me down, please." Her voice came out as a hoarse whisper.

He released an exaggerated sigh, then slowly lowered her until her feet rested on the step below. "Easy now, feuerzeug." He cleared his throat as he moved his hands away.

Her knees buckled. She reached for the banister.

His hand closed on her shoulder, firm and strong. Keeping her from falling again.

Sparks skittered through her. She wanted to turn into his arms. Wanted....

Nein! She turned to face him. "You're telling me to take it easy? You must be a professional flirt. I was with you and PJ this afternoon. When did you break up? Was it when you walked her to the door? If so, that was the *friendliest* breakup I've ever seen."

He shook his head. "Not then. In your onkel's barn. By text message. Long overdue, I might add."

Abigail stared at him. "You broke up with her by text message? Really? That was low." But maybe it was preferable to whispering a vague "Trust me, it's better this way."

"She broke up with me, I think. I guess I'm not sure who broke up with whom, but I'm pretty sure it was mutual. I planned to do it in person."

There was nein pain in his voice. Nein regret, either. Just...relief.

Should she say she was sorry? She searched his expression, but she didn't see any signs of suffering. Still, it was the polite thing to do. "I'm sorry."

His smile was crooked. "I'm not."

She frowned. "Why are you telling me? I have a boyfriend, remember?" Wait. Did she? Hurt slithered through her at the memory of Mark's words, and the look in his eyes.

Sammy's hand left her shoulder. She instantly missed his touch.

"Because I think I like you." There was something vulnerable in his expression.

"Trust me, you don't." She pivoted and marched the rest of the way down the stairs.

But she wanted him to.

⸞

"Jah, I think I do," Sam whispered to himself.

Spending the nacht here was probably a bad decision all around, but Sam looked forward to an evening of banter with Abigail. Of getting to know her better. Of possibly beating her at Scrabble, even if he ultimately lost to Ruthie.

And he was free to enjoy it all without guilt. The breakup with PJ had lifted a weight from his shoulders, a burden whose heaviness he hadn't even realized till now. He could truthfully tell Mamm he wasn't courting an Englisch girl. But he would make sure she understood that he wasn't courting Abigail, either.

Yet.

Even though he wanted to jump into this new relationship with both feet, and with arms wide open, he would be wise to take things slow. To make sure he wasn't on the rebound. To give Abigail time to accept that her relationship with Mark was over.

They needed to become friends, first and foremost.

And then…then, if der Herr willed…maybe more.

Sam smiled. Warmth filled his heart.

Followed by guilt.

If der Herr willed…. The expression implied that he put Gott first. He didn't. He wanted to, but it was easier putting himself first. Following his own preference. Perhaps that sign from Gott he'd looked for earlier was meant to help him get his priorities back in order.

"You gonna stand there all nacht, bu?" Darius's voice intruded on his thoughts.

Sam jerked out of his musings and focused his gaze on the man standing at the bottom of the stairs with a rectangular box in his hands.

"Uh...."

"Ruthie suggested you and I play a game of checkers while she and Abigail fix supper. But you're acting rather befuddled. A maidal can do that to a bu—mess with his mind. And I need to finish chores and close up the barn for the nacht."

"I'll help you." The frigid air might clear Sam's head. He'd need his wits about him this evening, for sure, as he dealt with newfound freedom, an intriguing girl, and her onkel—a man who saw entirely too much.

In fact, he probably should spend time in prayer, asking Gott first for forgiveness, and then for guidance.

And he would. But maybe he should also talk with his brother-in-law, David Lapp. He was a preacher. Surely, he'd have wisdom to offer about PJ, their sinful relationship and recent breakup, and Sam's unexpected feelings for a girl he barely knew.

Or maybe Sam should wait and talk to Daed.

He went downstairs and followed Darius into the kitchen, where Ruthie sliced onions on a wooden cutting board, while Abigail kneaded a floury mixture on the counter. Sam forced his gaze away from the motions of her body.

Darius put on his work boots. "We're going out to finish the chores."

Sam laced up his tennis shoes and headed out the door. His breath steamed in the cold air.

"What about a coat?" Darius called.

"Left it at home this morgen. I'll be fine." Sam strode down the steps.

Darius chuckled and muttered something Sam didn't catch, but Ruthie laughed.

I'll be fine. Spoken too soon. His arms made pinwheels as his feet threatened to slide out from under him. But he regained his balance, then continued toward the barn at a slower, more careful pace.

Lord Gott.... Sam blew out another breath that steamed in the cold air. *I don't know where to start or how to pray. I'm so sorry for... for everything.* Gott knew, didn't He? *Danki for freeing me from PJ.* A text-message breakup was legitimate, ain't so? But they'd broken up before. And gotten back together. A sense of doubt niggled at him. *Help me to be strong and to wait patiently for You to guide me in the direction You want me to go. I've followed my own path for too long and gotten into too much trouble as a result, and I'm sorry. Help me to seek You first.*

And, Lord...about Abigail...help me not to plunge headlong into a new relationship but to put You first. Not me and my desires but Yours alone, Lord Gott.

Sam didn't want to play the fool.

Not anymore.

Never again.

Chapter 9

Abigail's cheeks still felt flushed due to her onkel's muttered comment. *"That bu is twitterpated."*

Twitterpated!

Did he mean "infatuated"? Or "characterized by nervous excitement"?

Essentially the same thing. Right?

Abigail had watched the movie *Bambi* with some Englisch friends back in Ohio. Evidently her aenti and onkel had seen it, too. This surprised her.

If only she hadn't been sent away. If only Mark hadn't kissed her as he had, alerting his daed to what was going on between the two of them.

If only....

But there was something different about Sammy. Something that filled her with a sense of nervous excitement when she was around him. Something that made her aware of his every move.

Maybe she was twitterpated, too.

Nein. It was a simple case of the new girl meeting a handsome man. One who made her heart do cartwheels and her stomach flip.

Twitterpated. Jah.

Her hands shook as she set the dough aside and covered it with a clean towel to let it rise. She didn't kum here to find a new romance. She came because she was forced.

Another sigh.

Mamm didn't even want her.

Aenti Ruth finished chopping the onions and started cleaning a green bell pepper. "Did you write home, like I asked?" She seemed to have read Abigail's mind.

"Jah. Told Mamm I arrived safely, had nein news, and would write again sometime. I mailed the letter in town."

"Gut. I know she would've been worried not to hear from you."

Right. Abigail shrugged. "I'm sure she hasn't given me a thought. She has four new stepdochters and two new stepsohns. The big family she always wanted." Bitterness clogged her throat. She went to get a can opener.

"You stop with the 'poor me' attitude right now, Abigail Susanne. Your mamm loves you and wants the best for you. That's the reason she sent you here. Because you needed to get away from that bu and find a new love."

Abigail froze. She slowly turned. "What do you mean?" Maybe there would finally be an explanation—a gut one—to help ease her hurt.

"There are things you don't know. Things you don't need to know."

Aenti Ruth knew and wouldn't tell her? Abigail drew in a shuddery breath.

"Sometimes, you just need to trust. You know the Gut Book says in Second Corinthians, *'For we walk by faith, not by sight.'*" Aenti Ruth scraped out the seeds from inside the pepper. "Of course, you have to live by faith, too. So, you need to trust that this is what's best for you. That's all."

Abigail frowned. "'This' is worthy of a sermonette but not an explanation?"

"Someday, you'll understand, and then you'll thank your mamm," Aenti Ruth stated calmly.

It made nein sense.

"How will I understand if nobody will explain?"

Sam followed Darius into the kitchen, where they were greeted by the tempting aromas of fresh-baked dough and melted cheese. Two rectangular baking sheets of pizza—one pepperoni, one ground venison—were positioned at the ends of the table, which was set with four square plastic plates in assorted colors: bright pink, sunshine yellow, lime green, and turquoise blue. Mismatched, like the plates at home, since the haus fire had destroyed the dinnerware and everything else about a year and a half ago. In the center was a bowl of tossed salad: lettuce, grated carrots, diced celery, and shredded purple cabbage.

Sam's stomach rumbled.

Ruthie poked her head through a doorway. "Dinner's ready. Wash up, and we'll be right there."

A thump sounded upstairs, and Ruthie disappeared again.

Sam glanced at Darius. The older man calmly removed his hat and coat, then hung them on a wall peg. Next, he took off his boots. Sam followed suit, lining up his tennis shoes and tucking the laces neatly inside. As Sam stood, he heard another thump. Darius didn't react to the noise but headed to the sink and started washing up. After a moment's hesitation, Sam headed for the room Ruthie had disappeared into.

Nobody was there. A third thud sounded directly overhead. Sam went upstairs. He peeked in the first bedroom—Abigail's. Vacant. He moved to the next doorway. Abigail and Ruthie were shoving a dresser against the wall.

Sam cleared his throat. "Why didn't you ask for help?"

Abigail swiped a hand across her forehead, leaving a trail of dust just below her hairline. "We handled it just fine, danki."

Ruthie grabbed a broom and began sweeping the floor.

Sam looked around. "Is there anything else I can do to help?"

"Nein, we're gut." Abigail tugged the quilt taut to smooth a wrinkle.

"Go wash up for supper," Ruthie told him as she swept several dust bunnies into a dustpan.

Sam stepped aside. "After you."

Ruthie shook her head. "You head on down. We're going to wash up first, but we'll be down in a minute." She left the room and headed down the hall, probably to the bathroom. Sam heard a door close.

He glanced at Abigail, but she'd turned her back to him and was staring out the window into the darkness. The ice was still coming down.

He made a move toward her, but when she stiffened, he thought better of it. She must be watching his reflection in the window. *Okay, then.* He would respect her boundaries, physical and emotional. He headed for the stairs.

⌒

Abigail breathed a sigh of relief when Sammy left the room. The top step creaked as he started downstairs. She waited a minute or two, then turned away from the window. She heard the bathroom door open down the hall, and then the top step creaked again. Aenti Ruth must be on her way to the kitchen.

Or had Sammy changed his mind and decided to kum back to tease her? Abigail froze. She wasn't in the mood to take his taunts and provocations tonight.

She'd managed to stand her ground that morgen, but about the time she'd started stressing over the locations of their beds, her courage had left her. She *couldn't* be attracted to him.

Well, she could be. He was a handsome man. But his gut looks were tempered by his personality, which she couldn't figure out. The man who'd caught her at the barn when the fire began seemed a different man from the one who'd cared for her afterward. And he behaved differently around PJ than he did around her.

Who was he, really?

It'd be fun to find out.

Or maybe she should run in the opposite direction. Home, to Mark. But then, Mark's parting words to her replayed in her mind. *"Trust me, it's better this way. Don't write me. I won't respond."*

How could he say those things? What had his daed told him that made him so willing to abandon her at the bus station? Considering they'd been planning to marry, didn't she deserve some answers? Some closure?

It seemed not.

She shook her head, forcing her thoughts off him and their failed relationship in order to refocus on the present.

She hadn't heard any other sounds in the hall, so she tiptoed to the door and peeked out. The landing area was empty. She went to the bathroom and washed up, then hurried downstairs and into the kitchen. Onkel Darius and Sammy were already seated at the table. Sammy's head was bowed, presumably in prayer. Aenti Ruth was setting cloth napkins made from scrap material at every place.

Abigail assumed her place as Aenti Ruth slid into her own seat. They both bowed their heads. But Abigail didn't close her eyes. Instead, she stared down at her fisted hands.

Maybe she should write Mark. Surely, he didn't mean what he said.

Or should she let it go, as Aenti Ruth had suggested? Trust that Gott had her life in His hands?

She picked at the hem of her apron. "It's the will of der Herr" seemed too trite a consolation. What did that mean, anyway? That she should sit back and let life happen to her because she had nein control? Did Gott manipulate people in the same way Abigail used to play with her dolls when she was young?

She could imagine His line of reasoning. *Let's take Abigail away from her home and family and send her off to another state, a new community, and have her start over from scratch. Nein friends. Only an aenti and an onkel for family. Nein boyfriend. Nein job.*

Abigail didn't think very much of this Gott right now.

"Amen," said Onkel Darius.

"Amen," Sammy parroted.

Abigail started to raise her head as the pizza was being served, but she felt a stab of guilt for failing to pray. She quickly lowered her gaze. *Danki for this meal. Amen.* She looked up again.

Onkel Darius arranged three anchovies on his slice of pizza, then passed the bowl to Sammy, who eyed it warily. "What's this?"

"Anchovies," said Aenti Ruth. "My friend says they are a must for pizza, and they can be added after baking. When I learned that Abigail was coming to live with us, I wanted to make sure I had a wide variety of appealing foods for her to choose from."

Hold it. Aenti Ruth had known in advance that she was coming? How could that be, when Abigail herself hadn't found out until they'd left her at the bus station?

Nein. There had to be some misunderstanding. Otherwise, the obvious implication was that her abandonment was premeditated. Planned. Plotted. Prearranged. And Mamm *had* to have been in on it. Her being sent away wasn't because Mark's daed had caught them kissing, but because of something else. And Mamm hadn't seen fit to warn her. She'd just written to Aenti Ruth—a woman Abigail hadn't known existed—and made the arrangements.

Through tear-blurred eyes, Abigail watched Sammy pick up an anchovy. It dangled limply from his fingers for a moment. Then he put it on his piece of pizza. "So, Abby, you like anchovies?" He met her gaze, his eyes narrowing with concern as he studied her expression.

She shook her head and blinked her tears away. "I've never had them before, but they look...um...interesting." *In a disgusting sort of way.*

Stop with the "poor me" thing, Aenti Ruth had said. Well, right now, Abigail was feeling entitled to indulge in a little self-pity. Mamm obviously didn't want her. Mark didn't love her enough to fight for her.

They weren't worth crying over. Not now, at least. Abigail would cry later. When nobody would see or hear. She wouldn't let anyone kick her when she was down.

She squared her shoulders.

A second later, she noticed Sammy staring at her with worried eyes.

She gave him the steadiest grin she could muster.

She was stronger than she thought. She could do this.

But Sammy's sympathetic gaze didn't waver. After a long moment, he picked up another anchovy, then reached over the table and put the dangly thing on her plate.

"Here you go, feuerzeug. We'll brave these waters together."

Chapter 10

Later that nacht, Sam stood outside Abigail's closed door. The haus had been quiet for about an hour, but he couldn't relax enough to fall asleep. He was bothered by the personality shift he'd witnessed in Abigail. She seemed to have done a complete turn-around from the girl who'd argued with him in the schoolhaus. The girl who'd told him off at McDonald's. Even the girl he'd kept from falling down the stairs. He was probably more worried than he should be, all things considered, but he wanted to fix the problem if he could. He didn't know Abigail well enough to expect that she'd want to talk to him, but he had to give it a shot, even if she slammed the door in his face and locked it.

He held up the lantern and glanced at the doorknob. There was a lock. Odd, for an Amish haus. But then, he'd noticed light switches on the walls, too. They didn't work, of course, but this must have been an Englisch haus at one time.

He knocked softly, and quiet footsteps sounded from inside the room. He raised the lantern higher as the door opened a crack. Abigail peeked out, and her eyes widened. "What do you want?"

"Can we talk?" He tried to match her whisper.

She hesitated a moment. "Jah. Just a second." She shut the door. There was a rustling noise, and then the door opened again. She came out wearing a long white nacht-gown mostly covered by a robe. The braided rope of her beautiful golden-brown hair fell over her left shoulder, secured by a pink band. Sam's free hand twitched involuntarily with a sudden urge to finger her tresses, to find out if they felt as soft as they looked. He curled his fingers into a ball to keep himself from touching her.

A girl like her…the effect she had on him was light-years away from the influence of PJ. There were girls guys dated, and girls guys married. Abigail was definitely among the latter.

She shut the door behind her. "Where?"

Sam glanced over the upstairs railing, down at the dark first floor. "Do you think we'd disturb your aent and onkel if we talked in the kitchen?" Then they'd have a table between them. Even though Abigail seemed more the marrying type, Sam was still a red-blooded male.

Abigail frowned. "Maybe the sewing room would be better. The way their whispered conversation carried the other nacht, coming through the floor vents—" She slapped her hand over her mouth and looked toward the open staircase. "Maybe the barn."

He raised his eyebrows and nodded at her bare feet. "Ice is still coming down. You really want to go outside?"

Abigail gave a sheepish grin. "The sewing room it is, then."

Sam went down the hall and into the room. He set the lantern in the middle of the sewing table.

Abigail quietly shut the door behind her, then walked around to the opposite side of the table. *Wise girl.*

She folded her arms over her chest. "What'd you want to talk about?" Her voice shook a little.

He hesitated. When he'd gone to her room in his tired but sleepless state, it made perfect sense: He would simply ask her what was wrong, she would tell him, and he would fix it. End of story. But now, with her standing before him, and the lantern's glow casting shadows all around….

Maybe he should pretend she was his sister. He could tease her to the point where she became so upset, it prompted a verbal spill. Then he would fix the problem. Or, if he couldn't fix it, at least she would feel better after having had her say.

Sam looked down. Abigail wasn't his sister. He clenched and unclenched his fists. "I'm sorry I teased you so much. I didn't mean to upset you."

Abigail blinked. "I would've let you know if you had. I can hold my own."

He scratched his neck. "You seemed a little sad at supper. Depressed, actually. And—"

"You think that it's all about you, don't you? That the only reason I could possibly have for being sad is because of something you did."

Put that way, it did sound rather egotistical. But she'd completely misread his intentions. He opened his mouth, but nein words came to mind. He pressed his lips together again.

"I've got news for you," she went on. "It's *not* all about you."

Waking her to talk had been a bad idea. He hadn't expected to invite an attack. And he still didn't know what to say.

Sam frowned. "I just wanted to help. Wanted to give you a chance to talk. That's all."

"By apologizing for upsetting me? Why not simply ask me what's wrong?"

Could it really be that simple? He raised his eyebrows. "Okay, then. Was ist letz?" He braced himself, in case it did turn out to be all about him. His shameless flirting, maybe. His giving in to Ruthie and Darius's insistence that he stay the nacht, even though Abigail clearly didn't want him there. His…something.

Her pink tongue peeked out as she moistened her lips. His mouth dried, and his heart rate increased. Gut thing there was a table between them.

Abigail pulled out a chair, wincing as the legs scraped against the wood floor. Then she sat down, propped her elbows on the table, rested her chin in her palms, and stared at him. "You're not my best friend."

"Nein…but I'm a gut listener." Well, he could be, if he set his mind to it. He listened to the lectures at school, took notes, and retained enough information to carry A's across the board. Not that his academic success would impress her. "Talk to me, Abby."

She looked away. Lowered one of her hands and traced a figure eight on the table with her fingertip. And stayed silent. But he could imagine the proverbial gears in her head turning. If he got her to open up, he might experience information overload.

He still didn't know what to say, so he pulled the chair away from the pedal sewing machine and sat down across from her. And waited.

"You can't put a bandage on this wound, even if you are an EMT." Her voice was so quiet, he could barely hear it.

Maybe this was about being abandoned at the bus station. Or being forced to break up with her beau, and then having the wound reopened when she learned of his breakup via text message.

She traced a second figure eight. And then a third.

Would it help if Sam shared something about himself? He was hardly an expert at relationships. PJ had always shared whatever was bothering her without requiring the slightest encouragement. If she was mad at him or upset at her mom or angry at the world in general, she ranted. It made her easier to figure out. And he could usually tease her out of her foul mood. When all else failed, engaging in a heavy make-out session usually worked, but it always left him feeling guilty.

Neither of those was an option now.

Sam didn't know what to do, what to say. So, he watched Abigail trace figure eights. Over and over and over.

He wasn't being the comforter he'd imagined.

Well, he could pray. Gott knew Abigail's thoughts. He knew what troubled her.

Sam bowed his head. Closed his eyes. *Lord Gott, I don't know what's wrong. I don't know how to fix it. But You do. Help me to be a friend.*

She needs to hear the words.

Sam's prayer stumbled to a stop. What?

Silence. But he knew what he'd been told.

Now to obey.

Still, he hesitated. Praying out loud was discouraged, as a rule. A man's conversations with Gott were personal. Not public.

He scratched his neck again. Swallowed. Cleared his throat. And reached for Abigail's hand. His fingers brushed hers before settling atop them. She didn't pull away.

Guide my words, please, he prayed silently, then continued out loud: "Lord Gott, please reach out to Abigail and comfort her in the way that You alone can. Help her to know she has friends here who care for her. Heal the hurt that she feels over being forced away from her home, away from her family, away from her beau, and help her to embrace the future that You have for her. We give You all the glory and honor and praise. Amen."

Abigail swiped away a renegade tear. Then another. She hadn't meant—hadn't wanted—to cry. She curled her free hand into a fist, pressing her fingernails into her palm. Relishing the pain. How had Sammy known exactly what to pray? He'd met her just a little over twenty-four hours ago, and already he knew more about her than Miranda had learned in a week.

Abigail had thought Miranda was her friend.

She pressed a hand to her face again, then stood. "Danki."

Sammy watched her, silent.

"I…I can't formulate the words to express what I'm feeling right now. I need time."

Sammy's lips parted. Then his mouth shut. He nodded. Pushed to his feet. "Okay. Whenever. I mean, if you want to talk—"

"It's just…something Aenti Ruth said." Abigail's throat tightened. She wiped her face again, ashamed of her waterworks. Mamm would have called her a big boppli.

Sammy leaned over the table toward her. "What did Ruthie say?"

"That…that Mamm wrote to tell her I was coming. Which means she knew ahead of time. They arranged it all. It wasn't about the kiss. They set it up in advance, and nobody bothered to tell me. And the only thing Mark had to say was, 'Trust me, it's better this way.' What's better? Kicking me out without a warning? Don't I deserve an explanation?"

Sammy blinked. "The kiss? Wait. What kiss?"

She rolled her eyes. "You are such a man."

"Danki." He frowned. "I think."

"They told him why. Not me! I'm the one affected, the one who had to move across the country, the one who had to leave her family and friends, the one who...." She choked, coughed. And turned away, stumbling blindly toward the closed door.

"We knew you were coming for close to a month, I'd say. Ruthie came to talk to Daed about it, to get permission, and...."

She glanced over her shoulder, and a whimper escaped her lips.

"Ouch." Sam cringed. "I didn't mean to say that."

Another tiny moan forced its way out, and she turned to face him fully. "See? Even you knew. You. And I'm the one involved here." She jabbed her finger in his direction, then pressed it to her heart.

"I'm sorry. You need some answers."

"You think?" Her throat threatened to close. She made for the door.

Her hand gripped the knob, but nein matter how hard she tried, she couldn't make it turn. So, she kicked the door as hard as she could. Her bare toes stung. She winced as a fresh round of tears burned her eyes.

Sammy's hand folded around hers. "Easy there, feuerzeug. Calm down, or you're going to hurt yourself and wake your onkel and aenti." He rotated the knob and pulled the door open. Then he released her hand and stepped away.

Abigail looked up at him. Concern and confusion warred in his blue eyes. She swallowed the lump in her throat. "Danki for being a friend."

"Anytime, feuerzeug."

She stood there, forcing herself to breathe. Willing the tears to stop. "I'll get over it, ain't so?"

"Jah, you will." His gaze searched hers. "In time. And maybe Gott has in mind to use this for a better future. It might be part of His plan for you."

"Danki." She rose up on tiptoe, pressed her lips to his cheek, and fled to her room.

⌒

Sam gazed down the hall at Abigail's closed door. He raised his hand and touched the tingly spot she'd kissed. Bristly whiskers poked his fingertips. The same whiskers that had pricked Abigail's soft lips. Funny how a simple peck on his cheek from Abigail meant more to him than the passionate kiss on the lips he'd gotten from PJ earlier that day.

Danki, Gott, for giving me the words to say. More words than he'd expected. Could der Herr use Abigail's hurt for the best? Maybe He had some reason for removing her to Missouri for a while.

Sam picked up the lantern, returned to his room, and quietly closed the door. He probably wouldn't get any sleep to-nacht. His heart ached for Abigail, for the treatment she had endured from her immediate family. Would it do any gut for him to call them and ask for some answers? He grabbed his cell phone from the dresser and pressed the power button.

They probably wouldn't tell him anything. After all, who was he to them? Ruthie wouldn't even satisfy his curiosity when he asked. And she knew him. Loved him. Accepted him as a member of her family, ever since he'd started going out with her oldest dochter, Leah—before the accident that claimed the lives of Leah and her two sisters.

Sam hadn't dated Leah long enough to fall in love with her. He'd started courting her in an attempt to settle down after being involved in a car accident in Pennsylvania—one that had left his best friend dead. Sam and Leah were barely past the beginning stages of their relationship when she died. They'd courted long enough for Ruthie to consider Sam as her future sohn-in-law. Long enough for him to be deeply saddened by Leah's death. He'd dated PJ for a much longer stretch, but his heart wasn't involved. She'd been new and exciting at a time when he was torn, questioning everything he'd been taught, and searching for answers.

He returned the cell phone to the dresser and touched the German Bible lying next to it. Despite all Sam's searching and rebelling, Gott had turned out to be the answer all along. Sam was still learning that truth. Still prone to relying on his own abilities and resources to fix his problems. Still used to doing what he wanted.

And now he wanted to fix Abigail's problems.

He couldn't. Not in his power. But Gott could.

How had this girl managed to tie Sam's insides in knots so quickly?

Muffled sobs came from the adjacent room.

Sam sat on the edge of the bed and stared at the wall separating his room from Abigail's. He wanted to hold her, the way he had earlier. Wanted to comfort her, the only way he knew how.

He didn't have the right.

Chapter 11

When Abigail got up in the morgen, her head felt stuffed with fuzz, as if she'd taken a heavy dose of painkillers. Her throat hurt, and her nose ran. Probably a result of crying herself to sleep last nacht. She stumbled across the hall to the bathroom and splashed water on her face, then peered into the small hand mirror hanging on the wall. Her eyes were red. If only she were allowed to wear makeup, as the Englisch did. Then Aenti Ruth wouldn't know she'd been crying, and Sammy would find her more attractive.

She should have better control of her emotions. Spilling everything to Sammy the way she had, crying like a boppli…. Shame ate at her. What must Sammy think of her?

It was behind her now. She'd mourned, until a strange, unexpected sense of peace washed over her. Which was probably the only reason she'd fallen asleep.

Maybe it meant she would soon be allowed to return home. When she did, she'd give Mamm a piece of her mind.

But, nein. That would be disrespectful. And Abigail had been raised to obey without question.

Would Mark answer her letters if she wrote? He'd said he wouldn't, but he'd also indicated he loved her, though he'd never said the words. If that were true, he would reply, ain't so? How could he blindly accept this arrangement? A twinge of anxiety threatened her sense of peace.

Nein. She wouldn't worry.

Surely, Mamm was missing her help in a haus full of stepkinner. Nein doubt her first letter to Abigail would be filled with apologies and pleas for her to kum home. Then Abigail would forgive them all, and everything would go back to normal. She'd return to her family and friends, resume working at the quilt shop, and prepare to marry Mark.

Though, she would miss her aenti and onkel...and even Sammy, strange as that seemed.

Abigail washed her face once more, pinned up her hair, and secured her kapp. Time to take on the day.

She went back to her room and made the bed, then peered out the window at the shimmering, ice-covered world. The tree beside the haus was coated with frozen rainwater. Beautiful. It would surely be a gut day. She wouldn't think about anything or anyone at home and would just enjoy her first church Sunday in this district.

She went downstairs to help Aenti Ruth with breakfast. The aromas of frying bacon and brewing koffee filled the kitchen. Abigail found Aenti Ruth setting the table with the same plates they'd used the previous evening.

"Ach, Abigail. You're up. Gut morgen. Can you check the oatmeal and see if it's about done? Darius and Sammy will be in soon." She glanced toward the window. If she'd noticed Abigail's bleary eyes, she'd chosen not to say anything. "That is, if they don't get sidetracked by that infernal car. Why some buwe won't be satisfied with a perfectly gut horse and buggy, I'll never know. But Darius was—and still is—the same way. Fascinated with those machines."

Abigail didn't understand the fascination, either. She ran a wooden spoon through the thickened, bubbling oatmeal. "It's ready." She turned the gas down, then picked up a fork and started flipping the bacon slices. "I think these are done, too. Are you cooking eggs?"

Aenti Ruth pursed her lips. "I wasn't sure how Sammy would want them. Fried? Over easy? Scrambled? Poached?" She shrugged. "He's never eaten breakfast here before. Well, other than at the frolics, with everyone else. And I never noticed what he ate, only that his plate was always piled high."

"I'll make scrambled eggs, if that's okay." They were Mark's least favorite. And right now, she didn't want to make anything that he liked. She got out a small mixing bowl and started cracking eggs into it.

Aenti Ruth moved to the window and peeked outside. "Church wasn't canceled, despite the weather. We'll walk over after breakfast. You need to meet the other young people and make some friends, since you're settling here."

Abigail's chest tightened. "Who said I'm settling here?" She knew who, though. What she didn't know was *why*.

Aenti Ruth didn't respond. Other than with pursed lips. And those spoke volumes.

⌒

Sam stomped his too-tight, borrowed work boots on the porch and then followed Darius into the haus. The aroma of bacon made his stomach rumble. He stopped inside the door to hang up his borrowed coat and hat, then took off the boots and lined them up next to his tennis shoes. His toes wiggled in relief. It would be gut to get home later today and take a bath, change clothes....

Hold it. The caravan of buggies coming down the road and pulling into the field next door meant today was church Sunday. He wasn't dressed for church, so he'd need to go home sooner than later. He should've considered that last nacht. He would have to walk home and would miss out on standing with the other single men in the lineup, trying to catch the eye of a certain someone as the maidals filed into the barn.

His gaze shot to Abigail. She'd cried most of the nacht. Without his comfort. He'd wanted to go to her, but he couldn't. Every time he would move toward the door, he would sense Gott saying a firm nein. So, Sam had knelt beside his bed and prayed for Gott to hold her. To love her. To reassure her.

Her eyes were still bloodshot.

Catching someone's notice had never mattered much to him before. After all, he'd grown up with all the local girls. Was somehow related to more than half of them.

But he rather wanted to catch Abigail's eye. At least, until the fascination wore off. It always had in the past. So, this strange attraction was bound to do the same. Eventually.

"Do you have some extra clothes I could borrow for church?" The words were out before Sam could censor them.

Darius stopped, turned around, and tugged at his beard. He scanned Sam from head to toe, eyeing his T-shirt, blue jeans, and belt. "Can't say that I do."

Ruthie studied him, too. "Well, you do have an extra white shirt, Darius. It might be a bit snug around Sammy's shoulders, but too big everywhere else. And you have another pair of suspenders. He'd have to wear them with his jeans, though, because I'm certain you don't wear the same size pants." She shrugged. "Beggars can't be choosers. If Sammy's in church, that should be enough, ain't so?"

Sam shifted. "It's probably better if I go home to shower and change into my own clothes. That way, Daed won't have to field criticism. I'll hurry, though, and try to get back before the lineup."

Darius chuckled. "Don't want another man getting first dibs, for sure." He shook his head. "Twitterpated."

Abigail's face flamed. Sam pretended not to notice, though his neck heated. He headed for the sink and washed up with a bar of homemade soap, then wiped his hands on the rough, line-dried towel. "Hate to run, but—"

"You *are* eating breakfast before you go," Ruthie stated. "If you slip in late to the service, so be it. Your daed and the other preachers will understand. As for Abigail, nobody is going to do any talking to her until afterward, so as long as you are there…."

Abigail cleared her throat. "I *am* right here, you know. And I have a beau—"

"Nein, you don't." Ruthie aimed a hard look at her niece. "And the faster you get that through your head, the better. Sammy is as gut as they kum. Better than most."

"I wouldn't say that," Sam protested. He could think of plenty of men who were better. As well as plenty of reasons why he wasn't what Ruthie claimed.

Abigail stiffened as a look of irritation crossed her face. And the glare she shot at Sam indicated she wouldn't be pushed in his direction.

Which rather hurt. He wanted her to make her own decision, to be sure, but he didn't want her to choose another man as an act of rebellion against Ruthie.

He sighed.

He didn't want an arranged marriage, either.

He wanted to marry for love.

Someday.

Not here. Not now. Not her.

Because, despite the undeniable sparks between them, love was not present. Only attraction.

At least on his part.

What she felt for him was another matter entirely. And right now, he strongly suspected it wasn't attraction.

Although, she *had* given him a kiss….

His heart rate increased at the memory. Of its own volition, his hand rose to touch his cheek. It still tingled.

Sam's gaze caught Abigail's. And held it.

He would do whatever he could to earn another kiss.

⌒

Abigail finished her breakfast, then bowed her head for the after-meal prayer before getting up from the table. She collected her dishes and was about to carry them to the sink when Sammy laid his silverware across his plate and looked up at her. "Ser gut. Danki." His gaze shifted to Aenti Ruth, including her in the thanks. "Scrambled eggs are my favorite." Then he bowed his head for a moment before shooting to his feet. "I'd best go home so I can get ready." He put on his tennis shoes and went out the door, coatless and hatless.

As she finished clearing the table, Abigail peered out the window and watched as Sammy stepped off the porch. He glanced skyward, then brushed something off his cheek, and that's when Abigail noticed the water dripping from the eaves and the tree branches. Was the ice melting already? Apparently the forecast for warmer temperatures he'd mentioned yesterday had been accurate.

She moved to the sink, plunged her hands into the hot, sudsy water Aenti Ruth had prepared, and started washing the dishes, her mind focused on the man who'd just left. He made her think and feel things she'd never experienced with Mark. And his insightful prayer last nacht still touched her heart. She could still recall the prickly sensation on her lips when she'd kissed him.

Behind her, Aenti Ruth wiped the table as she hummed a melody Abigail didn't recognize. It certainly wasn't anything in the Ausbund.

Abigail glanced out the tiny window above the sink and saw Sammy break into a jog as he turned onto the road. Why was she so attracted to him? Or maybe it was just appreciation for his friendship.

Aenti Ruth touched Abigail's arm. "He is a gut man."

"I'm sure he is. He seems to be, anyway." Abigail averted her gaze from the window as Sammy disappeared from sight. "But—"

"But nothing," Aenti Ruth snapped. "Hurry and finish so we can go next door for church." She pivoted on her heel and left the room.

Why wouldn't Aenti Ruth tell her the real reason her family wanted to separate her and Mark? Abigail tried to distract herself by concentrating on finishing the dishes. When she was done, she tossed the pan of soapy rinse water on the dormant rosebush outside, then returned to the kitchen and hung her dishcloth by the sink. The dishes would air-dry, since it was the Lord's Day.

Even though church was being held next door, Onkel Darius hooked up the horse and buggy for the short journey across the slush. He stopped in the circular drive between the buildings so that

Abigail and Aenti Ruth could get out before he went and parked the buggy. Aenti Ruth carried a platter of cold sliced ham into the haus, while Abigail approached the other single girls grouped together next to the barn.

As she came nearer, the buwe standing on the other side of the double doors all stopped talking. After a moment, the girls fell silent, too. Everyone turned to stare at her. One of the buwe whispered something to the bu beside him.

Anyone who'd been around the previous nacht might recognize her. Might've even heard Sammy call her a feuerzeug.

Abigail's stomach hurt. She wanted to shout, "I didn't do it!" But she could imagine how that would go over.

One of the girls, a tall, slender blonde, stepped forward with a welcoming smile. "Hi! You must be Abigail Stutzman. I've heard so much about you. I'm Bethany Weiss. I'm sure we'll be close friends."

Abigail managed a nod, but she didn't trust herself to open her mouth. She forced her lips into an expression that she hoped resembled a smile.

"You can sit by me. I'll introduce you around." Bethany scanned the others standing nearby and rattled off a list of names, none of which registered with Abigail. Then she took Abigail's hand and pulled her forward as Abigail murmured "hallo" in the midst of the other murmured welcomes.

"You'll get to know us, eventually." Bethany held on tight when Abigail attempted to pull away. "Have you met any of the guys yet?"

Abigail started to shake her head, but then she nodded. "Sammy." His name came out as a croak. She cleared her throat. "I don't know his last name. He's a firefighter."

"Sammy Miller, then. I'll introduce you to everyone else after church. It's time to line up to go in now." Bethany maintained her grip on Abigail's hand and held her back as the other girls formed a queue. She leaned closer and whispered, "I always know who's courting whom, but only because I watch everyone closely. My daed's the bishop, so nobody tells me anything. They're afraid I'll run to Daed. I wouldn't, but…." She shrugged.

"So, you knew I was coming to Jamesport." Abigail hoped her voice didn't betray the bitterness she felt.

Bethany nodded. "I've known for about a month. Mid-January, I think I found out. The news of your coming created quite a buzz. We're all excited you're here now, and we can't wait to get to know you." She released Abigail's hand and got into line.

Abigail had never minded the tradition of lining up, because she'd always had someone who paid her special attention. She'd always had Mark. Even at the last service she attended, at home two weeks ago, he'd winked at her. And she caught her usual buggy ride home with him after the singing.

But now…. "'How queer everything is today,'" she murmured. "'And yesterday things went on just as usual.'"

"What?" Bethany turned and stared at her.

"A line from *Alice in Wonderland*." Her face warmed. Way to make an impression, quoting children's literature.

Bethany muttered something, but Abigail didn't catch it because she was startled by the angry sneer of a man standing nearby. He was tall and gut-looking, but when his brown eyes met hers, they narrowed into a glare that seemed to shout hatred.

She shivered.

There was a scuffling at the end of the line, and Abigail glanced back to see Sammy slide into place. He was a carbon copy of all the other men—white shirt; black hat, vest, and pants—except for the mischief in his eye when he met her gaze.

Chapter 12

Sam followed the other single men into the barn and took a seat on the right near the back. The women had already gathered on the left. He scanned the room for Abigail and found her sitting between his cousin Gizelle and Bethany Weiss. Bethany's golden head and Gizelle's strawberry blonde one were angled toward Abigail's darker honey, as if one of them—probably Bethany—were whispering something, and the others were straining to listen. Bethany Weiss could talk the ears off a stalk of corn.

"You doin' okay?"

Sam glanced to the side and met the gaze of his close friend Caleb Bontrager. "After the fire, you mean? Jah. Not much I can do about it now, anyway. Worked on my car yesterday. A never-ending job, it seems."

Caleb chuckled. "Get a horse. Much more trustworthy."

Sam grinned. "But not near as much fun." He shifted slightly and saw the preachers making their way into the barn through a door at the front. He blew out a puff of air and tried to prepare himself mentally for the long service ahead.

Sam's brother-in-law, David, was the first preacher in the lineup. As David reached the front and turned to take his seat, his dark eyes scanned the group gathered in the barn. He usually spoke in Englisch if there were visitors at the service, even if those visitors were Amish, since the German dialect varied from community to community.

David's gaze lingered on the area where Abigail was seated. He'd probably identified her as someone unfamiliar. Or maybe he'd noticed the bishop's dochter whispering at a time when everyone was supposed to be quiet.

The service began with the opening hymn…every verse of it. And not just three or four, like in the Englisch hymnals, but dozens. Today, with Sam itching to get out of the dusty barn, off the uncomfortable backless bench, and into the fresh air and sunshine, the time would crawl by. A picnic lunch by the pond with Abigail would be nice, but after a day of freezing rain and ice, it was still much too cold and muddy. Some other day, maybe.

Of course, a one-on-one picnic would indicate that they were courting.

Sam released a long sigh and listened to the rise and fall of the voices around him. He started to join in, but his voice broke—an aftereffect of having a breathing tube stuffed down his throat following that car accident a year ago. He'd expected to be healed by now. A couple of other men glanced his way, not bothering to hide their derisive grins. Definitely not a gut singing day. But then, it never was—the reason he usually remained silent during the hymns. The same reason he'd stopped going to singings altogether after Leah's death.

He sighed again. He wouldn't embarrass himself by going to the singing to-nacht, either. Especially since Ruthie and Darius would want Abigail to attend, and Sam didn't want to make a fool of himself in front of her.

On the other hand, if he went to the singing, he might be able to drive Abigail home—taking the long way, since she lived next door to the farm where the singing would be held. They would have an opportunity to talk. To get to know each other better.

The sudden silence was deafening. Sam shook himself from his thoughts and forced his attention to the front of the barn.

David stood behind the makeshift pulpit. "If you have your Bible and want to turn with me to John one, verse twenty-nine…." Around the barn, pages rustled. David picked up his own Bible and began reading aloud. "*The next day John seeth Jesus coming unto him, and saith, Behold the Lamb of God, which taketh away the sin of the world.'*" He paused and looked around the room. "What is sin?"

Sam resisted the urge to roll his eyes. *Not another sermon about how important it is to remain separate from the world.* He expected more from his brother-in-law, who usually preached messages that reached deep into Sam's heart.

"Sin is a debt. It is an expression of enmity, and it is depicted as a crime."

David had gone for the jugular. Not exactly a cut-and-dried sermon, after all.

Beside Sam, Caleb squirmed on the backless bench.

"Sin is a debt we owe but can never pay to a God who is under no obligation to offer us terms to pay it back—even if we could. Sin is enmity. We, of our own choosing, have lashed out against our Creator, disregarding His authority, kindness, and mercy. And we all are criminals guilty of breaking God's law. God deserves justice, just as we would if someone committed a crime against us."

Sam's gaze shot to Abigail. She glanced over her shoulder, and when her gaze rested on him, he cringed. Jah, he wanted justice. He wanted the person who'd started the fire in his family's barn to pay. Big time.

David picked up his open Bible and stepped out from behind the pulpit. "Let me paraphrase John one, verse twenty-nine, so we can better understand what Jesus has done for us. 'Look! The Lamb of God, who has paid our unpayable debt, who comes and brings peace between enemies, and who, though innocent, was condemned and punished as guilty for crimes He didn't commit!'"

Anguish flooded Sam. He leaned forward, balancing his elbows on his knees and resting his chin in his palms. All his deeds…all his thoughts…all his crimes…. His eyes burned with tears of conviction. *Jesus, danki for what You've done for me. I'm so sorry for everything.*

As the service ended, Abigail stood and arched her back, trying to stretch the taut muscles. Her right knee throbbed, probably due to her having spent hours on end in the same position. And probably due in part to the bad weather yesterday.

As she hastened to the haus, the bishop's dochter chattered next to her all the way, explaining how the food line worked and who usually brought what. But Abigail tuned her out. The names meant nothing to Abigail. She already knew about church Sunday dinners. The details of that tradition didn't differ too drastically from one district to another. Besides, she didn't need to get to know everyone here. She planned to go home, nein matter what Aenti Ruth said.

Abigail picked up two pies from the kitchen counter—one apple, one chocolate cream—and carried them out to the front porch. Against her will, her attention darted to Sammy, who stood talking with a group of buwe.

Sammy seemed to sense her eyes on him. He glanced up, his gaze landing on her. A smile curved his lips.

Abigail's face heated, and she looked away. Her traitorous knee buckled as she stepped down onto the first stair. She bit back a cry at the sharp pain that shot through her leg, and with the hand holding the apple pie, she attempted to grab the railing. Except that there wasn't any railing. She tumbled the rest of the way down the stairs and landed in a puddle of cold slush. Her breath exited her lungs with a whoosh. At least she'd caught herself before doing a face-plant in the gooey mess. A belly flop was bad enough.

The chocolate cream pie had exploded all over, and the impact of her fall had sent muddy water spouting everywhere. On her lips was a mixture of whipped cream, chocolate filling, and soil. *Yuck*. On the ground next to her sat the apple pie. It had somehow remained intact, but it was soggy from being splashed. Burning with embarrassment, Abigail struggled to a sitting position and rubbed her knee, wishing she'd wrapped it instead of allowing her pride to get in the way. A slight limp would've been better than this shame.

An older woman stooped and picked up the ruined pies. She hesitated a moment and studied Abigail with pursed lips, her gaze skimming her face, then traveling downward to the mud-covered dress Abigail had borrowed from Aenti Ruth. "I'll tell Orpah." The woman stood, hurried up the stairs, and went inside.

Who was Orpah? And why did she need to know what had happened? Abigail blinked back her tears. Hadn't she cried enough last nacht?

Sammy crouched by her side and touched her hand. "Are you okay? Overdid it yesterday, ain't so? You need to get checked out."

"Nein, I'll be fine," she insisted. "I...I just need to rest. I didn't bother wrapping my knee this morgen."

Onkel Darius strode over to them. "I'll get the buggy and take her home," he told Sammy. "You can check out her knee there. We don't need everybody seeing beneath her dress."

"*Nobody* is going to see beneath my dress." Abigail struggled to stand. Failed. Her knee refused to cooperate.

Sammy straightened. "She needs to go to the ER."

Onkel Darius frowned. "You haven't even looked at it. Get Ruthie. I'll be right back." Then he started for the field where the buggies were parked.

Sammy eyed Abigail for a second. Then he bent without a word and slid one arm under her knees. Tucked the other arm around her back. And hoisted her up.

Abigail's breath caught, and her heart pounded into a gallop, as he cradled her against his firm chest. She wrapped an arm around his neck...and then he lowered her to the porch floor at the top of the stairs. At least she was off to the side, so the women could walk past her easily as they carried the food outside.

Sammy's fingers brushed against her cheek as he pulled away. "Stay here, feuerzeug. I'm going to get Ruthie." Abigail shivered as he climbed past her and went into the haus.

What a way to make an impression. Her first church Sunday in this community, and she had to fall down some stairs and make a fool of herself. Her stomach churned. She looked at her filthy hands. At her borrowed dress, soaked with muddy water. At the smears of chocolate and splatters of whipped cream competing for space on the fabric. As if all that wasn't bad enough, her right knee throbbed hard enough to make her vision blur. She tugged at the hemline of her dress to straighten the fabric.

The haus door opened, and an older woman stepped out and approached Abigail. "Bless your heart, child. I've taken a tumble like that a time or two, but never with a pie in my hand. Aren't you just a sight?" She shook her head. "Ruthie is carving a venison roast for me. The girls and I don't have much strength in our hands anymore, and we didn't get it sliced yesterday. They sent Sammy down to the cellar for a couple jars of pickles. Seems nobody brought any, and the other women are all too busy."

Abigail squirmed. She should be inside, helping.

"Don't you worry none," the woman said, as if she'd heard Abigail's thoughts. "It's just that Zelda and Yenneke and I don't get so much done anymore. I haven't been down in the cellar since I put up the garden produce last fall. I'm sure the cobwebs are multiplying like rabbits. Probably why they sent Sammy down there. A man doesn't mind a web sticking to his face so much."

Abigail's heart began to warm at the woman's kindness. She was a welkum distraction from her pain and embarrassment.

Just as Onkel Darius drove up in the horse and buggy, the haus door opened again, and Sammy came outside. "Food's all out, Orpah," he said to the older woman.

"Danki, Sammy. Stop by later this week, and I'll make some cookies." Orpah looked at Abigail. "You want me to go along with you to the ER?"

Abigail stared at her. Why would she want a stranger to accompany her to the ER? She didn't want to go, period. But with someone she didn't know? She shook her head. "I'll be fine, danki." She still planned on talking Sammy out of taking her there, anyway.

Orpah nodded, then turned to go back inside. "Nice to finally meet you, Abigail. Kum visit us sometime. I'd love to get to know you."

Abigail tried to push herself up to a standing position. The pain in her knee rivaled the feeling she'd had when she'd torn her ligament.

Sammy watched her a second, then scooped her up in his arms again. "You shouldn't be walking. If you want to stop by my haus on the way to the ER, I have some crutches you can borrow. They're in the…never mind."

A sense of guilt worked through Abigail. If only she'd seen the fire sooner, she might've been able to keep it from spreading. Might've been able to save Sammy's crutches, and the rest of the contents of the Millers' barn.

Aenti Ruth came outside. "Sorry I was so long in there. Had to help clean up a mess." Her gaze fell on Abigail. "Speaking of messes, honestly, Abigail! You're filthy. What happened?"

"I—"

"I'm taking her to the ER." Sammy pulled Abigail tighter against his chest. "She needs a professional evaluation."

With a hitch of her breath, Abigail wrapped her arm around Sammy's neck. Just to be safe. "I'm fine. I just need to bandage and ice my knee." But really, crutches would be nice. They'd make walking easier until the pain subsided. Not as nice as being held against Sammy's chest, though. Her pulse accelerated.

Darius pulled up in the buggy and climbed out. "You can take her to the hospital." He extended the reins to Sammy as he approached the buggy and placed Abigail in the seat. "Ruthie and I will walk home."

"Danki." Sammy grasped the reins and climbed in beside Abigail.

"The ER is for true emergencies," Abigail murmured. "Why not a walk-in clinic, if I 'need' a professional evaluation?"

"Here's her purse." Aenti Ruth handed Abigail's black clutch to Sammy.

He set the purse on the seat between him and Abigail. A Bible's width—according to Daed, that was the proper distance to separate her and a bu in a buggy. Seemed Sammy had been told the same thing.

"Danki, Ruthie. I'll bring her back as soon as she's released." Sammy glanced at Abigail. "This *is* a real emergency, Abby. And there aren't any walk-in clinics around here."

"You can't leave without something to eat." Orpah reappeared, holding a brown paper bag. "Zelda made you some sandwiches. BLTs, she said. I put a couple of bananas in there, too." She handed the bag to Sammy. "Take gut care of my maidal, now."

Odd how this complete stranger seemed to have adopted Abigail in a matter of minutes.

"Danki." Sammy's fingers grazed Abigail's as he handed her the bag. He looked back at Orpah. "Jah, I'll take care of my girl." The corners of his mouth curved in a slight smile.

A strange shiver worked its way up Abigail's spine.

⌒

Sam's cheeks heated at the Freudian slip he'd just made. He cleared his throat and glanced at Orpah, then looked to Ruthie. "Uh…I mean, your girl." Then he clicked his tongue at the horse.

"Please, just take me back to my onkel's," Abigail whispered as they neared the end of the circular drive between the haus and the barn. "I'm okay. Really."

"You might be okay, Abby, but I think you need to have this checked out. You don't want to risk any long-term damage."

She opened her mouth, as if to voice another objection.

"Nein. I'm not giving in on this." He shook his head and turned the horse toward town.

"I hate for you to give up your Sunday," she muttered.

"I could have called for an ambulance, but it would have taken twice as long to get you to the hospital. And I still would've kum along."

She huffed. "I'm not your responsibility."

"Jah, you are."

She lapsed into silence and folded her arms across her chest. Shutting him out.

"You might want to eat your sandwich with caution. Zelda's cooking is…adventurous, to put it nicely. Last time she served me a BLT, it was blueberries, liver, and turnips."

Her face showed not even the flicker of a smile.

"Honest."

He'd eaten the sandwich, anyway. Even though it ranked among the most unusual things he'd ever tried, he hadn't wanted to hurt Zelda's feelings.

Abigail still ignored him.

He fell silent. Whether she was sulking or trying not to cry in spite of the pain, he didn't know; but he decided to give her the quiet she seemed to want.

When they arrived at the hospital, Sam lifted Abigail out of the buggy and carried her inside. "Incoming!" he called to Michelle, the middle-aged nurse seated at the reception counter. "Where do you want her?"

Michelle pushed the button that automatically opened the doors at the end of the waiting room. "Exam room one. What happened, Sammy?"

"Knee injury. She's torn a ligament in the past, and she's had several recent falls that may have reinjured the knee. We thought it might be bruised or sprained, but…."

"We'll get it checked out." Michelle led the way into a small room with two empty beds separated by a curtain. "Here you go, honey." She gestured to the second bed, the one nearer to the window. "You're lucky he's the one who responded. He's one of the best local EMTs."

"You're a bit biased." Sam winked at the nurse, then looked at Abigail. "I was on call when Michelle was involved in an accident." He lowered Abigail onto the bed, then released her and stepped back. "I'll wait in the lobby, feuerzeug."

She nodded. Still wordless. But the fear in her eyes tore him up.

It hurt to turn and walk away. But he couldn't remain in the room with her. For many reasons.

Chapter 13

After what seemed like hours of extensive poking, prodding, and X-rays, Abigail was fitted with a plain white cast for a fractured patella, then wheeled out of the ER with a pair of crutches propped across her lap. The doctor said she could have the cast cut off in a month, provided her knee had started healing, at which point she'd exchange the plaster for a leg brace.

It could've been worse, she supposed. The pain wasn't as bad as when she'd torn her ligament. But her wounded pride hurt almost as much. And she wouldn't be in a big hurry to see the people of this community again. At least she could conceal herself at Onkel Darius's.

The nurse pushing her wheelchair stopped at the curb and waited for Sammy to get his vehicle. When he drove up in a horse and buggy, she snorted. "How am I supposed to help her into this contraption?"

Sammy dropped the reins, hopped out of the buggy, and came over. "I'll lift her in, Cynthia. Thanks for your help."

"Why didn't you hire a driver?"

Sammy gave her a patient smile. "It's Sunday, Cynthia. I couldn't interrupt anyone on the Lord's Day."

But he could have. Still, it was probably better he hadn't. Abigail didn't need any more strangers seeing her humiliation.

Would Mamm let her kum home, now that she was injured?

"I'm picking you up again, Abby." Sammy spoke softly as he lifted her in his strong arms. Arms that felt way too comfortable, way too safe—and already way too familiar. Was it bad she didn't want to leave the warmth of his embrace? Was it bad she looked forward to it, considering that, just a little over a week ago, she'd been held in Mark's embrace? The embrace that led to a passionate kiss—her first from him—and had her bending over backward...until Mark's daed walked in, furious beyond words, and Mark dropped her in the dirt as he stammered an excuse.

Abigail closed her eyes, as if to block out the memory. When she opened them again, she got a view of the horse making a contribution to the ecosystem—if such a thing existed on the asphalt parking lot. Sammy tucked her crutches in the backseat of the buggy, then climbed in beside her.

"Take care of yourself now, honey." Cynthia grasped the handles of the wheelchair once more and began pushing it back to the confines of the hospital, while Abigail braced herself for the embarrassment of facing the world after this latest incident. Could she go back in time and start over? Arrive in Jamesport with some idea of why she'd been put on the bus, some clue as to whom she'd be meeting, say no to Miranda's invitation to the "party," and prevent both the tumbles she'd taken since arriving? Maybe face this new district with self-confidence, and wow its members with something other than her clumsiness and her gossip-generating presence?

"Pride goeth before destruction, and an haughty spirit before a fall." The oft-quoted caution from the book of Proverbs floated through her mind.

It seemed a lot of things went before falls. Like pies. But she couldn't blame her fall on pride or a haughty spirit.

Or maybe she could. She'd refused to wear the knee wrap, after all.

Somewhere in the buggy, a rooster crowed. Abigail twisted around, looking for the stowaway bird.

Sammy pulled his cell phone out of his pocket. "PJ picked the ringtone. It's for the phone shanty." He slid his finger across the bottom of the screen as the rooster crowed again. "Sam speaking. Hallo, Ruthie....Jah....Ach, you did?" His eyes narrowed as he glanced at Abigail. "And...?"

They were talking about her. Abigail's heart constricted with worry.

Sammy was silent for a long moment. He furrowed his eyebrows and pressed his lips into a thin line. A muscle jumped in his jaw before he spoke again. "Danki, Ruthie. I...jah, we're on our way home. She has a broken kneecap, and they put a cast on. The doctor gave her a few pain pills and wrote a prescription for more, but everything's closed...jah. Okay. See you soon." He pressed the screen again, then wedged the phone between his leg and Abigail's purse.

When he didn't volunteer any details of the conversation but sat in stony silence, Abigail picked at the fabric of her dress, pleating it with her fingers. Did she really want to know what her aent had said? What else could go wrong in her life? Her stomach knotted as Sammy drove out onto the main road and started back the way they'd kum.

"Just say it, okay?"

Sammy jumped.

She hadn't meant to snap.

"Ach, Abigail." It was the first time he'd uttered her name without drawling it out in a caress.

Something in her belly flopped like a dying fish.

Then he grasped her hand, his fingers threading through hers with an intimacy she hadn't expected. Probably trying to offer her strength, like when he'd touched her hand while praying for her the previous nacht. She stiffened, bracing herself for whatever had upset him.

He let out his breath in a long exhalation. "Ruthie tried calling your mamm. The phone shanty in your barn."

As if she didn't know where it was located.

But, suddenly, judging by Sammy's choice of words, she didn't want to know what Aenti Ruth had told him. It was all too apparent she wouldn't be going home to convalesce.

She wouldn't be going home at all.

She bit her lip to keep her emotions in check. A wail danced on the edge of her tongue, just waiting for a chance to escape.

Nein. Don't say it. Just don't.

Sammy glanced at her, then stroked the back of her hand with his thumb. "Your stepdaed answered. Said he has nein dochter named Abigail...." His voice cracked. "And he doesn't want to hear your name mentioned again. You don't exist to him."

⌒

Sam felt a stab of pain on Abigail's behalf, along with a niggling suspicion that maybe she hadn't been completely candid in telling him about her banishment. What kind of parents disowned their child for nein reason? None that he knew.

Abigail's eyes widened with pain, and she jerked her hand free from his. Folded her arms across her chest once more. And started rocking back and forth, slowly, the way Mamm had cradled Sammy's littlest sister when she was a colicky boppli.

Abigail's bottom lip quivered, but she raised her chin, as if she were determined not to succumb to any more rejection-induced injuries.

Sam wished she would give in to the grief so he'd have an excuse to take her in his arms and hold her.

How he wanted to. He drew in a shuddery breath, unsure of how to proceed. Taking her home to Ruthie and Darius was a given. But, beyond that, he didn't have a clue what to do. Between having a broken kneecap and being on strong painkillers, she wouldn't attend the singing that nacht. And with emotional pain compounding her physical injury, she probably wouldn't want company. Still, dropping her off at her new home and leaving her there seemed wrong.

He peered at her out of the corner of his eye.

She was in the hands of der Herr. A far safer place to be than in his.

Lord, comfort her. The simple prayer seemed inadequate. He lowered his head and glanced her way again. A tear ran truant down her cheek and dripped off her quivering chin.

Would the pills the doctor gave her be strong enough to dull her physical hurt as well as her emotional pain?

⌒

Yesterday had been the worst day of Abigail's life. Until today.

The only highlight? Being carried in Sammy's arms, close to his heart. Kind of how she'd imagined Gott carried His kinner. In His hands. Held close. Loved. Protected. Safe.

So much for being protected and safe in His arms. And she certainly wasn't close or loved. She'd been rejected by Gott as surely as she'd been rejected by Mamm. And for what reason? What crimes had she committed to warrant this punishment?

None that she could think of.

Gott is love. Right.

She blinked her burning eyes and swiped at her damp cheeks, but she didn't even attempt a fake smile as Sammy parked the buggy in front of Onkel Darius's haus. Nor did she allow herself any pleasure as Sammy lifted her out of the buggy and carried her inside.

As he deposited her lengthwise on a couch, Aenti Ruth appeared in the doorway. "Ach, you poor dear." She fluffed a pillow and tucked it under Abigail's right leg.

Sammy nodded at Aenti Ruth and then walked out the door. He closed it behind him. Leaving Abigail. With nein gut-bye.

Abigail fingered the hem of the pillowcase. Was she supposed to keep her knee elevated? The memory of the doctor's muttered instructions had faded in the wake of the heartbreaking news Sammy had shared. The nurse had given her a sheet of handwritten instructions, which Abigail had stuffed in her purse. She would read them when she was in a more rational state of mind.

Not such an emotional one.

The door opened again, and Sammy came back in, carrying her purse in one hand, her hospital-issued crutches in the other. He dropped her purse on the end table and propped the crutches against the wall.

Okay, so he hadn't left without saying gut-bye.

His gaze rested on her, concern lingering in the depths of his eyes.

Then he shifted his attention to Aenti Ruth as he retrieved his cell phone from his pocket. "Give me the number for her family's phone shanty. I'm going to talk to her stepdaed." His tone left nein room for argument.

Abigail's heart stuttered. Would Sammy reject her, too, once he learned the truth—whatever it was?

Chapter 14

S am stepped onto the porch, ignoring Abigail's whispered "Nein." Why didn't she want him to call her parents? Was she hiding something? He hated the suspicion that rose like smoke and feathered out inside him.

The phone on the other end rang once. Twice. Three times…seventeen times. Didn't they have an answering machine? He was about to end the call when he heard a breathless "Hallo?" The speaker sounded young; whether male or female, Sam couldn't tell.

Sam cleared his throat. "This is Samuel Miller. May I speak to your daed, please?"

There was a loud bang, followed by a series of rhythmic slams. The phone must have been left dangling from the cord.

Somewhere in the distance, a voice yelled, "Daed! Phone!"

The receiver stopped swinging. Seconds—minutes—crawled by.

Sam strode across the wraparound porch and turned the corner to the other side of the haus.

"Leo Swartz speaking." The man's voice was brusque.

"Samuel Miller," Sam stated, in the most authoritative tone he could manage. "Listen, what's going on?"

"I'm sure I don't know—"

"And *I'm* sure you do know. What did Abigail do to warrant being sent away? Seduce your sohn?" Okay, that might have been over-the-top. Still, Sam made no attempt to soften his voice. "Did she refuse to kneel and confess to some wrongdoing? Why did you send her away from home and then disown—basically shun—her?" His anger threatened to boil over. "She's hurt. She needs her mamm—"

121

Leo Swartz slammed the phone down, hard enough to make a sound that hurt Sam's ear.

Sam called the man back.

The phone rang and rang and rang.

"This isn't over," Sam growled. Not that Leo Swartz could hear him.

Not that Sam would worry if he did.

Would Abigail's stepdaed be more likely to talk if Sam showed up in his driveway demanding answers? Or would he be waiting, ready to use the business end of a pitchfork on him?

Maybe Sam should've taken the time to pray before contacting Abigail's family. Daed would've scolded him for arrogance. Presumptuousness. Disrespect of an elder.

He would've been right.

Let go. I've got this. My ways are not your ways, nor are My thoughts your thoughts….

Sam shook his head. That sounded like a Bible verse. But he didn't know the Scriptures well enough to recall where it had kum from.

Daed would know.

Sam's breath hitched. As a preacher, Daed was privy to all kinds of information. Why hadn't Sam thought of that before?

Daed would know.

⌒

Monday morgen, Abigail awoke in the daybed in her temporary bedroom—the small, cramped all-season room off the kitchen. She couldn't easily climb the narrow staircase to the second floor, so she'd been moved to this location, where Aenti Ruth usually hung the laundry to dry when the weather was too wet. A door opened to the backyard, where there was an out-haus for the men. Since the sole indoor bathroom was on the second level, the out-haus was Abigail's, too. *Oh, joy.*

Had her stepdaed given Sammy any answers? If so, Sammy hadn't shared them. Instead, he'd jumped off the porch and run as if he couldn't get away from her fast enough. He'd disappeared before Aenti Ruth could get to the door and yell after him.

Had whatever she'd done been that bad?

Abigail swallowed the lump in her throat as she hobbled on her crutches into the kitchen. The egg basket waited on the counter. Time to collect. She grasped the basket with her right index and middle fingers and started for the door.

"Where do you think you're going?" Aenti Ruth asked from behind her.

Wasn't it obvious? Abigail glanced over her shoulder. "The eggs…?"

"And just how do you imagine you'll carry the basket of eggs and fight off any overprotective fowls while maneuvering on crutches?" Aenti Ruth's hands went to her hips.

Abigail eyed the crutches, then looked up with a smile as she lifted one crutch like a sword. "En garde!"

Aenti Ruth chuckled. "Funny. But I'll handle that job until your mobility is back. You start the oatmeal." She took the basket from Abigail and went outside.

Abigail made her way to the pantry and began assembling the necessary ingredients, plus her favorite oatmeal toppings: raisins and brown sugar. Her stomach rumbled.

The sound was soon muffled by the roar of an engine in the driveway.

Abigail peeked outside and recognized the pickup truck as the one she'd ridden in with Sammy on Saturday. He'd kum back! She tried to tame her singing, dancing heart as she measured oats and then water into the saucepan. Why did she feel this strong attraction to Sammy, anyway? Because he'd gone from acting rude to treating her nicely? Because he'd prayed for her with great understanding? Because he'd held her in his arms?

The door opened, and Sammy came in. He wiped his feet on the mat, then crossed the room to her, smiling broadly. She tried to ignore how well his Englisch clothes fit him.

"I thought I'd check on you on my way to school. You need to take it easy, you know."

Abigail shrugged. "What'd he say?"

"Your stepdaed? Pleasant man." Sammy rolled his eyes. "He hung up on me. So then, I thought my daed would know, since he's a preacher."

"Did he?" She stepped closer, catching a whiff of piney soap or aftershave. It smelled gut.

Sammy's gaze dropped to her lips. She shivered. After a long, sizzling moment, his eyes shot up to meet hers. A question appeared on his face.

Her heart pounded. *Jah, please.* She needed his arms around her. Needed his lips on hers. Needed the rush that would tell her she was loved, desired, wanted.

The question died with a hard shake of Sammy's head. But he didn't move away. Instead, he reached out with a trembling hand… which stopped centimeters short of touching her cheek. He let his hand fall to his side with a heavy sigh.

"All Daed said was, 'It isn't my story to tell.' That, and 'what a tangled web we weave when first we practice to deceive.'"

Abigail frowned. "What?"

The corners of Sammy's mouth turned up, but the chuckle that accompanied his subtle grin was humorless. "My reaction, exactly. He knows, and he wouldn't say." He leaned closer. "So, who practiced to deceive? And why?"

⌒

It was hard for Sam to turn and walk away, leaving Abigail standing, confused, in the kitchen. But he didn't want to be late for class. Plus, if he stayed any longer, he would take her in his arms. Press his lips to hers. Kiss her until his knees buckled, and….

His body warmed.

She didn't need heartbreak; she needed answers. Promises. Commitment. None of which he could offer. Not when all he had was uncertainty. Confusion. And crimes. Things he would have to take responsibility for, sooner or later.

Later was better.

Right now, he had more important things on his agenda. Such as figuring out who really set fire to his family's barn. Sam needed to find out if the fire chief had questioned Miranda and her friends.

But, first and foremost, he wanted to understand the mystery that was Abigail Stutzman.

Chapter 15

Abigail glanced at the door as Aenti Ruth came back inside, one hand clutching the egg basket, the other hand holding a stack of dirty seed trays. "Here, Abigail. Something else you can do. Plant tomato seeds after breakfast." She set the stack of trays on the counter next to the sink. "I shook out the bugs, but it wouldn't hurt to wash them after the dishes are done. In the meantime, I'll set up a card table and bring down what you'll need to cut out your dresses."

Abigail eyed her aent. "Isn't February a little early for starting seeds?"

Aenti Ruth shook her head. "It means they'll have a gut start when we plant them outside. Your mamm doesn't start her plants indoors?"

"Nein. She always plants them straight into the garden. Says she doesn't see the point in doing something twice when once is enough. Maybe we would've had fresh tomatoes for longer if Mamm had done it differently." Abigail took a tray of warm biscuits out of the oven and slid them into a towel-lined basket, which she carried to the table and set near the butter and honey. "Breakfast is ready." She crossed the room to the door and rang the dinner bell.

"Danki." Aenti Ruth nodded. "Ach, don't forget, I'm going to Osceola for a few days to look after my cousin who just had surgery. My ride will be here after breakfast." She glanced at the battery-operated clock on the wall. "You'll need to make sure the meals are ready for Darius. The laundry can wait until I get home." She looked at the cast on Abigail's leg. "You'll be okay, ain't so? If you need help, send Darius next door for Orpah."

"I'll be fine." *Hopefully.* Abigail ladled oatmeal into three bowls.

Onkel Darius opened the door and stepped inside. "Nice sun-shine out there, Ruthie. Gut day for a trip, jah? But we'll sure miss you." He washed up at the sink, then sat at his place at the table.

As soon as Abigail had delivered the bowls of oatmeal, she and Aenti Ruth took their seats. Onkel Darius bowed his head for the silent prayer. A moment later, he looked up and met Abigail's gaze. "I'm working in town all this week, remodeling one of the old shops. I'll be back in time for supper, but I'll need a lunch packed every day." He quickly ate his breakfast, then stood and glanced at his frau. "If you'll pack my lunch, I'll get the horse ready to go."

Aenti Ruth stood and helped Abigail clear the table. While Abigail washed the dishes and the plastic seed trays, her aent sliced the leftover biscuits in half and made them into peanut-butter-and-jelly sandwiches.

"My ride should be here any minute," said Aenti Ruth. "I'm going to run upstairs and get the sewing supplies you'll need. Have Darius or Sammy bring down the treadle sewing machine." She hurried for the stairs.

Minutes later, Abigail heard a vehicle skid to a stop outside.

Aenti Ruth reentered the kitchen with her luggage. She dropped a pile of fabric on the card table.

Darius poked his head inside. "Driver's car just missed the cat." He grinned at his frau. "Bye, dear." Then he turned to Abigail. "See you to-nacht." He grabbed his lunch and left as Abigail bid her aenti gut-bye.

After she planted the tomato seeds, Abigail set the trays on the table in front of the south-facing window, then scrubbed her hands to prepare for her next undertaking. She spread out the smooth, rich material on the cardboard cutting board used for sewing. She loved the dark mauve color. How would it look on her? She'd held up a swatch at the fabric shop and asked Aenti Ruth, but her aent had merely shrugged and muttered, "Charm is deceitful, and beauty is vain, but a woman who fears der Herr shall be praised."

The other fabrics Aenti Ruth had purchased for her were a dark green and a grayish-blue. Neither of those was Abigail's top choice, but her aent had deemed them functional. Even the beautiful shade of mauve had gotten the same label. *Functional.* At least Abigail had been given some say in the color.

How would Aenti Ruth label her and her situation with Mamm and her new stepdaed? Dysfunctional? Abigail shook her head and forced her mind to concentrate on the task in front of her.

She'd just finished cutting out three dresses when she heard a car drive in. Aenti Ruth must've forgotten something. Abigail hobbled to the door and pushed it open.

Miranda got out of the front passenger side. The driver was a male, and another young man was sitting in the backseat.

Miranda started toward the porch. "Hey, Abby. I heard about your 'introduction' to the community. How embarrassing." She giggled. "Anyway, my boyfriend and I are heading to Trenton. Want to come along with us? We were going to stop at McDonald's and hang out awhile."

Abigail tightened her fingers around the doorknob and peeked at the car. "Who's the other guy?"

"That's my boyfriend's Amish cousin. He asked me to invite you. Said he saw you at church yesterday, but you didn't come back for the singing. He's interested, definitely, or he wouldn't have asked. Come on. You weren't doing anything, anyway, were you?"

Abigail thought about the dresses. She couldn't do much more with them until Onkel Darius brought down what she needed from upstairs. She sighed. "Nein barns to burn, right? The last time I went with you, I ended up being accused of arson."

Miranda held up her hands. "Sorry. Really. I had no idea they'd do something like that. Except they were mad at Sammy for something and wanted to get even with him." Miranda laughed. "You should've hurried when I told you to come. Then you wouldn't have gotten caught."

"Why were they mad at Sammy?"

Miranda shrugged. "They don't tell me everything. But we're just going to Trenton today. No burning barns, houses, sheds, or anything else. Just a chance to go on a date with a cute Amish man, if you like that type." Her eyes skimmed Abigail, and she laughed again. "Who knows? I might be able to take credit for introducing you to your future husband."

Abigail was about to object, saying she was already promised to someone, but then she remembered she no longer was. When would she get that through her head?

"Come on." Miranda nodded toward the car. "I can't wait for you to meet Hen. You'll love him."

Hen? "What kind of a name is Hen?" She immediately regretted the rude comment.

Miranda giggled. "I know, right? He says it's biblical. Ask him about it."

"I need my crutches." Abigail started to turn, then paused. "We'll be back by suppertime, right? I'm supposed to have a meal ready for my onkel when he gets home."

"I'm sure we'll be back in plenty of time. Grab your crutches and come. It's time you started making friends around here. And Hen is kinda nice. Exciting."

Abigail hobbled inside and grabbed her crutches, then realized she ought to leave a note for Onkel Darius. She found a pen and a pad of paper.

Went out with Miranda. I'll be home by supper.

Abigail

She propped the note on the counter, then went outside and followed Miranda to the car.

"I've been craving a McCafé Mango Pineapple Smoothie. Ever had one?" Miranda asked over her shoulder.

"Nei—no."

"I'll ask Hen to buy you one. They also have Strawberry Banana and Blueberry Pomegranate, if either of those appeals more."

"They all sound tasty."

Miranda climbed into the front seat of the small car, which rivaled Sammy's broken-down vehicle in appearance. At least this one ran. Abigail opened the back door and lowered herself onto the seat, then carefully brought her crutches in and shut the door.

She turned to her "date" and found herself face-to-face with the man who'd glared at her in front of the barn yesterday. His brown eyes still appeared cold. Angry. Or maybe that was his natural look.

Why had he requested they invite her?

Abigail silently chided herself for passing judgment. She would have issues, too, if she were a man named Hen.

⌒

Sam's last class that day was canceled, leaving him with two hours to kill before the start of his evening shift on the ambulance. He certainly didn't mind. This would give him time to stop and talk to Abigail. Or, if Darius happened to be around, maybe they could work on the car. And maybe Darius would open up some about Abigail's situation, if Sam asked some carefully worded questions.

As he crossed the parking lot to the truck he'd borrowed from Viktor, his pager went off. "Jamesport station, structure fire…." The address was on the outskirts of town. An Amish farm, maybe. Sam couldn't be sure. He turned onto the highway in the direction of Jamesport. Seconds later, the song "Dancing Too Close to the Fire" broke the silence. It was the ringtone PJ had selected for the fire department.

Sam glanced at his phone long enough to read the text message, then grabbed the emergency light from the seat beside him. He turned the light on, then reached through the open window to attach it to the roof as he floored the gas pedal.

Ten minutes later, Sam rushed into the fire station, threw on his bunker gear, and was on the engine when it pealed out of the garage, siren screaming.

His stomach churned at the sight of black billows of smoke marring the clear blue sky. Flames shot from the roof of the barn and flickered in the loft windows. At least it wasn't the haus. He scanned the pasture. A group of animals huddled together a fair distance from the burning building.

An Amish woman he recognized—a distant cousin of his—was closing the goat pen as Sam jumped down from the engine and started unwinding the hose. "Jesse's in the barn!" she shouted, then added something else that Sam couldn't make out in the chaos.

Two of his fellow firefighters donned oxygen masks and ran toward the barn. Before they could enter, Jesse staggered out of the open door, carrying a woman in his arms. Sam saw her skirts. Her kapp. And the cast on her right leg.

Abigail.

So, she *was* involved. And she'd lied.

Sam's lips flattened in a thin line as he helped hold the heavy hose shooting water onto the blaze. The ambulance screeched to a halt in the yard behind him, followed by two cars from the county sheriff's department.

He couldn't leave his post to yell at Abigail.

But someone else would yell. The fire chief or the sheriff.

She wasn't getting off easy this time.

～

Huddled on a metal bench on the front porch of yet another home, Abigail coughed and blinked her burning eyes. The Amish man who'd deposited her there had ordered her not to move, then brought his frau to stay with her while he ran back and joined the effort to fight the blaze. Not that he really helped. Right now, he stood talking to one of the firefighters, gesturing with his hands.

How had Abigail gotten here? Another barn fire. Another instance of her so-called friends dumping her and then fleeing the scene, leaving her to take the blame. But she had nein memory of anything.

Well, she remembered climbing into the beat-up car beside Hen and riding to a town whose name she couldn't recall. They went to McDonald's, and she and Miranda sat at a table while Miranda's boyfriend and Hen placed their orders. Hen brought her a Mango Pineapple Smoothie. She took a few sips of the tasty, tropical-flavored beverage, and then she started to feel dizzy. Fuzziness filled her head. Maybe she was allergic to mangos.

But that didn't explain how she'd ended up at the site of another barn fire. At least Sammy wouldn't be here to condemn her. But she would still get the blame. Guilty until proven innocent…and she had nein proof of her innocence.

Her crutches were missing. Had they been incinerated in the barn fire? Or were they still in the backseat of Miranda's boyfriend's car? Abigail still didn't understand how she'd gotten here, or how she'd left McDonald's, for that matter. Her right leg ached. She didn't have any more pain pills from the doctor—and nein way of getting any. She would take an aspirin when she got back to her onkel's haus.

The woman seated on the bench next to her cradled her belly, stroking it. Was she pregnant? Abigail's mamm blamed the loss of a boppli bu on the stress she'd experienced from a barn fire that started when lightning struck the roof.

Abigail swallowed the lump in her throat. *Gott, be with this woman and her boppli. And help me…help me.*

Seemed He already had. If that man hadn't carried Abigail out of the barn, she would have died in the fire. Did somebody want her dead? Her heart pounded. She stared at the inferno across the drive.

Had Miranda's boyfriend and Hen started the fires? It seemed likely. At least Abigail could identify them, even if she didn't know the boyfriend's name.

Steam rose from the barn as the firefighters sprayed water to put out the flames shooting high in the air. The Amish man who'd rescued Abigail was still talking to one of them. He took off his hat, slapped it against his leg, and put it back on his head as he gestured toward the haus. Toward Abigail.

The firefighter readjusted his grip on the hose and glanced her way.

Her heart lodged in her throat.

Sammy.

Chapter 16

S am cringed as he watched Jesse march over to the law enforcement officers who'd just arrived and start complaining loudly while pointing in Abigail's direction. Ryan and Trevor, the EMTs who'd responded, were already there, crouched in front of Abigail. Their bodies blocked Sam's view of her cast but not of her pretty face. He half wished he'd been on call as an EMT. But this way was better, because he wouldn't be in close contact with Abigail in the aftermath of another fire. Another fire *she'd* started.

He studied her. Pale face. Darting eyes. Open mouth taking rapid breaths. Probably had a sore throat due to smoke inhalation. Where were her crutches? Had they been lost in the fire?

Sam turned his back on the proceedings so he could focus on putting out the blaze. But this barn, like the others before it, would be a total loss. And the community had yet to rebuild his family's barn. The project was scheduled to begin next week, as long as the load of supplies Daed had ordered arrived on time.

Sam resisted the urge to peek over his shoulder at Abigail. She might be stressed, but she was in gut hands. Ryan and Trevor were two of the best.

As much as Sam wanted to lash out at her and demand to know *why*, he didn't want her to be guilty. He liked her. She was sweet, and beautiful, and…a feuerzeug.

His heart sagged.

Steam rose from the smoldering ashes. The area stank of smoke and damp burned lumber. Sam adjusted his grip on the hose, then watched to make sure the remaining embers had been extinguished.

When the group had deemed it was safe, Sam glanced at Jerrod, another volunteer firefighter. "I'll be right back," he told him. "Need to talk to someone."

Jerrod nodded.

Sam stalked toward the porch, where Abigail sat with the two officers. Everything was quiet. The officer named Kyle scribbled something in his notebook. He looked up as Sam approached and held out his hand, but Sam ignored him and stared at Abigail. Hard. "What are you doing here?"

"I…I don't know." Spoken as a sob.

Sam glanced at the usually stern-faced Kyle.

Kyle closed his notebook and looked at Abigail. "I'll be in contact." He slid his pad and pen into his pocket, nodded at Sam, and strode away.

So, whatever excuse Abigail had given, the officers had accepted it. For now. They weren't arresting her.

Ryan rose to his feet and motioned for Sam to follow him. They moved a few yards away, and Ryan told him quietly, "We're taking her to the hospital. She says she has no memory of anything, other than going to McDonald's with Miranda; Miranda's boyfriend, Zane—she didn't know his name, but we all know who he is; and Hen. We're going to have her tested for predator drugs and possible sexual violation."

Hen? Nausea rose in Sam's throat.

"Sam!" Jerrod called. "We're going."

Sam started walking backward. His gaze shot to Abigail. Her head was bowed, her soot-smeared face framed by several loose strands of honey-blonde hair. The least of her concerns. Hen may be Amish, but he wasn't someone to trifle with. He was dangerous. Operated outside the parameters of the Ordnung. And of the law.

If he had violated Abigail….

Sam's breathing accelerated. He went to rake his fingers through his hair but ran into the stiffness of his fire helmet.

"Sam!" Jerrod called again.

Sam glanced at Ryan. "Can you cover for me awhile? I'll meet you guys at the hospital. Make sure she's okay, then take her home. And then I'll report for my shift."

Ryan nodded. "You'll owe me." He grinned, but his eyes showed concern. He knew about Hen. *Everyone* knew about Hen. It was a small town. The problem was finding proof. And Sam couldn't provide that without....

He turned and ran for the fire engine.

～

The doctor's mouth flattened. His eyes softened with sympathy. "I'm sorry, but you tested positive for Rohypnol."

Abigail stared at him. "What's that?"

The doctor's chest rose and fell. "A more common name for it is the 'date-rape drug.' Does that help explain anything?"

Date-rape drug? Abigail swallowed the lump in her throat. That meant the invasive tests the doctor had mentioned earlier would be necessary.

She clutched the fabric of her dress, right above her bosom, as a flashback replayed of the anger in Hen's eyes when he looked at her. It hurt to know Miranda was in on the scheme and did nothing to help her.

Shortly after the doctor left the room, a nurse entered with a tray of several medical instruments. She set the tray on the counter, then reached inside a drawer and pulled out a thin aqua gown, which she handed to Abigail. "Take off all your clothes, then put this on, open in the front, and lie on the bed." Her tone was clinical. She laid a blanket next to Abigail before she, too, left the room.

Abigail whimpered as she undid the pins of her dress and peeled off the garment. After draping herself in the horribly immodest hospital gown, she lay down, as instructed. When the nurse and the doctor reentered the room, Abigail squeezed her eyes shut and gripped the edges of the bed with her fingers. And prayed. If only someone was there with her to hold her hand. To comfort her.

The nurse gave Abigail a pat on the shoulder.

It didn't help.

Tears snuck out the corners of Abigail's eyes. Dribbled down her cheeks and into her ears. Shame and embarrassment filled her.

"You're one of the lucky ones." The doctor pulled off his gloves as the nurse helped Abigail to sit up. "No sign of sexual violation. I'd suggest steering clear of whoever it was that drugged you. You may not be so lucky next time."

An adage Abigail had heard somewhere flashed through her mind: *Fool me once, shame on you. Fool me twice, shame on me. Fool me again, shame on both of us.* There wouldn't be a "next time," for sure.

Her friendship with Miranda was over. As for Hen…she would avoid him at all costs. She'd given both their names to the officers who'd questioned her. Would Miranda and Hen retaliate? As if leaving her drugged in a burning barn wasn't bad enough.

Abigail fought to control her tears as she got dressed again. Then the nurse helped her into a wheelchair and pushed her out to the waiting room. She would need someone to drive her home, but she didn't know whom to call. With her clumsy cast, it'd be hard getting into a buggy. And she'd lost her crutches. Somewhere.

She wiped at her stinging eyes and blinked, trying to clear the blurriness. When she refocused, Sammy stood in front of her, looking worried. She blinked again.

"Are you okay?"

"Okay is…." Abigail cleared her throat. Looked away and swallowed. "All things considered, I could be worse."

"Did he…hurt you?"

"The doctor? Or Hen?" Abigail hated that her voice shook. She'd never been so humiliated, so violated.

Sammy frowned. He glanced up, over her head, and nodded at the nurse. When he looked down at Abigail again, his gaze was full of understanding. He pulled in a deep breath. "Let's get you home, Abby."

"I didn't do it." Unshed tears clogged her throat. "I was drugged."

"She's in shock, Sammy," the nurse told him. "Go get your vehicle."

Sammy started backing away. "I'll be right back."

Abigail watched him retreat through the lobby and out the glass doors toward the parking lot. Then he broke into a jog and vanished from view.

"He's a good man." The nurse sighed. "So sweet of him to come for you. He sure thinks a lot of you."

Jah, right. He thought she was an arsonist. She wiped her nose on the wadded tissue in her hand, then tilted her head back to look at the nurse. "I lost my crutches somewhere. Maybe in the fire."

The nurse smiled sympathetically. "I'll tell Sammy to stop by my house and get a set from the shed. I have an ever-growing collection, thanks to my accident-prone husband and sons."

Abigail tried to smile back. "Thank you for your help."

Viktor's big pickup appeared outside, and Sammy came around to open the passenger door.

The nurse wheeled Abigail outside. "A truck, Sammy? Not much better than a buggy." She locked the brakes of the wheelchair.

Sammy shrugged. "My car's broken down. Haven't had time to work on it, so I'm borrowing the truck from a relative." He scooped Abigail into his arms and deposited her in the front passenger seat.

"I think you just wanted an excuse to hold her," the nurse teased him.

Abigail's face heated, and the warmth only intensified when Sammy winked at her.

"Whatever works." Sammy shut the door, then stood there a moment, talking to the nurse. When the nurse turned to push the chair back inside, he ran around the front of the truck and climbed behind the wheel. "Jen just gave me directions to her place. She's got some crutches you can use. What happened to yours?"

"I don't know. I had them with me at McDonald's." Abigail's voice cracked.

Sammy expelled his breath forcefully. But all he said was, "Jah."

Abigail closed her eyes. "I hate—"

"Don't say it." His fingers grazed her hand. Hesitated. Then settled in, intertwining with her fingers. "It's not all bad. I'm here."

Again, sparks ignited. Keeping her eyes shut intensified the sensation, somehow. Abigail's heart pounded as tingles raced up her arm. Warmth worked through her.

Sammy made a couple of right turns before bringing the truck to a stop. He pulled his hand away. "I'll be right back, schnuckelchen."

Beautiful girl?

Abigail's eyes popped open. Nobody had ever called her that before.

Not even Mark.

⌒

Sam retrieved a pair of crutches from the shed behind Jen's place and tossed them in the back of the truck before he climbed into the cab again. "I'll adjust them for you when we reach your onkel's haus," he told Abigail. "Or Darius can, since I need to get to work."

"I didn't mean to keep you from your job."

Sam shook his head. "You didn't. I chose to make sure you were safe. But, just so you know, this isn't over. I have plenty to say to you." He frowned as he turned the truck onto the main road. After the first fire, she should've known better than to go anywhere with Miranda.

"I'm surprised you haven't said anything yet." Her tone was wry. "My onkel is working in town. He won't be home till supper." She paused. "You can rant to your heart's content."

Sam glanced at her. "Were you…raped?" His voice broke.

"Nein." She shook her head emphatically.

Sam released the breath he hadn't realized he was holding. Turned left down a dirt road. "Since your onkel isn't home, I'll take you next door."

Abigail stiffened. "To Miranda's? You think she might have my crutches?"

"Forget your crutches. I meant to the neighbors on the other side. You shouldn't be alone. I'm dropping you at The Hen Haus."

"*Hen?* Nein."

Sam winced. "Not *that* Hen. It's the home of three old mauds: Orpah—you met her—and Zelda and Yenneke. They'll welkum the chance to get to know you. I'll leave a note for Darius, telling him where to find you."

Abigail grabbed the door handle as the truck passed a slow-moving buggy. "But—"

"Please. I need to know you're taken care of." Sam reached for her hand again. It was soft and warm. "The ladies will love having you there. Trust me."

"Why not take me to my onkel's and leave me to fend for myself? I don't deserve anything more." Abigail looked away but left her hand cradled in his.

"Because." Sam swallowed. "You've been hurt enough, and my yelling won't help anything. I'm upset, and I might say and do things I don't mean to. Like kiss you senseless."

Abigail's breath hitched.

"I need time to cool off." *In more ways than one.*

In spite of his words, he couldn't keep his fingertips from trailing across her palm to her wrist and then back again.

She trembled. "Maybe I'd be okay alone."

Was that a tentative invitation?

He slowed at the Zooks' driveway. Then set his jaw and drove past.

With the sparks shooting between him and Abigail, he didn't dare accept.

He parked the truck in the circular drive outside the home where yesterday's church service had been held. Seconds later, the haus door opened, and a gray head poked out.

"Ach, feuerzeug." He sighed and slid his hand away from Abigail's. "If you play with fire, you're gonna get burnt. And you, schatz, are playing with fire."

Chapter 17

Abigail cringed. Sammy's comment hit too close to home. When would she learn? Two barn fires in four days, and she was at both of them. Plus, she'd basically thrown herself at Sammy while he was on the rebound from PJ. Just because she was lonely.

There must be some reciprocal interest on his part, or he wouldn't have acknowledged the temptation to kiss her senseless. And the fact that he wasn't willing to take advantage of her when she was in serious need of comforting spoke volumes about him as a man.

When Sammy came around and opened the front passenger door for Abigail, all three residents of The Hen Haus had lined up on the front porch. A tabby cat wended its way around their ankles.

Sammy reached for Abigail, sliding his hand behind her knees. The pressure put her in mind of the unwelkum doctor's exam, and she shifted away. "I can get out on my own. With the crutches."

Sammy held up his hands in surrender. "Of course." He retrieved the crutches from the bed of the pickup and handed them to her, then stood back and waited with a dubious expression on his face.

His obvious doubt was strong motivation. She'd do it by herself if it killed her.

She peered down from her perch on the seat. Higher up than in a buggy.

This might very well kill her. She'd refused Sammy's help before realizing that she would have to bend almost in half to set the crutches on the ground.

Should she tell him to turn around, so he wouldn't see her make a fool of herself—again? Of course, if she fell, she would need his help getting up. Or should she swallow her pride and tell him she'd changed her mind?

Nein contest.

She released her grip on the crutches, letting them clatter to the ground. "Oops."

Sammy smirked and stepped forward. "May I?"

"Jah, but you don't need to carry me inside."

Sammy chuckled. "Wouldn't dream of it."

One of the mauds on the porch released a loud sigh. "Ah, young love. How romantic."

It wasn't love. And there was nothing romantic about being stuck in a huge truck with nein way of getting out, short of falling on one's face. All because she'd stubbornly refused Sammy's offer of help.

Sammy stepped forward and settled his hands on her waist. She wrapped her arms around him and clasped her hands tightly behind his neck. Her body brushed against his, and every nerve ending sprang to life.

He exhaled sharply, then lowered her to the ground, released her, and stepped away so fast that her head spun. He pushed the crutches into her arms and turned toward the porch. "Ladies, this is Abigail." He cleared his throat. "Darius will kum for her later. I have to get to work."

Abigail took a wobbly step forward, then glanced back toward the truck.

Sammy shut the front passenger door. Hesitated. Then turned around and looked at her. "Stay out of trouble, feuerzeug."

There was no denying the sparks between them, but she could never trust her life—or her heart—to a man who believed her to be guilty. She'd seen the censored expression on his face when he first discovered her that afternoon. And this time, he hadn't told her he believed her.

"I didn't start the fire. Fires. Either of them."

Sammy ignored her protests. He ran around the front of the truck. Jumped in. And drove off. He was out of sight before she reached the very steps she'd fallen down the day before.

When she'd maneuvered her way up to the porch, Orpah embraced her. The other two mauds were sighing and fanning their faces with their hands.

"I didn't start any of the fires," Abigail said again. She needed these ladies to know she was innocent.

"Of course you did." The shortest and plumpest of the three women opened the screen door, then stepped aside to let the others enter the haus.

"You mean 'didn't,' ain't so?" the third woman asked, stooping to pick up the cat. Abigail recognized her as the one who'd gathered the ruined pies the previous day.

"I think Zelda meant what she said." Orpah pulled Abigail closer. "There's more than one type of fire, you know. And the one between that man and this woman...it's lit. Definite heat."

⟵⟶

Sam entered the Zooks' silent home and looked around. Cuts of fabric, abandoned on a card table. Abigail's note, propped on the countertop. He picked it up and crumpled it in his fist. Then smoothed it out and read it. Nein mention of going to McDonald's. Just Miranda. Evidence of guilt or innocence? He slid the paper into his pocket.

But the note wasn't intended for him. With a sigh, he pulled it out again and put it back where he'd found it.

He picked up a pen and a pad of paper with the words "Shopping List" at the top.

Darius,

> *Abigail is at The Hen Haus.*

> > > > *Sam*

So much more he could say. Should say. But it'd be better for him to relay it in person. Confronting Abigail when her onkel was there seemed a wiser course of action, considering Sam's growing attraction to her. Maybe he ought to kum courting instead of condemning.

She *had* to be innocent. Unless she'd been orchestrating fires long-distance before she arrived. Granted, Jen had mouthed something about Abigail's having been drugged. Sam wanted to find Hen and rake him over the coals for hurting someone he cared about.

He propped the pad of paper where Darius would see it, then turned and went upstairs to Abigail's room. The two plush hearts from McDonald's rested on top of the dresser. He reached for the one that said "I Luv You." She'd called that one "sweet," and he wanted to do something to cheer her.

She'd been sleeping downstairs, in the all-season room. Or so he'd been told.

He left the heart lying in her temporary bedroom, in the middle of her pillow.

⌒

"You sit here, Abigail." Orpah led her to a glider rocker with a footrest. "Put your foot up, dear. It's my turn to make dinner, but Zelda volunteered to cook to-nacht so we could talk. Your onkel can join us for the meal."

It was kind of nice to have someone fussing over her. If only Mamm cared enough.

"How's your mamm, poor thing? I do feel sorry for her, although, in a sense, she made her own bed." Orpah pulled up a stool and sat next to her.

Abigail stared at the older woman. "What do you mean? How do you know about my family?"

"Deborah shouldn't have married Obadiah in the first place," Orpah went on, ignoring her questions. "He was on *the list*, you know. It's truly a wonder you lived."

"Was I sick?" Abigail bit her tongue to stop the flood of other questions that threatened to spill out of her mouth. She didn't want to scare Orpah into silence.

But instead of saying anything more, Orpah studied Abigail a moment, then blinked and looked down. "I see." Her voice was quiet, her tone resigned. "I have said too much." She started to stand.

"Nein, wait." Abigail reached for her. "Please." Her voice cracked.

Orpah sighed. "You weren't sick. We all were afraid you'd be still-born, like your brothers and sisters before you. Or that you would die soon after birth. But there was nothing wrong with you, praise Gott."

She'd known about only one boppli Mamm had lost—a bu, whose stillbirth Mamm blamed on a fire. There were more? An unfamiliar sadness washed through her at the thought of brothers and sisters she would never know. She'd asked Mamm and Daed countless times why she was an "only lonely." Why hadn't they told her the truth? Too painful to talk about, maybe.

It was gut that Orpah seemed willing to answer questions. Abigail would take advantage of the older woman's talkative mood while she could. She propped her injured leg on the footrest. "What list was Daed on? And why?"

Orpah frowned and rubbed her arms briskly, as if to warm herself. She glanced over her shoulder, then lowered her voice to say, "There was a list of families that showed who was related to whom, and how closely. The bishop forbade it, saying it took matters out of Gott's hands. But the list is out there. Somewhere. And it proved your mamm and daed were second cousins. Deborah was warned, but she chose to believe the lies instead of accepting the truth."

"How could they not have known they were second cousins?"

Orpah stood, grabbed an afghan, and draped it over Abigail's legs. "That's all I'd better say for now."

"But how do you know Mamm?" She'd never lived in Jamesport, as far as Abigail knew.

"It's a small community." Orpah shook her head. "May I get you something to drink?"

"I'm fine, danki." Sitting there while an elder waited on her went against everything Abigail had been taught.

"Have some water, at least. You need to stay hydrated." Orpah left the room.

Abigail heard clatters coming from the kitchen. Was Zelda really as adventurous a cook as Sammy had claimed? Abigail hadn't eaten the BLT Zelda had fixed for her yesterday, and she wasn't sure what Sammy had done with it.

A few moments later, Orpah returned, carrying a glass of water. "Here you go." She handed it to Abigail. "You're in luck. Zelda is making your onkel's favorite supper. Dill pickle soup."

Abigail raised her eyebrows, not bothering to hide her skepticism.

Orpah leaned closer. "Really, it's Zelda's most palatable concoction," she confided quietly.

Abigail heard the front door open.

"Mamm?"

The voice belonged to Onkel Darius.

"In here," Orpah called back. "With Abigail."

Abigail almost dropped her glass. Water sloshed over the edge. "Onkel Darius is your sohn?"

Orpah bit her lip. Glanced at Onkel Darius as he walked into the room. Then nodded.

"And he's my mother's brother. Which means...." Abigail swallowed. "You're my...grossmammi?"

Chapter 18

Sam gulped his koffee as he strode across the parking lot to the borrowed pickup. It'd been a quiet shift on the ambulance. Only one call, to a residence where a woman had fallen and couldn't get up. She'd refused transport.

He glanced at his cell phone. 11 p.m. He doubted Abigail was still awake. He'd second-guessed his decision to place that plush heart on her pillow every time he'd thought about it. He didn't want to spook her.

The truth was, his treatment of her frightened even himself. They had known each other only four days, and already he'd staked a claim. Started acting overprotective. Was thinking about courting. All because she had a pretty face and ignited sparks in him.

Love is a choice. How many times had he heard that? *Feelings fade, but marriage is forever. Choose wisely.*

He was nowhere near ready to choose to love anyone. Especially forever.

Darius's farmhaus came into view. Sammy slowed the truck and pulled to the side of the road. Cut the engine, then sat there for a minute, staring. He really needed to talk to Abigail. Should he toss pebbles at the porch windows to try to wake her?

A figure in white crossed the yard with jerky movements. He could recognize Abigail anywhere, even without crutches. She disappeared into the darkness of the barn.

Sam's heart lodged in his throat.

His car was in there. The new parts he'd bought for it. His Tablet. Some of his school supplies.

149

He forced himself to shrug off his concern. Abigail was innocent, wasn't she? Maybe she'd heard a noise and was going to investigate.

Sam jumped from the truck, shut the door as quietly as he could, and took off at a run. Darius didn't have a dog to alert anyone.

Nacht insects droned around his head. Somewhere in the area, a chorus of bullfrogs croaked along.

Sam slowed and sniffed as he entered the barn. He didn't smell gasoline, or the sulfur of a lit match.

From deep in the shadows, there came the sound of a car trunk slamming shut.

Sam headed in that direction, past several stalls of nickering horses.

A lantern-style flashlight—his own, from his car—rested on an antique wicker chair. Next to the chair, sitting on a hay bale draped with a blanket—also his—was a vision in white. Her face was buried in her hands, but nein sobs shook her shoulders. Her hair was braided in a rope that hung down her back. And her crutches lay on the ground next to her.

Sam stopped and stared at her. At least she wasn't playing with matches.

"Abby." Her name came out on a sigh.

She jerked her head up, her eyes wide. "Ach, I didn't hear you kum in. What are you doing here?" She glanced down at her nacht-gown, drawing the fabric closer to her body. "I'm not modest."

He couldn't admit the reason he'd initially stopped: that he liked her—too much—and wanted to be around her. "I saw somebody in the yard. Wanted to make sure this barn wasn't the next target."

"I hope you don't mind, I borrowed your blanket and flashlight. I thought this would be a gut place to think." She paused. "What you said about weaving a tangled web of deceit…that's the truth of it."

He studied her expression. It was a mixture of confusion and anger, with a touch of wry resignation. "The truth of what?"

"You said The Hen Haus ladies were three old mauds who never married."

"They are." He inched closer, then dropped down and sat cross-legged at her feet.

She exhaled a sigh. "Onkel Darius is Orpah's sohn. Which makes her my mamm's mamm. My grossmammi."

Sam's mouth dropped open. He closed it. "Wow. You sure?"

"Jah. Onkel Darius and Orpah admitted it. And all these years, Mamm told me I had nein family." Abigail's voice held an unfamiliar hardness.

"I had nein idea. Though they've lived next door to each other for as long as I can remember. And Darius has always taken care of Orpah and the ladies." Sam rubbed his chin.

"Why lie and cover it up? Because Orpah had two kinner outside of marriage?"

Sam shook his head. "Nein, she couldn't have. Orpah is...nein." But he had nein explanation. If only he could question Daed and get some answers. His mind scrambled in different directions—crazy pathways that provided nein answers, only more questions. He looked around for a distraction and saw the notepad in Abigail's lap. "Writing a letter?"

Abigail shrugged. "Onkel Darius said Mamm called the shanty and complained about the letter I wrote on Saturday. She received it today, and she wants 'more than a line or two.'"

"After your stepdaed said he has nein dochter named Abigail?" Sam hitched an eyebrow. "Some failure to communicate, I think."

"Lots of failures." Abigail lowered her head again. "I don't know what to do. Write and pretend nothing's wrong? Pretend I didn't just find out I've been lied to all my life? Or ignore the request for a letter, since, to them, *I don't exist?*" She looked up at him, her eyes hard and angry. "Or maybe tell Mamm what I think about her and all her deceit."

"If you go that route, you should rip up the letter rather than send it." Sam grinned. "I wish I'd done that a time or two." Especially in regard to his brother-in-law.

"You? Mr. Perfect?"

He winced at the heavy sarcasm. "Hardly perfect, Abby."

"An EMT. An Amish firefighter. The one everyone calls to fix everything. The one I'm supposed to marry, since they took Mark away from me." She bolted to her feet, grabbed the crutches, and hobbled toward the exit.

⸺

Abigail had traveled a whole five feet when Sammy grasped her by the upper arm and swung her around so seamlessly, she didn't even wobble. It was almost a twirl, like she used to do as a child. Skirt flaring, hair flying. Unbridled joy.

Except she had *nein* joy now.

Her heart pounded as she stared up at him.

"Nobody expects you to marry me." His voice was too calm. Too controlled.

Why had she expected him to take her in his arms and kiss her the way she longed to be kissed—the way Mark had once done?

But Mark didn't want her anymore.

And apparently, neither did Sammy. Despite the "I Luv You" toy he'd left on her pillow.

Fresh fury surged through her, filling the hidden crevices.

"*He's a gut man, Abigail. He'd make a gut ehemann, Abigail. You couldn't do better, Abigail.*'" She hated that her voice broke. That her throat clogged with tears.

"Calm down, Abby."

Calm down? She wanted to stomp her foot. But her stomping foot was in a cast. She clenched her jaw, instead.

At least Sammy knew better than to call her "feuerzeug."

"You're overreacting."

Abigail tried to shove him away.

He didn't budge. Instead, his hand loosened and trailed down her arm, setting fire to her skin under the thin sleeve of her nachtgown. Rendering her a trembling mass, like gelatin. "You're a bigger drama queen than my *boppli* sister." His fingers encircled her wrist.

Thankfully, he hadn't compared her to PJ. Though he could've, with gut reason.

"Breathe. Breathe." He tugged her close, his other arm curving around her waist. He drew her back to the blanket-draped hay bale and pulled her down beside him before releasing her. The crutches fell to the barn floor with a soft thud. He slid closer to her, so that the space of an imaginary Bible between them was reduced to maybe a millimeter.

Her anger faded, replaced with…desire. Longing.

Her breaths came in spurts as Sammy's free hand, the one that wasn't holding her waist, touched her neck and gently cradled her head against his strong chest.

She lifted her face toward his.

Sammy closed his eyes. He bent his head forward. But he didn't close the distance. Instead, he…prayed? A moment later, a sensation of calming peace washed through her, dissipating the anger altogether.

Who was this man, and how did he calm her storms so effortlessly?

⌒

Sam's prayer was a single word. *Gott*…. That was all he had. But as he repeated it in his mind, he felt the stiffness and tension leave Abigail's body. She relaxed against him and wrapped her arms around his waist.

He didn't know how long he'd held her, praying that single word, when she shifted slightly. But she didn't pull away.

"I feel so safe in your arms," she murmured.

That was gut. But then, safe was probably the last thing she should feel.

"Like you could protect me from anything."

Except himself.

"Can I stay here forever?" She sounded drowsy. Relaxed.

Something inside his heart warmed and opened, letting her in. He tightened his embrace and rubbed his hand up and down her spine, over and over. And over.

Her breathing changed. Softened. Became more regulated.

Had she really fallen asleep in his arms? He frowned. What next? He couldn't hold her all nacht, as much as he wanted to. Nor could he leave her here in the barn, to sleep on the hay bale. He needed to get her inside.

"Abby." He started patting her back.

"I think I love you," she murmured, burrowing closer. "Stay with me to-nacht." Her hand slid up his chest.

His breath hitched.

But she was probably dreaming of Mark. Believed she was speaking to him.

Had she ever slept in Mark's arms? Exactly how close had they been?

Sam felt a tiny prick of jealousy. He touched a hand to her upper arm and started to shift her away from him.

Abigail swayed and startled, her eyes popping open. She blinked at him.

He wanted to kiss her. Wanted to make her forget the other guy.

His stomach tightened. Quivered.

"We should get you to bed, feuerzeug. I need to go home." Before he did something they both would regret.

"I'm awake." Her voice was husky. Sleepy.

Jah, right.

Sam pushed to his feet.

A clatter sounded near the barn doors.

"Meeting someone here to-nacht, Abby?" He didn't turn to look at her.

"What? Nein!"

"Shh!" He groped for the lantern but touched something soft.

Abigail gasped.

"Uh, sorry." He quickly moved on, until his fingers closed around the handle of his flashlight. He turned and started toward the sound.

A snap. And then silence.

Sam stopped and stared into the darkness. He held the flashlight high above his head as he looked around.

Nein indication that anyone had been there.

But, wait. There were Abigail's original crutches, propped against Sam's car.

He went to the barn door and looked outside. Whoever had been there was gone. Disappeared.

Sam returned to the crutches. One of them had a piece of paper rubber-banded to it.

He freed the paper and unfolded it carefully. It was a page ripped from an Englisch translation of the Bible. Exodus 22:18 was underlined. *"Thou shalt not suffer a witch to live."*

Chapter 19

Still half asleep, Abigail rose unsteadily to her feet. She heard Sammy growl, and saw the bouncing glow of the lantern-flashlight as he ran out the barn door. Leaving her in the dark. Alone.

Where was he going? And why?

She stumbled after the bobbing light, stopping when it abruptly disappeared—as if he'd turned it off. Or turned a corner.

"Sammy?"

Nein answer.

She reached inside her pocket for her tiny handheld flashlight, whose dim glow had gotten her out to the barn. It wasn't nearly as powerful as Sammy's, which was why she'd borrowed it from the collection of miscellaneous items in the trunk of his car. She'd remembered seeing him retrieve it from there the nacht of the first fire.

She turned on the flashlight. The faint beam bounced off Sammy's car, straight ahead. She should probably return his blanket, too, but she hadn't written the letter, and thought she might still like to write it from her "desk" of hay. Though she still didn't know what to say. Whether to lash out or to play nice.

Maybe she'd talk to her long-lost grossmammi and ask her for a suggestion. How well had Orpah known Mamm? Maybe she'd like to include a note of her own. *The gig is up, Deb.*

Okay, that wasn't nice.

It was gut to know Abigail had family here.

Wait. Was her daed from here, originally? If so, he probably had relatives in the area. More aentis and onkels. Cousins, maybe.

Lost in thought, she'd almost passed the car when she noticed a strange shadow. She stopped and shined the light directly at a pair of wooden crutches leaning against the hood.

Not just any pair of crutches. *Her* crutches. Somebody had returned them. But why?

Her heart stuttered at the realization: Whoever had brought them was probably intending to light the barn on fire. And leave her crutches at the scene, in an attempt to implicate her in yet another arson.

"The sheriff is on his way."

Sammy's voice came out of nowhere. Abigail swung the flashlight around, but he stood beyond the reach of its pitifully dim glow.

"You should go change out of your nacht-gown." His voice was stern.

She looked down at her admittedly flimsy gown. She hadn't bothered putting on a robe, since she'd assumed she would be alone. "Sammy—"

"And wake Darius. He needs to be out here when the sheriff arrives."

"Stop ordering me around already! Can't you ask nicely? Try. The results might surprise you." She would have folded her arms across her chest, if she weren't juggling crutches and a flashlight.

Sammy sighed and stepped into the circle of light. "Sorry, Abby. There was a note…a threat. I'll tell you more when your onkel joins us." He came closer and handed her his lantern-style flashlight. "This one's brighter, if you want to use it."

She ignored the proffered light. "You mean, someone is threatening *me*?" Her fingers tightened around the handles of her crutches. She would kum out swinging at the enemy, if she could. Except, the enemy was missing. "Who? Miranda?"

Sammy's brow wrinkled. "Miranda? I doubt it. But maybe Hen."

"Why?" She looked down at her cast, at the crutches. She'd make an easy target for anyone who might want to hurt her.

"I don't know." Sammy's gaze dipped to the bodice of her nacht-gown, then shot up to her face again. "You would feel more comfortable in your normal clothes when speaking with the sheriff and his deputies. That fabric is thin...probably see-through, if you were to stand in the headlights of the squad car." He looked away.

"Are you saying *you* can see through my nacht-gown?" Abigail hugged herself, suddenly self-conscious. If only she'd grabbed her robe.

"Uh...through? Nein." He kept his eyes averted. "I wasn't looking. But I have two little sisters, and Mamm has been trying to teach them about modesty. I don't want anybody ogling you."

Abigail pulled in a shallow breath. "Okay."

"And wake your onkel. Tell him to kum."

"Back to issuing orders? You were doing *so* well."

"Nein need to wake me." Onkel Darius entered the barn holding a flickering kerosene lantern. "Abigail, go do as Sam said, then set out cookies and make tea. Sam, explain yourself."

〜

So much for explaining the situation to Darius and Abigail at the same time. As Abigail turned her dim flashlight on and left the barn, Sam set the lantern-flashlight on the hood of his car, then held out the page torn from the Bible. "This was attached with a rubber band to her crutches—the ones she lost somewhere between being drugged at McDonald's and being pulled from a burning barn."

Darius paled. "And you've already called the sheriff?" He sounded incredulous, upset, and a little confused. As if he thought Sam shouldn't have involved any authorities over a set of returned crutches.

"Jah. Read it." Sam raked his fingers through his hair.

Darius reached for the paper, but Sam pulled it back. "Don't touch it. Bad enough it's going to have my fingerprints all over it."

Darius rolled his eyes but dropped his hand to his side. His eyebrows rose as he scanned the paper. Then he pressed his lips tightly together.

"What?" Sam leaned back against the vehicle.

Darius shook his head. "Best be getting up to the haus."

"Your body language is screaming that you know what this is about."

The older man frowned. "Maybe. Maybe not. But you shouldn't have called the sheriff. This needs to be handled among our people."

"The way everything else has been handled, right? By getting swept under the rug? Just like the truth that Orpah is your mamm?"

Darius shifted. "Secrecy is how the preachers and the bishop at time told her to handle it. I've a feeling the current preachers might've chosen a different way, but it hasn't been addressed again. Water under the bridge, and all that."

Sam stared at him. "Seems that water hit a dam and flooded. And now Abigail's caught in it."

"She is, jah. Deeper than she knows. And in more ways than one." Resignation colored the older man's tone. He pulled at his beard, his expression unreadable.

"Don't you think she should know?"

Darius shook his head and walked out of the barn.

Sam wasn't sure if that meant Darius believed the secrets should stay secret, or if he was simply lamenting the mess those secrets had made.

All he knew was what he believed—that Abigail deserved answers. And Sam intended to make sure she got them.

He grabbed his flashlight and Abigail's writing supplies, then followed her onkel across the yard and into the haus.

In the kitchen, two lanterns were burning. A steaming teakettle sat on the stove. On the table were a basket of assorted tea bags and a jar of instant koffee, along with a plate of cookies—oatmeal raisin and peanut butter, from the looks of it.

Sam laid the stationery and pen on the table, then went to the sink to wash up. Darius handed him the hand towel when he was finished with it.

A moment later, the door to the all-season room opened, and Abigail emerged from her makeshift quarters. She'd put on a gray dress but left her head uncovered, her hair still braided. Her feet were bare. Sam grinned when he caught a glimpse of her toenails, painted with pink polish. Verboden, but it was a popular "hidden sin" for girls to engage in. That, and lying out in bikinis on hot summer days. His sister Rachel and their cousin Greta had done that once. Until Daed had kum home unexpectedly, caught them, and read them the riot act.

Abigail's dress concealed the curves that her thin, clingy nacht-gown had revealed, tantalizing and teasing him, making it a challenge to focus elsewhere. It would be interesting seeing Abigail in a bikini… if she had that vice.

Darius selected a tea bag from the basket, tore off the packaging, and lowered the bag into an empty mug. As he moved toward the stove, car headlights flashed through the window. With a heavy sigh, he bypassed the stove and headed for the door. He opened it a scant foot, then stood there, blocking the doorway with his body.

"Had a call about a prowler?"

"False alarm, officers. Sorry for the inconvenience. Seems we're all a bit antsy, with the recent fires and all."

Sam gaped at him. He could barely contain his outburst, but he remained silent until Darius closed the door. "What do you mean, false alarm? There was a threat on Abigail's life."

"She's not a witch." Darius calmly returned to the stove and filled his mug with steaming water.

⌒

"Someone called me a *witch?*" To Abigail, that was worse than a death threat, for some reason.

"Now, hold on a minute, Abigail." Onkel Darius pointed to a chair. "Fix yourself some tea and have a seat."

Abigail pressed a hand to her stomach and glanced at the mugs she'd set out. At the basket of sachets. At the stove. She sat without getting herself any tea.

Sammy did, too. Then he popped up and filled a mug with hot water. He grabbed a pink packet from the basket—a sample of hibiscus tea sent by the company Aenti Ruth ordered from—and dropped onto the wooden chair again. Then he studied the package, both sides, as closely as if he expected to be quizzed about it.

Onkel Darius rotated his mug so the handle faced the way he preferred. "The officers aren't equipped to deal with this situation. It's a simple matter of misinterpretation. I believe the exact words your mamm used were 'bewitching Mark.'"

Abigail stared at her onkel. That made nein sense. Courting was expected and encouraged. Marriage, too.

"We had to present your mamm's letter to the bishop and the preachers to get permission for you to kum here. Someone must have overheard us talking about it and misunderstood, and felt compelled to threaten you. I'll have a talk with the preachers as soon as possible." Onkel Darius shifted the basket of tea.

Sammy frowned. "What's wrong with Abigail attracting Mark— 'bewitching' him, as you called it?" His gaze alighted briefly on her as he asked the very question that she'd been forming in her mind but hadn't managed to verbalize. "I mean, I understand. She's a…a feuerzeug." His voice lowered to almost a whisper. Then he shook his head. "Are you going to send her away from here for 'bewitching' me, too?"

Abigail's eyes locked on Sammy as her heart sped into a gallop.

His lips quirked. "*If.* I meant *if.*" A blush colored his cheeks.

Onkel Darius shook his head. "Her bewitching *you* wouldn't pose a problem. But with Mark, it does. He's her brother."

"*Step*brother." Abigail shook her head. "His daed married my mamm. Technically, not a problem. We weren't raised as siblings. We lived in the same haus for barely a week, and apparently Mamm had made the arrangements to…banish me…well before that."

Darius sighed. Looked at the tea steeping in his mug. Then lifted the bag by the string and squeezed it out. "Ruthie and your mamm didn't think you needed to know. But this whole thing has been a rotten egg from the start. It's at the point where you touch it, and it's going to explode. And it would've been avoided, completely avoided, if your daed—"

"My daed?" Abigail leaned back and folded her arms defensively across her chest. To shield herself from the blow that was sure to follow. Not that physical protection could fend off an emotional injury, but she couldn't keep herself from doing it.

What was it Orpah had said about a list?

Keeping his gaze fixed on Onkel Darius, Sammy tore open the packet of hibiscus tea and dropped the bag into his mug. His mouth flattened into a thin, straight line. His blue eyes darkened into storm clouds.

"Ach, Abigail. I hate this." Onkel Darius's voice broke. He inhaled a long, deep breath and closed his eyes a moment. When he opened them again, he reached for her hand.

The rushing noise in her ears hinted she'd reached the very rockiest of bottoms. She pulled her hand away from her onkel and scooted her chair back. Out of his reach. Closer to Sammy, her defender. "Just say it."

Hopefully, the news he was about to share wouldn't cause her to shatter.

Onkel Darius took another deep breath. "Mark is…he's not your stepbrother. He's your half brother."

Chapter 20

Sam raised his eyebrows. "That explains things. Well, some things, anyway." His gaze shot to Abigail. She sat still, with her lips parted slightly. Looking far calmer than he would have expected, considering that her onkel had just delivered a message that would rock anyone's world.

She got up, grabbed her crutches, and went into the all-season room. Shut the door softly, with a click.

Not with the slam Sam had braced himself for.

Her reaction really didn't fit. Where was the spitfire who'd fought everything from beginning to end, every step of the way? Sam had expected denial. Anger. Arguing.

Not calm acceptance.

Or maybe what he'd witnessed was just the eye of the hurricane.

Darius took a sip of his tea. Apparently, Abigail's response hadn't fazed him at all.

It was beginning to scare Sam. Terrify him, actually.

He cleared his throat. "So, her daed cheated on her mamm?"

Darius sighed. "Jah, but...not exactly. Not so cut-and-dried." Darius set his mug down. "They weren't married yet. And our mamm was against Deborah's being with Obadiah, due to *the list.*"

Sam wasn't sure how to respond, or even if he should. He glanced at the door to Abigail's room. He wanted to go to her. To be with her when this volcano blew. Not sit here and discuss who'd cheated on whom.

Darius took another sip of tea and then glanced at Abigail's empty seat. "Guess she needs time to think this through. Decide on her own if it's fact or fiction. I'm going to go to bed. I'll stop by Preacher Samuel's tomorrow and have a talk with him about this 'witch' stuff. And the flood, as you so aptly called it, that Abigail's caught in." He twisted his lips as he stood and picked up the torn Bible page from the table.

"I suppose I'll go home." Sam eyed Abigail's door again. Maybe he'd tap on the window from outside.

"Pretty late." Darius glanced at the battery-operated clock on the wall. "After mid-nacht. You're welkum to stay here again, if you want. Upstairs, of course." He tossed the words over his shoulder as he left the room.

"Of course." Sam reached to extinguish one of the lanterns. Then he picked up his mug and took a tentative sip. He'd never had hibiscus tea before. It tasted pretty much like normal tea with a hint of liquid chlorophyll. He'd sampled some of that from the bottle Mamm had kept in her refrigerator after the birth of his youngest sister. Kind of grassy.

Sam drained the rest of his tea, forcing it down, though he didn't care for the aftertaste. It fit the way he felt following the conversation with Darius, and Abigail's unexpected reaction. Then he sat there, weighing his options.

Leave? Or stay?

～

It took a moment for the rhythmic pounding sound to register with Abigail. She pushed herself off the daybed, shuffled across the room, and opened the door.

A flashlight flickered on, illuminating Sammy's face.

She shut the door on him.

"Kum on, Abigail. We need to talk."

She pressed her back against the door. What did he want to discuss? She wasn't interested in revisiting her onkel's ridiculous statement. It was stupid to even consider the possibility that Mark was her half brother. He looked nothing like her. They had different parents.

Well, up until his daed had gone and married Mamm. Stepsiblings, jah. Half? Nein.

Sammy knocked again. "Abby, please."

She sighed and opened the door.

"May I kum in?"

She looked behind her, at the room now dimly illuminated by his lantern. At the daybed, piled with fluffy pillows.

"Or would you rather kum out here?"

Her knee ached from all the moving she'd done that day, and she had nein pain pills, other than whatever was left in the off-brand bottle stashed in the kitchen cabinet. And those weren't extra-strength.

"I need to sit." She hobbled back over to the daybed. "Have a seat. Somewhere."

Sammy entered the room and looked around. Not that there was much to see. A clothesline, coiled on a hook, for hanging laundry indoors when the weather was bad. The daybed. A couple of other wall hooks, one holding her white kapp, the other a borrowed dress. Her nacht-gown, draped over the rail of the daybed.

After a moment, Sammy joined her on the daybed, keeping a safe distance away. They were almost a cushion's width apart. He clasped his hands over his knees and studied her with a wary look in his eyes, as if he wasn't quite sure what to make of her.

Really, did he have to sit there in silence and stare at her, like some scientist viewing a microorganism under a microscope? She'd done that in school once. All the students taking turns peering through the eyepieces at cells from someone's mouth swimming around on a slide.

Fascinating.

Creepy.

Abigail shuddered. "What was it you wanted?"

"I wanted to talk to you about…." The wariness had spread to his voice. "About what your onkel said."

She stilled.

"Kind of…explains things. Some. Ain't so?"

"It's a lie." She crossed her arms over her chest again. "There is absolutely nein way Mark's my half brother. None."

She couldn't think of any evidence that would prove Onkel Darius right—or wrong. Other than a vague memory of a move when she was maybe three or four.

Sammy twisted toward her. "Why would your onkel lie about something like that?"

Abigail shrugged.

"I've never known him to speak falsehoods."

She glared at him. "Well, you have now. I just can't prove it yet."

He cleared his throat. "But…uh…why do you want to prove him wrong? You don't want to get back with Mark, do you? After he just let you go without a fight?"

She bended her left leg and pulled her knee against her chest. Expelled a heavy breath, as if that would blow away the deep, dark depression that had begun to settle on her like a storm cloud. "Guess I'm not worth fighting for. To him, to Mamm…to anyone."

Silence. Then, "I'd fight for you, Abby."

Right.

"Really, I already have."

He had a point. He *had* called her stepdaed—Mark's daed—demanding answers.

And he had run out of the barn in pursuit of whoever had left that awful note.

But she wasn't ready to give in.

"Aren't you the same man who chased me down, accusing me of setting fire to your family's barn?" She encircled her knee with her arms and rested her head in the circle of her elbows. *Breathe in. Breathe out. Repeat.*

Sammy sighed. "I didn't know you then. And I was wrong. The fires started before you got here."

They did? But…. "You still call me a feuerzeug."

"Jah. That's because…you're a schnuckelchen."

Beautiful girl.

A tear escaped from the corner of her eye. *Ach, Sammy. I think I love you.*

"And because I think I might be falling in…like…with you."

⌒

It was more than just "like." It was dangerously close to love. But who fell in love after only a few days?

Sam wasn't anywhere near ready to confess to *that*. Even if it were true.

"In like, huh?" A smidgen of wry humor edged her voice, lending it a sharpness Sam hadn't heard before.

He didn't know what to say. What to do. It was probably a mistake coming in here to talk with her.

This dead calm *had* to be the eye of the hurricane. And he was afraid of the emotional backlash that would eventually follow.

"So, is 'in like' as much as the affection you had for PJ? Or not quite that much?" Abigail's face was still buried in the curve of her arms, her voice muffled by the fabric of her sleeves.

Sam couldn't answer that. Not without giving anything away. "Just different," he muttered. It didn't really answer her question, but thankfully she didn't call him on it. Maybe she hadn't heard him.

She sighed, then raised her head. When she glanced at him, her eyes reflected a certain neediness.

She lowered her left knee. "Would you hold me? Please?"

Ach, jah. He scooted closer to her, till their legs touched, and wrapped his arm around her shoulders. She curled against him, her hand sliding across his waist, her head coming to rest on his upper chest. He put his other arm around her, thankful for the thick fabric of her dress instead of the tempting, clinging thinness of her nacht-gown.

Her sigh—this time, of contentment—sent tingles racing through him. As she traced his side with her fingertips, he shut his eyes and soaked up the pleasure, allowing himself to enjoy simply having her in his arms.

He didn't have the right to take things any further.

But how he wanted that right. The right to take care of her for the rest of his life. The right to hold her every day…and nacht.

The right to go through the storms with her. And to rejoice together in the rainbows that followed.

Okay, he'd admit it. At least to himself. To Gott.

He loved her.

Chapter 21

Abigail awoke Tuesday morgen enveloped in a sense of peace and safety. She stretched her arms, opened her eyes, and froze. Very slowly, she sat up and surveyed the strong shoulder and firm chest she'd been leaning against.

Then she met Sammy's eyes. They were wide with shock. Or was it horror?

Those were the primary emotions coursing through her right now. Along with a hint of guilty pleasure.

She scooted away from Sammy as he sprang to his feet. "I'm sorry, Abby. I didn't mean…. I didn't…. I was praying for you, and I fell asleep, I guess."

If only her prayers had the same effect. If only Gott would show her that He was listening. She cast Sammy a shy glance. "Danki. I like it when you pray for me."

But she didn't know what to do now. Onkel Darius was probably out in the barn already. Pray that he wouldn't catch Sammy? Jah, that was a given. She looked from the door leading out back to the door connected to the kitchen. Which one would make for a safer escape route?

Sammy took a step toward the back door. "I'm going to head home. I'll…return. Later. To work on my car. Or something."

"But, how…?" She shook her head and twirled the end of her braid around her fingers.

Sammy gave her a wobbly smile. "I don't know. We'll figure it out." Then he opened the back door and left. Without looking around to see if the coast was clear.

What would they figure out? And what didn't he know? Instead of answering her query as to how they would sneak him out, he'd left her with more questions.

Sneaking out hadn't been on his radar. He'd walked out boldly. Confidently. As if he belonged in her bedroom. Belonged with her.

If only she knew where she belonged.

She opened the window shades, one by one, letting them snap to the top. Then she watched Sammy retreat down the dirt lane between the haus and the barn, angling toward the road and his borrowed truck.

Until Onkel Darius stepped out of the barn and waylaid him.

Fear threaded through her. He'd been caught.

Time to start breakfast.

And then face the fallout.

~

Sam was hoping to make his escape before Darius realized he'd spent the nacht someplace other than upstairs. Not that he had done anything to be ashamed of. Jah, he and Abigail had fallen asleep. On the daybed in her room. But they'd slept upright and fully clothed.

Still, that might be enough to warrant a forced marriage.

And if that were the case, he would comply. Gladly.

As You will, Lord.

Darius didn't appear combative but relaxed. "You mind running back inside to get the egg basket? I forgot that Ruthie told me not to let Abigail collect the eggs until her leg heals. Or are you in a hurry to get home?"

"I can collect the eggs first."

"How's Abigail this morgen?"

Sam stiffened. "Quiet."

"Still in denial, then? She's not exactly one to hold back what she's thinking."

"I think denial is about right. She said you were lying." Sam almost cringed, delivering that message to a highly respected man in the community.

But Darius nodded. "I kind of expected that. Still, it's the truth. Obadiah even confessed to the bishop and the preachers, and knelt before the church, so it's known by the older generation. I'm sure it's being whispered about, with Abigail's arrival. But who knows if anyone will talk openly about it?" Darius sighed. "When Mark's mother, Judith, and her ehemann, Leo, decided to move to Ohio for a fresh start—away from Obadiah, away from the rumors—I told Obadiah not to follow. But he was adamant about seeing his sohn grow up, even if he couldn't acknowledge the relationship. And his decision meant that everyone had a constant reminder of the sin. His presence wouldn't let them forget. And now, Deborah is faced with having to raise her ehemann's sohn by another woman. When Obadiah died, they would've lost the farm and been forced to return here if Leo hadn't offered to marry her. But he insisted on sending Abigail away and essentially disowning her. He didn't want anything to start between her and Mark, and neither did Deborah, because word was bound to get out that they were really half siblings. Too much shame."

A new light shone in the older man's eyes. The secrets he'd been carrying must have been a heavy burden.

Maybe Sam should eliminate the secrets darkening his own life.

Later. Right now, Abigail was more important.

"Then why did you tell Abigail to write her mamm?" he asked. "And why didn't they send Mark away, instead?"

"Mark was needed for farm work." Darius surveyed Sam a moment, sadness seeping into his expression. "You never lost a child, sohn. I lost three that I'll never see, touch, or talk to again. I understand what Deborah is going through. She knows Leo wants Abigail cut off, but she doesn't want to take that final step. She loves Abigail. And her hope was that if Abigail came here, the secrets could stay secrets." He sighed. "She should've known better."

Sam grunted. "I'm not thinking too highly of Deborah or Leo."

Darius grimaced. "Leo always was sort of a dictator. But, on the brighter side, Abigail is here, with me and Ruthie. I'm getting to know my niece, and loving her like a dochter." Darius smiled. "Gott has a plan for everything. All things work together for our benefit."

Sam nodded, though he didn't completely understand that concept.

"Maybe you should call it quits with that Englisch girlfriend of yours, now that you're 'twitterpated.'" Darius chuckled.

"Already did." Sam shifted his stance. "I'll get that basket and collect the eggs before Abby decides to do it."

Darius raised his eyebrows and glanced over Sam's head.

Sam turned around. Abigail was maneuvering her way across the porch with her crutches. A basket dangled by its handle from two of her fingers.

He took off at a run. "Let me help you, schatz."

"I can do it." But her steps faltered.

"I could carry the basket for you, ain't so?"

She rewarded him with a smile that showed her dimples. And held out the basket. "Danki."

He took it from her, and their fingers touched. Sparks shot up his arm.

A soft blush colored her cheeks. So, she'd felt the same thing.

She still wore the gray dress from last nacht, but she'd pinned up her hair and tied a handkerchief over it. Only a few honey-colored strands were visible above her forehead.

"Is Onkel Darius angry?"

Sam glanced toward the barn. Darius had disappeared.

He looked back at Abigail. "I don't think he knows what happened, exactly. I mean, he gave me permission to spend the nacht here. Upstairs."

"You didn't make it that far." The color of her cheeks deepened, and she started across the yard.

"Nein, feuerzeug, I didn't. And I'm sorry if we get in trouble. But I'm also glad I could be there for you." He fell into step beside her, slowing his stride to match hers.

Too bad she had to use those crutches. For four weeks.

Four. Long. Weeks.

It would eliminate the option of romantic strolls down the road when he came courting. But there was always the checkerboard. Or maybe Darius would help him build a porch swing and it would be a gut spot for sparking.

They could also take a slow buggy ride to the pond where some Amish teens hung out—on a not-so-popular nacht. Or sit together on a blanket and stargaze....

His blood heated.

The next thing he knew, Abigail had balanced the crutches under her arm and was reaching for the latch of the chicken coop.

He should've moved ahead of her to open it himself, but he'd been lost in his daydream.

Sam turned at the sound of crunching gravel and a snorting horse. Bethany Weiss leaned out the door of the buggy as it approached. "Gut morgen! I was just at the schoolhaus, dropping off something Daed asked me to deliver to the teacher, and I thought I'd stop by to invite you to my birthday frolic, Abigail. You too, Sammy. Friday nacht."

The way her gaze skittered from Abigail to him, she probably figured he'd staked his claim.

She would be right.

"Sounds fun." Sam glanced at Abigail. "You up for it? I'll take you there and bring you back home."

Her blush intensified, and she glanced at the cast on her right leg. "I wouldn't be able to play volleyball."

Bethany nodded. "That's fine. There'll be plenty of other things to do. And you can always sit with me on the porch. I look forward to getting to know you better." She lifted the reins but stopped short of flicking them. "I almost forgot, Sammy—I heard the sheriff and the fire chief went to talk to Hen yesterday afternoon. He wasn't arrested, though. Do you think he was involved in the recent fires?"

Abigail lowered her head and tightened her grip on the crutch handle, her fingers going white.

Sam felt a stab of conviction. Here he was, kicking himself for thinking about courting instead of opening chicken-coop latches, and there was somebody at large who'd threatened Abigail's life only hours after drugging her and leaving her in a burning barn.

He looked back at Bethany and shrugged with feigned nonchalance. "I'm sure they have gut reason to question him."

Of course, he thought Hen was guilty—of arson and of drugging Abigail. And he wished Hen had been arrested. Miranda, too. And her boyfriend.

Maybe that would kum in time. Hopefully, before any more barns burned.

Bethany frowned, then clicked her tongue at the horse and waved gut-bye as she steered the buggy toward the road.

"She seems nice." Abigail opened the gate to the chicken enclosure and stepped inside.

Sam followed her. "She is nice…and very chatty. In school, she was always getting in trouble for outtalking the teacher. Not everybody likes to talk to her, though, for fear she'll take gossip home. Her daed is the bishop, you know."

"She mentioned that." Abigail edged the coop door open, letting the birds into the enclosure. "And she told me she doesn't gossip."

When they'd finished, Sam escorted Abigail back to the haus and set the basket of ten warm brown eggs on the kitchen counter. "I'll go feed and water the chickens, but don't expect me for breakfast. I'll go home, clean up, and kum back later."

"To work on your car." Abigail leaned the crutches against the wall and reached for the canister of oatmeal.

"Jah, that. And to court you."

⌒

The oatmeal canister landed on the counter with a thud. Abigail spun around and stared at Sammy. "What?" Her heart raced.

His grin was crooked. "I know you aren't over Mark yet, but I want to be first in line when you're ready to move on. Until then, friends?"

"Friends." Her voice shook. She wanted to be more than friends with Sammy. She liked being in his arms. Besides, Sammy awakened emotions she'd never experienced with Mark.

She glanced shyly at him, then looked away. "I'm ready to move on." Her cheeks heated.

He chuckled. "I'll be back later." He headed for the door.

"Wait."

Sammy stopped and turned around.

"Before you go, would you mind bringing down a few items from upstairs? Aenti Ruth said she would assemble a stack of supplies I'd need to make my new dresses."

"Jah, I'd be glad to. Just remember, if you get bored sewing, you can kum out to the barn and watch me work."

She grinned. "Danki."

Minutes later, the treadle sewing machine was set up near a window in the living room, and on a nearby table was the pile of sewing supplies. "Be back a little later, Abigail." This time, he drew out her name in the sexy drawl he'd used the first couple of times he'd spoken it. She'd missed that. His gaze skittered over her face, dipping briefly to her lips.

She trembled and pretended to focus on measuring out the oatmeal for Onkel Darius's breakfast.

The door closed behind Sammy.

Then it opened again, and he came back inside. Seconds later, she was being held against his chest in a bear hug.

She wrapped her arms around his torso and hugged him back.

He touched his lips to her hairline with a gentle kiss. "We'll figure it out, feuerzeug."

Then he was gone.

And she was left alone, reeling.

If only she were six inches taller.

Chapter 22

Sam was lying beneath his car, having just finished changing the oil, when he saw a set of boots and a cane kum to a stop. Sam slid out from under the car and stared up into the face of his brother-in-law.

David's expression was serious. Not gut.

"Was ist letz?" Sam pushed himself to his feet.

Despite his grave demeanor, David's dark eyes conveyed warmth. Kindness. "Your daed wants you to kum up to the haus. We're here to talk to Abigail."

"Darius was supposed to stop and talk with Daed this morgen."

"And he did. But that's not why we're here."

Sam chilled. "Are you here in an official capacity?" Had Darius gone straight to the preachers about Sam's spending the nacht with Abigail instead of confronting him and getting his side of the story first?

"Jah." David gestured toward Abigail's original pair of crutches, which still leaned against Sam's car. He raised an eyebrow.

"Abigail's. She lost them. They were returned last night, around eleven thirty or so." Sam glanced at the crutches. Then blinked. They were covered in dirt. And was that a tomato vine? He plucked off the greenery with a frown. The crutches had been clean the nacht before.

"Bring them with you. The plant, too." David started for the door. "Don't clean anything off."

"I'll be right there. Need to clean *myself* off, at least." Sam reached for a small pail of GOOP hand cleaner and scooped some out with his fingertips.

"You are a mess." David's smile looked grim. "See you at the haus."

After getting cleaned up, Sam wiped his hands with a rag, then grabbed the crutches and the vine and carried them to the haus. He left the crutches propped against the siding, the tomato vine on the porch floor beside them. Then stepped into the kitchen.

Abigail had gotten out a tray of cookies and poured several glasses of iced tea, but she hadn't taken any for herself. She sat at the table, arms crossed over her chest in a protective stance, her eyes wide as she stared at Sam's daed.

Sam's heart ached for the hurt she was feeling. And this time, he was probably the reason for it.

Daed looked up at Sam with a slight smile. "Hallo, Sohn. Working on that car of yours?"

Sam pulled in a long breath. "Jah. Still thinking about selling it. Need to get it running first." Selling would be the right choice. Like getting rid of baggage.

"Trading it in?"

Sam angled a sideways glance toward Abigail, then looked back at Daed. "Probably for a horse and buggy." He ignored the brief flare of hope in Daed's eyes. "David said you wanted to see me."

"Jah, for a witness. You haven't done anything to be concerned about, ain't so?"

Well, technically, he had. But he wouldn't bring it up unless Daed or David did.

Sam pulled out the chair next to Abigail and sat. "Witness for what?"

Abigail had started tapping her left foot on the floor, but he couldn't tell whether it was a nervous habit or a show of impatience. He suspected the latter.

Daed cleared his throat. His expression sobered as he turned to Abigail. "The ladies next door have complained that someone destroyed their greenhaus. Yenneke went out to check when she heard noises, and said she saw a lit lantern and someone swinging a set of crutches like crazy, smashing things. Destroying plants, breaking pots...." He speared her with a look. "Preacher David says the condition of your crutches points to you as the perpetrator."

"What?" Abigail squeaked. She glanced at the crutches leaning against the wall.

"Not those crutches," David said. "The ones from the barn." He looked at Sam. "Where are they?"

Sam couldn't believe the nerve of his brother-in-law. "On the porch," he said slowly. "What time did this allegedly occur? Because somebody returned the crutches to the barn around eleven thirty last nacht, and they weren't dirty then. They just had a note attached...a threat. We reported it to the police."

"Yenneke said the greenhaus incident happened around two in the morgen." David took a sip of his tea.

Abigail opened her mouth. Shut it. And shook her head. Her shoulders slumped.

She would be in trouble, whether Sam defended her or not. But he needed to do what was right.

Sam swallowed. "Abigail didn't do it. She was asleep at two in the morgen. And...and I know this for certain because I was with her."

◟◝

Abigail's face flamed. At least she had an alibi...but it might get her into deeper trouble than the greenhaus incident would have.

Preacher David choked on his iced tea, sending it splattering across the table. "Ugh. Sorry." He reached for a napkin.

Preacher Samuel reared back, the front legs of his chair rising off the floor. He grabbed the edge of the table to regain his balance. The chair slammed down again as his mouth settled in a flat line. He stared at Sammy. Speechless.

"Not what it sounds like." Sammy pushed several more napkins toward Preacher David. "We were talking, and then she fell asleep. I started praying and drifted off, too. Completely innocent."

Not *completely*. The emotions that had coursed through her were anything but innocent.

"You fell asleep, too?" Preacher David glanced up, looking from her to Sammy. "She could've sneaked off, for all you know."

"Um, nein. We were sort of...tangled...in each other's arms." Red crawled up Sammy's neck. He glanced at Abigail and grimaced.

"So, not 'completely innocent,' as you claimed." Preacher Samuel tugged on his beard and glared at his sohn.

Sammy's chest rose and fell. He frowned. Remained silent.

Abigail opened her mouth to protest, but then she shut it again. What could she say? Deny what Sammy had said—the truth, though there was more to it than the preachers knew—and be blamed for the destruction next door? Or stick to her alibi and allow them to believe that Sammy.... That she.... That they....

"Nein." Sammy straightened. "It is exactly as I said. We were both fully dressed. I haven't even kissed her. We were just talking." He exhaled noisily. "She's going through a lot right now. And we're friends. Becoming friends, anyway." He cleared his throat.

Preacher David leaned forward, his eyes on Sammy. "The crutches...how kum there are two sets? And what do you mean, one set was returned last nacht?"

Sammy nodded. "She took her original set of crutches with her when she went out with Miranda, then ended up being drugged and left in a burning barn. When she was released from the hospital, a nurse loaned her another pair, and then the original set showed up here last nacht. Someone left them propped against my car. Along with a threatening note." He leaned back. "She's hobbling around with a broken knee in a cast, and nein pain medication. Do you really think she would walk across a bumpy yard at two in the morgen and destroy someone's greenhaus? And even if she were physically capable of doing all that, what motive could she possibly have?"

Preacher David sighed, the sternness fading from his face. "None that I can see." He smiled at Abigail.

But Sammy's daed surveyed her warily as he continued to tug on his beard. "Drugged. Left in a burning barn." He looked at his sohn. "You went to the hospital?"

Sammy nodded.

Preacher Samuel turned his gaze back to Abigail. "Were you... violated?" He cleared his throat.

Abigail shook her head. But, really, the answer depended on one's definition of "violated." Hen may not have violated her, technically, but the memory of those invasive tests at the hospital made her wish she'd answered differently.

"So. You are being falsely accused. Of starting fires." Preacher Samuel's gaze moved to Sammy, then returned to Abigail. "And of destroying a greenhaus. Then, there's this 'witch thing' Darius mentioned. I think...."

Ach, she'd almost forgotten the "witch thing." She swallowed, hard.

"I think that it probably would be wise to send you to live at The Hen Haus for a while," Preacher Samuel finished. "Whoever has been targeting you will think you're being punished. And the three women there, your grossmammi included, will be able to testify to your whereabouts."

The preachers knew about her relationship to Orpah, too? Did everyone in this town know more than she did?

Preacher Samuel reached for a cookie. "I know Darius stops by there every day. Sammy, you still check in on the mauds, ain't so?"

"Every few days. I can—I will—stop more often."

"Gut." Preacher Samuel took another cookie, then stood. "Abigail, this is not a punishment. We want to figure out who's behind all this, in an effort to clear you. Do not leave the haus or yard for any reason whatsoever, unless Darius or Sammy or one of the preachers is with you."

"Haus arrest," Sammy muttered.

Haus arrest? Abigail smoothed her apron with her sweaty palms. At least the preachers believed she was innocent. And they were trying to protect her the only way they knew how. She smiled. Maybe Gott cared about her, after all.

Preacher David chuckled. "Haus arrest, huh? If that's what you want to call it, Sam. She can still attend Bethany's birthday frolic on Friday—we heard she was going with you. But you've been hanging out with that Englisch girl too much. Picking up her language."

"We broke up." Sammy glanced at Abigail. Grinned.

"Probably wise, since you're courting Abigail," Preacher David teased.

Abigail's cheeks burned.

Preacher Samuel smiled. "Now, that's gut to know. Looking forward to getting better acquainted, Abigail. And welkum."

"We're not courting, but danki." Abigail pushed herself to her feet and grabbed her crutches. Bethany *did* talk too much, if word had reached the preachers that Sammy was courting her. Wasn't courtship supposed to be a secret?

"We're considering courtship," Sammy amended.

Whatever that meant. Even though she'd told him she was ready to move on from Mark, all they'd agreed on was friendship.

For now.

⁓

Sam didn't want Abigail to feel pressured, but he also wanted his daed and David to know he had definite interest in her.

He looked over at Daed. "When are you moving her next door?"

Daed shrugged. "Need to talk with the ladies to get their approval. But if they agree—and I'm sure they will—then to-nacht."

Sam nodded, then glanced at Abigail. "Want me to run upstairs and get your things?"

Her cheeks reddened. "Uh, nein. Danki. I'll manage."

Right. He glanced at her cast. She wasn't supposed to climb stairs.

"Rachel will kum over and help," David offered. He glanced at Abigail. "She's my frau. Sam's sister."

"I'll go talk to the ladies right now." Daed stood. "You get back to work on that car of yours, Sam, so you can sell it. Then we'll go to a horse auction."

Sam sighed. Nodded. And strode back out to the barn to resume working on his car. Despite what he'd told Daed, he wasn't in a huge hurry to sell it. But if the sale went quicker than he expected, Viktor would let him borrow his truck whenever he needed a vehicle. He could always call for a "Yoder Toter," too.

It would be nice to be able to take Abigail for buggy rides. At least that way, he wouldn't stick out at the youth functions. Though a buggy hardly provided an efficient means for responding to fire calls.

At least working on his car gave him an excuse to be near Abigail. Maybe at lunchtime, they could visit over sandwiches.

He'd just finished replacing the left brake lightbulb when Daed came into the barn. "Orpah and Zelda, at least, are happy Abigail is coming to stay. I tried to convince Yenneke that Abigail wasn't the one who destroyed her greenhaus, but I'm not sure I succeeded. She informed me that Abigail would be expected to help them clean up the greenhaus and start the plants as soon as everything was put back in order."

"I'll help with that." Sam glanced at his phone to check the time. "To-nacht, if they can get the supplies by then. But I'll be on call, so there's a chance I'll have to leave."

"I'm headed into town after lunch to get what they need," Daed said. "Want to kum?"

"I think I'll stay here and keep an eye on Abigail." Sam glanced toward the haus. "Trouble seems to keep finding her."

Daed gave a slight smile. The gleam in his eye said that he knew Sam wanted to stay for more than that reason alone. "She's had a hard time of it. And the gossip grapevine has gotten new life with her arrival. Never thought of it when Darius approached us to get permission for Abigail to kum and stay. To me, it seemed a gut idea to have Orpah's grossdochter kum. But Bishop Joe was against it from the start. Said it'd cause innumerable problems. Seems he was right."

"What do you mean, 'innumerable problems'?"

Daed shrugged. "Past problems have a way of messing up the present. Inviting Abigail here has threatened to uncover some truths that the past leaders wanted to keep secret. For gut reason."

Sam flexed his mouth. He wanted to blurt out that it was Abigail who had lured him away from PJ. Wanted to say he'd never felt this way before.

He sighed. "But this problem-causing grossdochter of Orpah's didn't ask to kum. And she still doesn't really know why her coming here is causing problems. Doesn't anyone care about her heart? Her feelings? The fact that she's been lied to repeatedly?"

Daed nodded. "Abigail has been hurt by a mishandling of the situation. I'm beginning to think we should make the path clear. Let me pray on the best way to do this."

Sam offered a tight smile as he looked down at his filthy hands. His heart was almost as dirty. Past sins had gotten hidden in the cracks and needed to be searched out. He reached for the rag hanging out of his back pocket and used it to wipe his grimy hands. He wished it were just as easy to wipe away every unclean thought he'd entertained, every sinful act he'd committed. Fortunately, Jesus had already done all that with His sacrifice on the cross. But Sam still couldn't forget. Couldn't forgive himself.

He sighed. What would Abigail think if she learned that he was as bad as Hen—and maybe even worse?

Chapter 23

Abigail stood at the foot of the stairs and gazed upward. She could do this. Really, she could. People used crutches to climb stairs all the time, ain't so? She'd managed the three steps down from the porch to the yard without a problem. Jah, she could do this.

But this staircase was narrow. And steep.

She eyed the white plastic grocery bag in her hand. Maybe she should've taken Sammy up on his offer to collect all her things from the bedroom and bring them down. But she couldn't bear the thought of his seeing, much less handling, her unmentionables. Aenti Ruth had bought them when Abigail arrived—lacy undergarments unlike anything Abigail had ever worn before. Aenti Ruth said that every woman needed a little something feminine.

Abigail liked the undergarments. They made her feel somewhat naughty. But they weren't for the casual observer. Or anyone else, for that matter. Just her.

That was why she couldn't let Sammy help her. Even though he'd probably seen his share of female undergarments. PJ seemed like the kind of girl who didn't mind showing them off.

Abigail ignored the burn of irritation that thought ignited in her gut. PJ was out of the picture, putting Abigail at the center of Sammy's attention. But for how long? He would eventually lose interest and move on to someone more exciting.

"Abigail?"

She didn't recognize the female voice that broke the silence. Then she remembered that Preacher David had said he would send his frau.

Relieved she wouldn't need to climb the stairs after all, Abigail turned around and headed back to the kitchen. There, she found a woman wearing a maroon dress and a black bonnet. Something about her seemed familiar. The eyes, maybe. They reminded Abigail of Sammy.

The woman tugged off her bonnet and dropped it on the table. "Hallo. I'm Rachel Lapp. David sent me over to help you pack up."

"Danki."

Abigail didn't want to pack up. Didn't want to be uprooted yet again. But she also understood why she had to. And she was looking forward to getting to know her grossmammi better.

"David mentioned you needed some things brought down from upstairs…?"

Abigail nodded, hoping her blush wasn't obvious. "Everything on top of the dresser and in the first and second drawers. Just put them in here."

Rachel took the limp plastic bag from Abigail, eyeing it dubiously. As if she doubted it could possibly contain all Abigail's belongings. For an average maidal, maybe not. For someone who'd been kicked out of her haus with nothing but the clothes on her back, it was plenty big enough.

"I have to finish a couple of dresses, yet," Abigail explained.

"Go work on your dresses, and don't worry about this. I'll help you with the sewing when I kum back down, if you want." Rachel smiled, then scampered upstairs with movements Abigail hadn't been able to manage since she'd torn her ligament the first time, over a year ago. She looked down at her casted leg. Would she ever be able to scamper again?

Even though Rachel was a woman, it was still somewhat unsettling to know she handled Abigail's personal items. It was too bad there wasn't a place for Abigail to store her things in the all-season room. That way, she wouldn't have needed someone else to retrieve them for her.

Abigail reluctantly went back to the treadle sewing machine in the living room. She aligned the green fabric with the faint line Aenti

Ruth had drawn in black permanent marker, and compressed the pedal.

A few minutes later, Rachel reappeared with the white plastic bag, now three-fourths full. She hadn't tied it shut, so it gaped open at the top when she set it on a chair. "How can I help?"

Abigail studied Rachel's face, looking for signs of censure. Mamm never would've approved the purchase of such frilly underwear. Strong and sturdy was better, she always said. But Rachel's expression was open and friendly. Maybe even a tad curious.

Abigail looked down at the fabric. "I don't know. All I need to do is sew the seams and finish the hem."

"I'll trim the seams, then press them flat—until you're ready for me to measure the hem." Rachel picked up the maroon dress Abigail had been working on when the preachers had interrupted her. "This looks like my dress. See? They match." She settled in the chair next to Abigail's. "So, you and Sammy are a couple."

It was a statement, not a question.

Abigail didn't know how to respond. She struggled to recall how Sammy had described their relationship to his daed—something that indicated he wanted to be more than friends. But that seemed rather forward to say to his sister.

"Don't get me wrong," Rachel went on, her eyes focused on the fabric in front of her. "We're worried about Sammy. We didn't have a problem with Leah. Sammy courted her for a short time, just so you know."

Abigail nodded. Ruthie had told her as much, when she'd shared the heartrending details of the loss of her dochters.

"But Mamm didn't feel she was the right girl for him. And then, after her tragic death, he turned around and started going out with that Englisch girl…." She sighed and shook her head.

"PJ," Abigail muttered.

Rachel abruptly raised her head. "That's right. He told you about her?"

"Um…we've actually met."

"Oh." Rachel raised her eyebrows. "Well, word has it you and Sammy are a couple now."

"'Word has it'? Who's been saying that?"

Rachel pinched her lips together a moment. "Bethany Weiss."

Abigail sighed. Nein wonder the other young people tried to keep their secrets from the bishop's dochter. Seemed she was at the center of the gossip grapevine.

"She's not the only one, though. I first heard the rumor the nacht Daed's barn was burned."

"Ach." Sammy had held Abigail's hand in the middle of his family's kitchen right after the first fire. There'd been a ton of witnesses.

"Rather quick, ain't so? You've been here, what, a week? Maybe a little longer? Not that I have any room to talk. My relationship with David moved fast. Only difference, we wrote each other about a year before we met." Rachel snipped the excess material as she talked.

Abigail wasn't sure what to say about the "speed" of the relationship, either. She faced the machine again and started feeding the fabric through. Her hands shook, and she fought to keep the material from sliding the wrong way.

The truth was probably the best place to start. "We're not courting. And even if we were, aren't those things supposed to be kept secret?"

"Jah, technically. But, in most cases, everyone knows. There is then occasional surprise, of course."

Abigail completed the final seam on the second dress, then handed the garment over to Rachel before picking up the third dress—a grayish-blue.

"I can see why Sammy would like you," Rachel went on. "I like you, too. An Amish girl who can pull my brother away from someone like PJ has a lot going for her." She set the dress aside and reached for the next one. "David said you were rather quiet. That you didn't try to defend yourself at all. He said that spoke volumes about your character."

Abigail simply hadn't known what to say. And David had looked to Sammy for the explanations he demanded. What did that say about her character, really?

Rachel returned her attention to the dress. "I'm worried about Sammy getting hurt…again. That might push him farther away from the Amish. And we've made so much progress drawing him in the right direction." Her voice firmed. "Maybe you two ought to call it quits, just for a while. Until neither of you is on the rebound."

⌒

When Sam had finished as much of the car repair as he could manage without Darius's help, he cleaned up and exited the barn, flexing his arms to work a kink out of his back. David Lapp's horse and buggy waited near the haus. Rachel had probably kum to help Abigail pack her things.

He hoped his sister would get along with Abigail. A favorable opinion on Rachel's part would go a long way toward softening Mamm's heart. If only he hadn't ruined Mamm's initial gut impression of Abigail by loudly—and falsely—accusing her of being a feuerzeug.

Sam wished he'd held his tongue instead of allowing words to fly uncensored from his mouth. He'd frightened Abigail, and his actions had ended up causing her physical injury, as well.

But, in his defense, she had run out of the burning barn. Had attempted to run from his family. What was he supposed to think?

Lord, help me not to judge by appearances. So often, things are not as they seem.

He climbed the porch stairs, entered the kitchen, and took off his boots. Hearing soft voices coming from the living room—mostly Rachel's, with a sparse comment from Abigail—he padded across the kitchen in stockinged feet and then stood in the doorway, watching.

Abigail balanced with her left foot as she stood on a low three-legged milking stool with her back toward him, her hands grasping the back of a kitchen chair for support. Rachel knelt at her feet, pinning up the hem of the green dress Abigail wore. Two other dresses lay pooled in a messy pile beside her. Pins stuck out like porcupine needles from the fabric. Three dresses. Ruthie had been generous. But Abigail deserved it, having lost so much.

If only Sam had the right to walk up to Abigail, gather her in his arms, and hug her from behind, as he had done on Saturday when she stumbled on the stairs. In that instance, it was an automatic move meant to keep her from falling, and he tripped all over himself due to unexpected attraction to her. Now, the gesture would be motivated by love—a feeling he wasn't quite ready to announce to the world. He wanted time to think about it, to get used to the idea, to see if the feelings lasted. Marriage was for keeps, and he wanted to be sure of himself before he laid claims.

Rachel noticed him and grinned. "We just need to finish the hems, and then she'll be ready to go."

Abigail wobbled slightly.

"Looks gut." Sam edged closer. He liked the way the green fabric clung to her curves, at least from behind. He circled around the stool to check out the frontal view. This dress definitely fit better than the ones she'd borrowed from Ruthie. Except that this dress wasn't pinned completely closed. Just enough to make sure it hung straight for the purpose of hemming. He caught the glimpse of a lacy bit of something peeking out the gap. His face heated, and he looked away. "You think Darius would mind if I helped myself to some koffee and a couple of cookies?"

Rachel sat back. "Sammy, first be a dear and help Abigail down."

Gladly.

Sam stepped forward and placed his hands firmly on Abigail's waist. Abigail shifted a little, her face turning pink as she released the back of the chair and reached for his shoulders. Her hands hovered there a millisecond, not touching.

She glanced at Rachel. Then looked back at him, gazing into his eyes. Her breathing quickened.

"Ready?" He hoped neither she nor his sister noticed the huskiness of his voice.

"Nein, not yet." Abigail's barely audible whisper somehow still had the power to make him shiver. She hesitated several more seconds, then settled her hands on his shoulders.

His fingers trembled against her.

He swallowed, wishing he could will Rachel out of the room, out of the haus, for a moment alone with Abigail.

"I think I'm ready now." Abigail's voice wavered, but her touch firmed, so that she was almost clinging to him.

Sam sucked in a gulp of air as he lifted her off the stool. Her soft curves pressed against him. Her breath feathered across his neck and ear. He settled her on the ground, making sure she was steady before he stepped away. Then he looked from Abigail's blush to Rachel's speculative gaze.

Had he done something wrong? Or too right?

His arms ached to embrace Abigail once more. To follow up in the way he longed to.

Sam pulled in another shaky breath, then retreated to the kitchen. Toward cookies and koffee.

And away from the sweetness of one too-beguiling female.

⌒

Abigail tried to still her trembling. She stared at the floor, afraid to look up. She didn't want to glimpse Sammy's backside in blue jeans, nor did she want to see the expression on his sister's face.

Probably a look of condemnation. After all, hadn't Rachel just warned Abigail to keep her distance from her brother? *"I'm worried about Sammy getting hurt...."*

And what about Abigail? She was the one who'd been rejected. Deemed unworthy of remaining with her family. Incapable of being trusted with the truth.

Not gut enough.

Not for her family. Not for Sammy. Not even for Gott.

Tears stung her eyes.

And now, someone—or several someones—thought she was a witch who deserved to die. Be burned, not at the stake but in a barn fire.

Her throat threatened to close up. One tear—two, three— escaped her eye and raced down her cheek.

She jumped when a hand gently smoothed her shoulder and traveled midway down her back. "You go get dressed, Abigail. I'll start the hems of the other two." Rachel spoke softly, gently. "And never mind what I said. I've never seen Sammy look at anyone that way before. *So romantic.* Maybe you're the one I should be worried about getting hurt."

Chapter 24

Sam stood in the kitchen and watched through the doorway as Abigail shuffled off to the all-season room, her shoulders slumped, her head bent.

She made nein acknowledgment of Rachel's comment. Sam was bothered by his sister's words, even though he didn't know the context.

Rachel turned toward the treadle sewing machine. She must've noticed him out of the corner of her eye, because she twisted around to face him. "Sammy?"

He crooked his finger to beckon her.

Rachel draped the dresses over the arm of the chair and came toward him. He stepped back to allow her entry to the kitchen.

"What was that about?" he asked, quietly, so Abigail wouldn't overhear.

She gazed at him with wide eyes. Feigned innocence. "I'm sorry?"

"'Never mind what I said'?" He hadn't meant to growl. "What, exactly, did you say to her?"

Rachel looked down. "That you both were on the rebound, and it might be a gut idea to take a break before starting anything new. I don't want you getting hurt."

"I'm not on the rebound." This time, he growled on purpose. "I broke up with PJ *after* I met Abigail."

Rachel winced. "Well, it's not like you didn't interfere with me and David." Her glance was pointed. "But, for what it's worth, I like Abigail. I told her that, too, before you came in."

Sam squeezed his eyes shut. Opened them again. "Okay. Got it. We want the best for each other." He found a smile. "And I was wrong about David. Maybe you're wrong about Abigail, too. I realize she appears vulnerable. It's understandable, considering what she's been through…what she's going through currently. But I was blessed with family who loved me and supported me, even when I made terrible mistakes. I know who my großeltern are, my cousins, all my kin. Abigail has only just met her grossmammi, and who knows if any of her daed's family lives around here? She probably has a lot of relatives she doesn't know about."

"I can't imagine not knowing my family." Rachel fingered her kapp strings. "Ach, wait. If she has a grossmammi around here, why doesn't she stay with her?"

He sighed. "She's about to. Orpah is her grossmammi."

Rachel's jaw dropped. "Nein."

"Don't ask, okay? Just don't ask. Because I don't know all the details."

Rachel sighed. "What a mess it must be. Kind of explains the new dresses and only half a plastic bag full of personal belongings, though."

Sam nodded. "There's so much about Abby you don't know. She's hurting."

"And you're a rescuer, ain't so? Ach, Sammy, not gut. You'll end up imagining you're in love with her—and that she's in love with you—when that isn't the reality."

"End up"? Too late.

He'd meant to convince Rachel that he knew what he was doing. Instead, he'd managed to alarm her even more.

"She's stronger than she appears, though," he added. "She's different. She doesn't need to be rescued so much as she needs someone she can count on." Sam forced a smile. "Don't worry. I'll be careful. I am capable of thinking things through, on occasion."

"On *rare* occasion." Rachel flashed him a teasing grin. "I told her I'd get this hemmed." She turned back toward the door—and froze.

Sam peeked over his shoulder. And gulped.

Standing less than ten feet away was Abigail.

~

Abigail spun around and headed for the sewing machine. Behind her, Rachel said something, but her words were lost in the mighty rushing wind filling Abigail's ears. Whispering the same two phrases.

You're a rescuer, ain't so?

You'll end up imagining you're in love with her.

Jah, Sammy was a rescuer. And the hope that maybe he loved her had crossed her mind. But she still had enough common sense to realize that a man's kindness didn't necessarily imply affection. Hadn't Leo been courteous to her while courting Mamm? All smiles and talk of being one big, happy family. Promises that he would honor the memory of her daed.

She plopped into the chair in front of the sewing machine and let the crutches clatter to the floor. Lined up the green fabric, then fed it over the stitch plate as she worked the foot pedal. A mindless task she hoped would help her to block out hurtful words. Painful thoughts.

It didn't work.

She'd been so excited for Mamm to marry Leo, mostly because it would mean living in the same haus as Mark. Seeing him every day. And every nacht. As if they were married, too.

"Trust me, it's better this way."

Why was it better for them to be separated? What if Onkel Darius was telling the truth?

"Trust me, it's better this way."

The memory of his whispered words washed through her mind with frightening clarity. Her foot slipped off the pedal, and she froze. *He knew. All along.* Mamm and Leo had entrusted him with the truth of his relationship to Abigail but kept it from her.

And that opened a window to countless more questions.

But she would process those later.

For now, she would spend every day with the grossmammi she'd never known. Maybe, between her, Onkel Darius, and the other two other ladies, someone could—would—fill in the blanks.

For now, she needed to be in control of her emotions, paste a smile on her face, and pretend everything was sunshine and cherry lollipops. Ignore the severe storms in her personal forecast for the immediate future. Large hail. Damaging wind. Dangerous lightning.

It was enough to make a girl want to seek cover. Protection.

And Sammy had proved himself able to provide both.

She snipped the thread, let the first dress drop, and reached for the second dress—the grayish-blue one. Repeated the steps.

Nein more relying on Sammy. Or on Gott. He didn't hear her prayers. Not the way He listened to Sammy.

Self-reliance was her only option.

"Abigail?" There was the gentle touch of a hand on her shoulder. She ignored it until it moved away. "I'll iron, then." Rachel picked up the discarded dress and walked off.

Rachel must have been talking all this time, and Abigail had completely blocked her out. Should she apologize? Ask Rachel to repeat herself? Abigail glanced over her shoulder and saw Rachel using a pot holder to lift the iron from the woodstove.

Sammy stood in the kitchen doorway, his mouth a thin line, his gaze intense. Unwavering. When Abigail's eyes met his, he didn't look away. Once again, he studied her as if she were some previously unknown specimen being viewed under a microscope.

She licked her lips. They'd gone suddenly dry.

His gaze flickered to her mouth. Lingered there.

Abigail swallowed. She wanted it, too. But that was probably a symptom of imagining herself to be in love with him. Either that or just wanting—needing—physical comfort.

Nein, to both scenarios. Nein.

Was it just her imagination? Or was it genuine attraction?

She jerked her attention back to the blue dress. To the machine, cold and unfeeling. Like she needed to be.

She was strong. She could figure this out and learn the new rules. Alone.

⌒

Sam hesitated in the doorway. He wanted to cross the room to Abigail, help her out of the chair, and take her for a stroll so they could talk. But something about her stiff posture informed him that asking a simple "Was ist letz?" would release the other half of the hurricane with frightening force.

It might be dangerous for her to rant while walking with crutches.

On the other hand, delaying their talk might result in releasing Hurricane Abigail on three unsuspecting elderly women.

He scratched his cheek.

Maybe it'd be best to let her simmer, and hope the storm would subside before making landfall.

He glanced at his sister. She mouthed something to him. "Talk to her"? He wasn't sure. He'd never been very gut at lipreading.

He shook his head but then crossed the room to Abigail. As he touched her shoulder, she jumped, causing the fabric to skitter crookedly on the table in front of her. "Kum...please. I need you." He bent over, picked up the crutches, and held them out to her.

Abigail glanced at Rachel. Sam did, too. She nodded, a smile on her face. "I can finish up out here. It won't take long."

Gut. Sam hadn't misunderstood her.

"Danki." Abigail sighed as she stood and took the crutches from him. "Where...?"

Ach. He didn't know. Her temporary room would offer the most privacy. And the most temptation.

"Don't you have some more packing to do?" Rachel nodded toward the all-season room.

"Jah." Abigail's voice shook a little. She scooped up a white plastic grocery bag from a chair.

Had Rachel meant to imply that they should go to her room to talk?

He scratched his neck. And followed Abigail through the living room, into the kitchen....

"Did you still want something to eat?" She looked around. "Cookies are in the cookie jar. I can make you some koffee or tea. Just let me go put this in my room." She started for the door.

"I need to talk to you." Sam swallowed his fear and followed her into the room, shutting the door behind him.

She set the grocery bag on a small table and turned to face him.

Sam cleared his throat. "What Rachel said...."

Moisture sprang to her eyes. Beaded on her lashes. Her chin quivered, even as she hiked it a little higher. "I realize you're a rescuer. But I don't need saving. And I know you don't love me."

Actually, he *did* love her. And she *did* need saving. In more than one way.

He opened his mouth to tell her just that. But then he remembered that Rachel had told her he was on the rebound. He closed his lips without a word.

Lord....

Talk to her.

Sam crossed the room in two strides. Took the crutches from Abigail. Gathered her in his arms.

She was rigid. Unyielding.

"I'm not on the rebound." It seemed important to make sure she knew that. Granted, she'd seen him with PJ. Knew how they interacted. But just in case.... "I wasn't in love with her."

The tension eased from her body. "I know."

Sam left one hand resting loosely on her back, as support if she happened to lose her balance. He looked at her a moment, studying her expression. It was a mystery. He raised his other hand and brushed his quivering fingertips lightly over her cheek. She trembled and leaned into his touch. His forefinger rested at the corner of her mouth, then traced it gently.

Her lips softened. Parted.

More than anything, he wanted to kiss her. But a man shouldn't kiss a woman like her without having very real intentions to commit.

Well, he had committed himself to her. And to Gott.

He let his hand slide down to her neck. Then stood there. Wordless. Gazing into her eyes.

She raised her head with an unspoken invitation.

His breathing became labored.

And he did what he had to do.

Chapter 25

Abigail couldn't contain the whimper that escaped her lungs when Sammy's mouth met hers. His kiss was soft. Teasing. Yet gentle, as if she were something valuable that might shatter unless handled with utmost care.

She wanted to cry at the sweetness of it.

Too soon, he pulled away and searched her eyes. Giving her every opportunity to step back.

She didn't have the strength.

She waited for what seemed an eternity. Then, with a groan, he slid his hand from her neck to the back of her head. Finally, his lips came back to reclaim hers.

Still tender.

She didn't want gentle. She wanted passionate. She pressed against him, wrapped her arms around his shoulders, and kissed him back with every bit of pent-up emotion inside.

After a startled hesitation, Sammy responded with a matching hunger that made Abigail's legs go weak. Gut thing one of her knees was supported by an unyielding cast.

She didn't know how long they had kissed when his hands moved to her back, pulling her nearer. Nearer…nearer. Without ending the kiss, he settled back on the daybed and took her on his lap.

Gut thing she didn't need to worry about keeping her balance on unsteady legs.

A shiver shimmied up her spine. She'd never been kissed this way. Never. She worked her fingers through Sammy's hair.

His mouth hardened, deepening the kiss. His fingers trembled against her, as if he fought to remain still.

She wanted more. More.

With another groan, Sammy broke away. He breathed heavily through parted lips.

She leaned into him, but he turned his head. Her lips brushed against his cheek, then landed near his ear. She rained tiny kisses along his jawline.

Sammy's hands shook. He found her mouth again for a few more minutes of passion, then broke loose long before she was ready. "We shouldn't have done that. I shouldn't have done that." His voice was ragged.

She blinked. She hadn't had enough. Still had a desperate inner urge for more. "Why?"

"Because you're the marrying kind, not the kiss-and-run kind."

That hurt, for some reason. "And you're…you're the 'kiss-and-run' kind?"

Sammy frowned. "I used to be." He shut his eyes. Sighed. "You deserve a lot better."

Disappointment filled her. She tried to squirm off his lap. If they weren't going to be kissing….

His eyes snapped open, and he gripped her waist. "Exactly how… intimate…were you with Mark?"

Abigail huffed. "Exactly how intimate were you with PJ?" If he wouldn't tell, he shouldn't expect her to.

He grimaced. "Way too intimate. I'm ashamed of—I hate—what we did. Things I should've waited to experience with you. Uh, with the one I marry."

Ach. She tried to hold the hurt at bay by reminding herself that she and Sammy hadn't known each other then. She summoned her courage. "Mark and I, we would kiss each other on the cheek. With an occasional peck on the lips. His daed caught us the one time Mark really kissed me." That kiss had been hard and angry. At the time, though, she'd mistaken anger for passion.

The real thing, with Sammy, was so much better. Beyond amazing.

She met Sammy's eyes. "But we planned to marry."

"Because you're the marrying kind." His smile wobbled. His gaze lowered to her mouth. Lingered.

Her lips ached in response.

Desire welled again.

⸺

Sam swallowed deliberately, trying to rein himself in. "Rachel's here. There's nein lock on the door. We'd better…." A tremor shook his voice. *If only.* "You'd best get up before she comes looking for us, and we give her the shock of her life." But, ach, he wanted her.

She scooted off his lap and stood, unsteadily, reaching for her crutches.

Sam dared to breathe deeply.

"I'm sorry. I don't know what came over me." She picked up the plastic grocery bag of belongings and stuffed a kapp inside. Then her black bonnet. Then the plush heart he'd left on her pillow—the one that read "I Luv You." And a few colorful wadded-up garments he couldn't plainly see. Her face flamed red.

"Hurricane Abigail." His voice sounded hoarse. He cleared his throat and stood.

She turned to look at him. "What?"

"I'd intended to ask you what's wrong."

She blinked. "What's wrong? Nothing. Except…." Her blush brightened.

Marry me. The words sprang, unbidden, to the tip of his tongue. He clamped his mouth shut to keep them unsaid. He and Abigail hadn't reached that point in their relationship. He should've waited till they reached it before kissing her like that.

"Kiss-and-run, jah?" Her voice broke.

Sam brushed his fingers over her cheek. "I'm not going anywhere, schnuckelchen. Not this time."

A look of relief filled her eyes.

"Not ever."

Maybe he shouldn't have said that. She might not want anything to do with him, once she found out certain things.

"What your sister said...." She sighed, so softly, he might've imagined it. "I'm afraid I do think ich liebe dich, Sammy. But I know it doesn't mean anything." She waved her hand dismissively. "I know you're a rescuer. That I'm lost, confused, and needy. But I think I need to find myself now. Learn to stand on my own two feet."

The passion had been Hurricane Abigail blowing through.

~

Abigail wanted Sammy to protest her words. To tell her that he'd meant everything he'd done. Every calming word he'd said. Every hug he'd given. Every prayer he'd prayed.

And she still wanted him to be her friend—nein, more than a friend. She wanted to tell him that she loved everything about him: his prayers, his calm, his friendship, his willingness to fight for her—for those he loved. And more. So much more.

Sammy stood completely still for the longest moment, his expression unreadable. Then he nodded.

Nein! Don't agree!

"But once you do—"

The door swung open. "There you are." Rachel came inside, carrying the three dresses. She held them up. "Hemmed and pressed. We'll carry them over to The Hen Haus like this so they don't get wrinkled. Sammy, are you coming with us?"

Sammy's gaze skimmed over Abigail. "Jah. You'll need me to help get her in and out of the buggy, ain't so?"

Abigail shut her eyes. She hadn't prepared herself for the pleasant torture of being in Sammy's arms again. And just after she'd technically broke up with him.

But Rachel had been right. They needed to be sure he wasn't on the rebound. Even though he'd said he wasn't. Abigail opened her eyes. "Maybe I could walk over there. The ladies believe I did, anyway, when I supposedly destroyed their greenhaus."

Rachel coughed.

Sammy shook his head at Rachel, whose eyebrows were raised. But when he glanced back at Abigail, his eyes showed relief. So, he didn't want to hold her, either.

Hurt flared. Tears pooled on her eyelashes.

A song Abigail didn't recognize came blaring from out of nowhere. The lyrics sounded like "Dancing too close to the—"

"Fire department." Sammy yanked his phone out of his pocket and glanced at the screen. "Structure fire." His gaze shot to Abigail.

"Finally, a fire I can't be accused of starting." As soon as the words crossed Abigail's lips, guilt nagged at her. She sounded hateful. Bitter. "Sorry."

Rachel gave her a puzzled look, then shook her head and turned to Sammy. "You're on call, ain't so?"

"Jah. *If* I'm available." But Sammy remained still, staring at Abigail. "Can't decide whether I should put out that fire or *this* one."

"This one?" Rachel glanced back and forth between them. "You mean…?"

"Um, Abigail might need to…." He hesitated. "Talk."

"Ach. Well, she can talk to me."

Sammy cleared his throat. "I probably should've said 'rant.'"

Ouch. Abigail tightened her grip on the handles of the crutches and pressed her lips together. He was more on target than she wanted to admit.

"Rant?" Rachel's tone held concern.

Abigail turned her back on both of them. "I *am* here, you know. While you're talking about me rather than to me." She bit her lip to stem the flow of angry words. Tears sprang to her eyes. Despite her blurred vision, she attempted to scan the room for any stray belongings.

"You go on home to David, Rachel." Sammy's voice had a hard edge.

208 Laura V. Hilton

More silence. Then, "But you're on call. And I have a message from David for the ladies next door."

"On call. If I'm available. I'm not avail—"

"Go…just go." Abigail forced the words past the lump that clogged her throat. Her tears were barely held at bay. "I don't need rescuing. Not from you. Not from anyone."

So untrue.

Another long silence.

Then Sammy released a heavy sigh. "Those poor ladies aren't going to know what hit them," he muttered. "See you later, feuerzeug."

Chapter 26

Sam didn't want to go. Felt it was wrong, in so many ways, to leave Abigail in this emotional state. But then, he'd volunteered to be her hero because he'd thought he could fix her problems. *Wrong.* It was becoming obvious that this was a situation only Gott could handle. Only Gott could fix.

Just like only Gott could fix the messes in Sam's past.

Sam left the haus, shut the door behind him, and stood on the porch. *Lord, help me to place Abigail in Your hands…and to leave her there. Help me to trust that You'll take care of the mess she's landed in. Please heal her. Heal her family.*

Did he dare pray for his relationship with her? He'd meant to talk to her. Not to get physical.

His eyes burned.

And if it's Your will, Lord, I want to marry her. Though I've known her just a few days, I love her. Help me to be the man I should be. Forgive me for my sins. And help me to make things right with the many people I've wronged.

Silence. He didn't sense any answers or words of comfort in his head. He didn't even feel at peace. The unrest made his stomach churn. He descended the porch stairs.

Lord, whatever I'm walking into…help.

The battle is not yours but God's.

One of the preachers had made that statement at church on Sunday. Said it was a paraphrase of a verse from the Old Testament. Was Sam really facing a battle?

Give me strength. Help me to rely on You.

Sam crossed the yard to the barn. His car wasn't completely fixed, but it ought to get him to the fire station and home again. Or close to it, at least.

His car jerked, shook, and grumbled its way to the station, but Sam made it there in time. He dived into his bunker gear, then raced for the engine.

Five minutes later, they screeched to a stop outside an all-too-familiar haus. PJ's.

PJ stood in the front yard with her smartphone in hand, appearing oblivious to the firefighters as she texted with someone. Cyber-flirting, probably.

When the blaze had been extinguished, the chief and another firefighter did a walk-through to determine the cause of the fire, even though PJ had told Sam—and everyone else within range—what had happened. She'd even snapped photos with her phone. Seemed to Sam she could've made better use of her time, by grabbing the fire extinguisher—or even just some baking soda—and putting out the grease fire before it grew and spread.

The damage was confined to the kitchen, but it was extensive: The walls, cabinets, and linoleum floor were ruined and would need to be replaced.

What was PJ doing home from school on a week-nacht? Was she on spring break?

Sam didn't ask. Didn't care.

PJ was history. Now that he'd met and fallen in love with the fiery Abigail, he couldn't imagine how he'd ever been attracted to PJ.

Well, that wasn't technically true. Her attire still screamed, "For a good time, call." Her low-rise short shorts and skimpy tank top were difficult to ignore. And it wasn't even that warm out. Mid-fifties, maybe.

Sam jerked his attention upward from her curves to her hair. She'd dyed it blonde with streaks of dark purple.

Jah, she was history.

Though he did still wonder what her initials stood for.

While Sam helped get the hoses coiled and back on the truck, PJ trailed him like a puppy on a leash. She ran her mouth constantly, but he tuned her out, concentrating on his work instead of her jabbering. Whenever she paused, he made a grunt that he hoped would pass for an acknowledgment.

Just when he was preparing to catch a ride back to the station, her hand landed, too possessively, on his thigh. He froze and stared at her. "What?" He shifted to free himself from her grip.

"Let's get together tonight. We can meet at the motel. Or my aunt's. Call me. I'll let you know where we are, since we can't stay here." PJ added an inviting smile.

Sam frowned. "We broke up last weekend, remember?"

PJ shrugged. "A big misunderstanding. You know that. It was nothing."

Nothing. Right. "Can't make it." He climbed into the truck.

"It'll be worth your while." She did a funny little chest wiggle as he reached to pull the door shut.

The guy next to him elbowed his side and chuckled. Someone else snickered.

Sam ignored them. "Sorry, Peej. I'm seeing someone else."

"I'll tell you my name." Her tone had turned wheedling.

Sam's partner dug his elbow into Sam's side again.

"No." Sam tuned out the chuckles of his friends as he grabbed the door handle. How long would he have to endure teasing from the other volunteers? Couldn't PJ leave well enough alone?

An emotion he didn't recognize filled her heavily made-up eyes. "This isn't the way I wanted to tell you, but…I'm pregnant."

⌒

Abigail maneuvered carefully with her crutches past Orpah and through the front door of The Hen Haus. Rachel followed her inside. Zelda stood in the hall, but Yenneke was suspiciously absent. Probably working in the greenhaus—or hiding in her bedroom—so she wouldn't have to face the girl she believed had wreaked havoc on her plants.

It hurt, being accused of yet another deed she hadn't done. What would happen if she was sent away from here? Where would she go?

Maybe she should kum up with a contingency plan of her own. The way things were going, it would likely be only a matter of time before the preachers approached her with somber faces and asked her to get on a bus and go away. Far, far away.

Maybe she could go to Florida. She'd heard the Amish who vacationed there did fun-sounding, unusual things, such as drive in solar-powered buggies. And ride bikes. And use electricity. She could get a job cleaning rental houses or waiting tables in a restaurant.

The painful thought of leaving Sammy eclipsed the initial twinge of excitement she'd felt.

"Where do you want these?" Rachel held up the plastic grocery bag of Abigail's belongings and her three dresses.

Abigail looked at her grossmammi.

"We'll put you in the room at the end of the hall," Orpah said, and Rachel headed in that direction. "The one on the right. It used to be Darius's. It's small, but there's a twin bed in there, and a chest of drawers. Your mamm's room was on the third floor, but I don't think you're ready for that yet."

Abigail wondered if she meant physically or emotionally.

And she had other questions, too, like how her mamm and onkel had lived here while nobody knew they were Orpah's kinner.

"Danki for…." What? For taking her in when she'd been falsely accused and forced to kum here to make things right? Abigail glanced away.

"Quite all right. Zelda and I know you didn't do it, and Yenneke will kum around, eventually. She says she heard a car engine that nacht. You don't have a vehicle; and even if you did, I can't imagine you driving one, with your leg in a cast."

Abigail nodded. "May I help with dinner? I'm supposed to earn my keep." *Earn forgiveness. Acceptance. Love.*

Love. Wasn't it supposed to be something freely given, not earned?

"Zelda's got supper tonight. We're having bean soup, I think." Orpah gestured to the living room. "For now, just sit and relax while I make you some tea."

"Danki." Abigail's knee had started throbbing. She moved into the living room and lowered herself onto the sofa, careful not to disturb the cat sleeping nearby. The menu sounded safe enough. And the pickle soup Zelda had made last time hadn't been bad, though Abigail wouldn't want to eat it on a regular basis.

Abigail looked around, taking in the setting of what would be her home for the foreseeable future. The floor plan was open, with a counter separating the living and dining rooms, providing her with a view of part of the kitchen. She caught an occasional glimpse of Zelda bustling about as she talked quietly with Orpah.

"I wonder if her young man will kum by to-nacht," Zelda was saying. "Maybe we could play Monopoly after dinner. It's my favorite game, and Sammy always makes it a challenge."

Abigail's hopes soared at the thought of a visit from Sammy. But she doubted he'd kum, since she'd all but told him to leave her alone. Maybe he would disregard her wishes. Or kum to check on the ladies, at least.

She could say with confidence that Mark never treated her like a prized possession, the way Sammy did. Nor did Mark's touch ever prompt shivers or sparks. He never held her while she cried, or offered to pray for her. He never asked her what was wrong when she "overreacted." And Mark never consumed her thoughts and dreams the way Sammy did. Yes, she and Mark had planned to marry, but all he'd said was that she'd make a gut frau. He'd never once told her he loved her.

She would like to hear that. Just once.

She'd assumed they were in love. Maybe not the stuff of romance novels, with sparks and fireworks, but mutual affection. Mark was a sought-after man. Handsome. Fun. Devoted to the Ordnung.

Was he courting someone new? Hopefully, he'd gotten over her as easily as she'd gotten over him.

⁓

Sam slammed his fist into his locker, relishing the pain. How could this have happened?

He turned around and noticed the other guys avoiding his gaze. At least he hadn't gotten the crude teasing and guffaws he'd expected.

Never had he expected *this*. PJ, pregnant.

Except…PJ's belly was flat. And the last time they'd gone all the way had been…when? Probably November, during her fall break from college. Four months ago.

Nein, they'd had a fight and had broken up then.

August.

A short time before he'd gotten saved.

Seven months ago.

Seven months pregnant, and still a flat stomach? Nein.

The boppli wasn't his. Nein way, nein how.

He dared to breathe deeply. His shoulders sagged as relief filled him.

Then his eyes narrowed. He clenched his fists. PJ expected the naive Amish bu to step forward and assume responsibility for someone else's boppli? *As if.*

But then, he could've gotten her pregnant at some point during their relationship. He hadn't, but the possibility had existed. And if that possibility had become reality, he would need to take responsibility.

What if PJ approached the preachers and demanded he make things right? The Ordnung would not permit him to request she get a paternity test, even if one could be done during pregnancy. If she really was pregnant. But why would she lie about something like that? It wasn't as if they'd ever planned to marry. Everything about the scenario was all wrong. She wanted Kansas City, nachts on the town, the glitz and glamour. The "high life." She would never want to marry a "former" Amish farmer. And Sam would never be able to afford her preferred lifestyle. He didn't want to.

He grabbed a bottle of water from the refrigerator and guzzled the cold liquid before heading out to the parking lot. If only there were someone at the station he could talk to or pray with. But the chaplain wasn't around; and if any of the other guys were men of faith, he didn't know about it. That wasn't discussed. Not like football. Baseball. Women.

Bile rose in his throat. He continued past his car and strode toward the road. It was a short walk to PJ's haus, and he had plenty he needed to say to her. Walking would give him time to organize his thoughts. Formulate his argument.

His steps slowed as remorse filled him for taking advantage of her. Using her for sex, when he'd known they'd never marry. She was just available. Willing.

He needed to think. Needed to pray before confronting her in blind rage.

The battle is Mine.

Sam turned around and started for his car. He'd go home and find Daed. He would pray with him. Offer guidance. *Ach, Lord. How can I confess that I had sex with a girl I didn't love—don't even like—and now am being falsely accused of fathering her child?*

PJ's claims could ruin his life. Okay, maybe "ruin" was a bit extreme. His life wouldn't be ruined. At least, not by this. Worst case, he would raise a child who wasn't his. Well, a boppli was a blessing, ain't so? He'd heard that often enough. And Mamm and Daed would be glad to help.

Sam slid behind the wheel, slammed the door shut and inserted the key in the ignition. The engine made some grinding noises and wouldn't turn over. Sam bit back a few curse words. Then scolded himself for even thinking them.

Time to trade in his car for a horse and buggy. Another thing to tell Daed. He was ready to join the church.

Lord, a little help? Please?

He heard the clip-clops of a horse, then saw the farm wagon coming down the road, as if it'd been summoned by his prayer. Sam jumped out of the car and stood there, waving his arms.

"Whoa." The driver slowed the wagon to a stop.

Shame kept Sam's gaze lowered. "I need a ride home. Please."

"And hallo to you, too, Sohn."

Daed? Sam looked up, surprised. *Danki, Gott.*

"I need…help." He barely squeezed the words past the lump forming in his throat.

Chapter 27

Abigail gave her bowl of "bean soup" a stir as she stared at the contents. She'd once eaten fifteen-bean soup with ham—a colorful mixture of proteins and vegetables whose variety paled in comparison to the dish before her: a glorious array of red, green, yellow, orange, blue, and purple in an amber base.

She pulled in a breath for courage. "Are these...um, jelly beans?"

Zelda grinned. "Yes, in maple syrup. It's a cold soup. My very own recipe."

Nein wonder Orpah had insisted on supplementing the meal with BLT sandwiches—real ones, using bacon, lettuce, and tomato.

And nein wonder Onkel Darius had declined the dinner invitation he'd received when he came to deliver a letter to Abigail from her mamm earlier that afternoon.

The letter was still stuffed in Abigail's apron pocket, unopened.

When the three ladies bowed their heads for the silent prayer. Abigail followed suit. *Lord, keep me from getting sick on this soup!* That seemed a safe prayer. She peeked through her eyelashes at the concoction. Maybe she should've prayed for it to disappear.

Behind her, a door opened and shut. There were footsteps, and then a shuffling sound. Followed by silence.

She hastened to finish her prayer. *Danki for Onkel Darius and for my newfound grossmammi and for Sammy. And danki for this meal, even if it frightens me. Amen.*

She raised her head and twisted around in her chair.

"Preacher Samuel." Zelda rose to her feet. "You're just in time for dinner. You must join us. We have plenty of soup, right, girls?"

"Plenty," Yenneke said dryly.

Abigail tried to smother a chuckle.

Preacher Samuel nodded. "Danki, Zelda. Sam's outside, unloading supplies for the greenhaus. We'll both be happy to stay for dinner, if that's all right."

Abigail felt a simultaneous thrill of joy and surge of panic. She wasn't sure how things stood between her and Sammy. Nothing like an unexpected dinner party to find out.

"We'll need more sandwich fixings." Yenneke rose to her feet and started for the refrigerator. The other two older women stood and started bustling about as Preacher Samuel hung his hat on a knob by the door.

In the next moment, Sammy entered the haus, his hat clasped against his chest, his lips pressed together. When his gaze locked on Abigail's, she almost didn't recognize him, for the acute pain in his eyes.

"Was ist letz?" Abigail reached for her crutches.

Sammy crossed the room in three strides and fell to his knees in front of her. A second later, his head was buried in her lap, his shoulders shaking.

Abigail dropped her hands to her sides. All movement in the room paused as every eye turned to Sammy, then shot to Preacher Samuel. He shook his head. "Not my story." The ladies nodded and got back to work.

Abigail feathered her fingers through Sammy's hair, wishing she could comfort him the way he'd comforted her so effectively before.

By praying.

She took a breath.

But Gott listened to Sammy, not to her.

Still, it was all she had.

She bowed her head, her fingers still trailing through his hair, and started a silent prayer. *Lord, I know You love Sammy. I don't know what's wrong right now, but You do. And he's hurting. Help him. Help me to be who he needs me to be. And, Lord, heal his pain. Please?*

Sam didn't know how long he'd knelt, crying, with his head in Abigail's lap, when certain details began to seep into his conscious mind. Mainly, her fingers filtering through his hair, the way Mamm would often soothe his hurts when he was a young bu. A sense of peace—faint yet distinct—filled him.

The battle is Mine.

Help me remember that, Lord.

He raised his head enough to mop his damp cheeks with his sleeves, then took Abigail's face in his hands, leaned forward, and kissed her. She responded, with a sweetness he could never get enough of. Too bad he wouldn't have a choice, if atoning for his sins required him to give her up.

With a sigh, he released her, then pushed to his feet and glanced around. The three older women returned to the table carrying plates of bread, strips of bacon, tomato slices, and lettuce. Daed washed up at the sink, something Sam needed to do.

Sam met Abigail's concerned gaze and shook his head. "I'll tell you later." Then he stepped up beside his daed at the sink.

Daed had listened quietly to Sam's predicament and had prayed with him, then suggested they wait before making any decisions or contacting PJ. Daed wanted to talk with the preachers first. Well, not the preachers, exactly, though some of them were. The group of men who had been meeting weekly for prayer and Bible study under the cover of darkness in a secluded cabin in the woods. The same cabin where Sam had first surrendered to Gott, the nacht his cousin Greta had returned after weeks of being held by two drug dealers/sex traffickers. Besides Sam, the attendees were Daed, David Lapp, Josh Yoder, Viktor Petersheim, and Viktor's grossdaedi Reuben. And Gott listened to them when they prayed.

Sam wanted to be counted among the prayer warriors.

He soaped up his hands and arms, washed his face, and rinsed off, then dried himself with the towel Daed handed him.

The ladies had rearranged the table and added a bench for him and Daed. To Sam's right was the chair where Abigail sat. He lowered himself to the bench and reached for her hand. Then he looked down at the colorful soup before him.

His stomach roiled. Only Zelda.

He worried about her mental faculties, but she hadn't been diagnosed with anything, to his knowledge. Or maybe she had, and she'd run out of medication.

Sam bowed his head to pray, determined to hang on to the faint sense of peace he felt and to simply enjoy this time rather than focusing on his failings. At least not until he had a Gott-given plan and divine permission to act.

Zelda gave a contented sigh as she dipped her soup spoon into her bowl of jelly beans and maple syrup. "I just love bean soup."

Abigail glanced at her, then looked away. Nobody else responded, all of them apparently busy assembling sandwiches for themselves.

"You know, Sammy, I have a story to tell you." Zelda swallowed her spoonful of soup and leaned forward. "I don't know what's going on with you, but I just thought of this, and I think you need to hear it."

"Maybe it's a word from der Herr," Yenneke remarked dryly as she cut her sandwich into fourths.

Preacher Samuel gave her a sharp look.

But Abigail could understand her sarcasm. Gott didn't speak directly to individuals anymore, did He? A measure of doubt crept in.

Zelda shrugged. "Once upon a time, there was a big, bad wolf that lived in a castle in a land far, far away. He had three pigs named Hansel, Gretel, and Rapunzel."

Orpah frowned. "I think you're getting your stories mixed up."

"Jah. Three totally different fairy tales." Yenneke took a bite of one of her sandwich squares.

Zelda glared. "It's *my* story. Now, hush and listen." Then she smiled at Sam. "Anyway, Hansel and Gretel were being fattened up on gingerbread houses so they could be eaten by the big, bad wolf."

Sam exchanged glances with Daed. Then he looked at Abigail. She appeared as confused as he was.

"Rapunzel the pig had a very long tail. She made a lasso out of it and threw it into a window of the tower where Hansel and Gretel were kept, and she rescued them so they wouldn't be eaten. The end." She nodded, then took another big bite of soup.

Certain now of Zelda's insanity, Sam pushed his bowl away, his appetite having escaped like the ill-fated pigs in Zelda's story. Everyone sat in silence for a long minute. Two minutes. Three.

Finally, Daed put down his soup spoon with a clatter. "Gut story, Zelda. And you are absolutely right." He turned to Sam and met his eyes. "The application is that Gott will make a way where there seems to be nein way."

Right. All the sugar in that soup must have gotten to Daed.

"Do you want to talk about it, Sammy?" Yenneke looked at him. "Nothing you say will leave this room." She fixed a warning glare on Abigail, as if she didn't quite trust her.

Abigail tightened her grip on Sam's hand beneath the table.

He clung to hers as if it were a lifeline. "The truth can condemn you."

⌒

Abigail's heart ached for Sammy. If only she could solve his problems as easily as he seemed to handle hers.

"You're right," Orpah said. "The truth can condemn you. Or the truth can set you free." She scooted closer to Abigail and gave her a sideways hug.

Abigail's throat swelled as hope rose. Maybe she would learn *her* truth while she was here. Hopefully, it would free rather than condemn.

Preacher Samuel nodded. "Absolutely right, Orpah. The truth can set you free. Jesus said so in the Gut Book." He ran his spoon through his jelly-bean soup in a slow swirl, then scooped out one bean. Put it in his mouth. Grimaced. Then took another bite. And another.

Abigail chewed her sandwich in silence. Everyone else seemed determined to stay quiet, too. Maybe they all were lost in thought. Or afraid to open their mouths in case what they really thought of Zelda's variation of bean soup emerged.

Sammy wasn't eating. He sat there, massaging Abigail's hand with his thumb, a pensive expression on his face.

If only she knew what bothered him. And how to fix it.

Lord....

She'd probably prayed more today than she had since finding herself abandoned at the bus station, her hand clutching a ticket that could lead to nowhere, tears streaming down her face as she watched her stepdaed and Mark drive away.

She'd prayed for Gott to intervene. For them to kum back for her. For it to be nothing more than a bad joke. For her to be loved. Wanted.

Trust me, it's better this way.

Would she ever get Mark's whispered words to stop playing through her mind like a broken record?

But he'd been right, she realized. They were half siblings. And she'd discovered a bunch of family members she hadn't even known existed who loved her. Onkel Darius. Aenti Ruth. Orpah.

Okay, maybe that wasn't a bunch. But it was three more than before. Mamm never mentioned she had a brother—or a mother—still alive.

Sammy dropped her hand and raked his fingers through his hair. His lips twisted in a frown, and he turned tormented eyes on her, then looked at his daed. "Gelassenheit."

Self-surrender? Abigail stared at him.

Sammy bolted to his feet. Stumbled toward the door.

Preacher Samuel hurried after him. "Now, hold on a moment, Sohn. We need to wait on direction from der Herr, not rush in where angels fear to tread." He turned back to the table. "Ladies, I'm sorry to leave so abruptly. Please accept my apologies."

"Of course," Orpah said. "But—"

The door shut.

Chapter 28

Dread weighed on Sam as he climbed into the wagon.

"What are you going to do?" Daed approached, his unfinished sandwich in one hand.

"I don't know." Sam drew in a shaky breath. "I mean, I thought I knew. It all made sense in there. I'd offer to marry PJ. She'd turn me down and tell me the boppli isn't mine, after all. End of story. But what if she doesn't?" And what if this was just a ploy to wheedle her way into his arms once more?

Daed climbed up beside Sam and clasped his shoulder. "We'll round up the prayer support."

"I'm surprised you haven't suggested that since I admitted to spending the nacht with Abigail. I compromised her, and we have to get married." It'd solve his PJ problems if Daed took him up on the thinly veiled suggestion.

But Daed shook his head. "You said you didn't do anything. That you both were fully dressed and just talking. It was an accident. I believe you. I also trust you when you say PJ's boppli isn't yours."

Sam's throat swelled. "Danki, Daed." It meant a lot, especially considering how many times he'd messed up in the past. Lied. Stolen.

He had a lot of sins to confess.

He raked his fingers through his hair, realizing he'd left his hat inside. Well, he wasn't going to go back inside for it now. He'd get it later.

When he returned, hopefully with answers. Resolution.

He took a deep breath. "Daed, I'm a horrible person. I—"

"You're a sinner saved by grace. I know what you've done, Sohn. Nein need to confess to me. You confess to Him." Daed pointed upward.

"I have, but I still feel guilty."

"Then you need to forgive yourself."

"But, Daed, you don't know what I've done."

"Jah, I do. And everyone else you've wronged does, too."

Really? And nobody had said anything? Nobody condemned him?

"I stole medication from the ladies...." Sam jerked his thumb over his shoulder.

Daed clicked his tongue, and Snickers moved forward, toward the road. "They know that. They chose to forgive you, and to trust you." He glanced at Sam. "Want me to go on?"

Not really. "Jah." He should find out how much Daed knew.

Daed pulled the reins, steering the buggy onto the road with a right-hand turn. "David knows you used the stolen medication to drug him. And that you threatened his life and vandalized the school-haus. He chose to forgive you, and to trust you. The whole community knows you partied, that you were the one who talked Ezra into going to Pennsylvania, where he died. They chose to forgive you, and to trust you. Several people have commented on the change they've noticed in you since last fall, when you bowed before Gott. Nobody's saying you're perfect. You still have plenty of room to grow. But you've changed—are changing. And it is opening the doors for us to share the gospel of the grace of Gott."

Daed had known all that, and said nothing. Sam was floored.

"But wouldn't it mean more to them if I confessed?" Sam bounced his fists on his knees.

"Jah, Sohn, it would. Especially if they saw you expressing genuine remorse."

"Then maybe we should pray about that, too." Should Sam confess to the medical director who oversaw the ambulance crews that he'd stolen drugs from some Amish ladies? It would cost him his career. Would probably mean doing jail time. Of course, that might solve his PJ problems....

His stomach churned as heaviness descended over him.

Lord, help me decide what to do. So much is at stake. With PJ. With confessing. And with Abigail....

Daed tightened the reins, and Snickers turned into the circular drive at Viktor's. "I'll be right back." Daed glanced at Sam, then climbed down from the buggy and headed toward the barn.

Sam had nein right even to think of a future with Abigail. Not when his life was so unsettled. Which meant he should apologize to her for leading her on. For teasing her. For playing with her emotions.

Something he hadn't intended to do.

He also hadn't planned on falling in love. But fall he did.

And the relationship was doomed because of his past.

His present.

He swiped his hand roughly across his eyes.

And his future.

⁓

"I'll do the dishes." Abigail rose and started stacking the empty bowls and plates. Sammy was the only one who hadn't finished his soup. She wished she hadn't eaten hers, but she hadn't wanted to hurt Zelda.

What was Sammy surrendering himself to? It didn't make sense.

"I'll dry." Orpah opened a cupboard and took out two lidded dishes. She scraped the leftover sandwich fixings into one.

"This won't get you out of helping with the greenhaus." Yenneke pursed her lips. "Preacher Samuel and Preacher David both say you didn't do it, but I know what I saw." She drained the skillet of bacon grease into a glass measuring cup on the stove.

Abigail bit back the argumentative words that sprang to her lips. Nodded as she met Yenneke's eyes.

Zelda pushed herself to her feet. "You saw our Abigail?"

"You saw crutches," Orpah put in. "And a shadowy person in pants." She spooned the leftover "soup" into the other dish.

Yenneke looked away. "I'll leave you to the dishes, then." She started for the door.

Abigail swallowed. "I'm sorry someone destroyed the greenhaus, Yenneke. It wasn't me, but I'll be happy to help put it back in order."

Yenneke paused, then turned around with a sigh. "I don't really think you would do such a thing. I just needed someone to blame." She approached Abigail. Touched her hand. Hesitated, then pulled her into a hug. "I'm sorry, too."

A second later, Zelda wrapped her arms around Abigail from behind.

Abigail hesitated a moment before she returned the embrace, but it made her uncomfortable. Neither Mamm nor Daed ever demonstrated their love in a physical way. Mamm almost seemed to hold her at a distance, though Abigail hadn't realized that until coming here and meeting Aenti Ruth and her grossmammi. Maybe because Mamm had lost other kinner, she'd been afraid to fully love Abigail.

Zelda pulled away and opened the refrigerator door. "Do we have any doughnuts?"

Yenneke released Abigail. "You've had enough sweets, Zelda. I'm going to go toss that snake out the window."

Orpah spun around. "What snake?"

"The one in her bed." Yenneke cackled. "Sorry. Just teasing. There's nein snake."

"You'll be the death of me," Orpah scolded her. "Nein snakes in the haus. We agreed on that the time one crawled out from behind the stove."

"I wasn't responsible for that." Yenneke grinned as she left the room.

Abigail giggled as she carried the plates over to the sink and set them in the hot, soapy water.

Zelda stood on tiptoe and stretched to see the top of the refrigerator. "I thought we had some doughnuts. Are you hiding them, Orpah?"

"You're diabetic, Zelda. You've had enough sugar with your bean soup, ain't so?"

Zelda frowned. "Mint tea, jah?" She reached for a mug as Abigail brought over the bowls and eating utensils.

Orpah nodded. "Drink it in the other room, though, please. Abigail and I need to talk."

Abigail's nerves danced as she glanced at her grossmammi. Did she really want to know? If everyone had gone to so much trouble to keep it secret....

Orpah picked up a dish towel and stood beside Abigail. "I'll dry while I tell you a story. Once upon a time...."

⌒

Sam's legs trembled as he entered the hunting cabin. His gaze shot to the ladder leading to the loft where he'd knelt last fall and asked Gott to forgive his sins and save him. Peace had filled him then.

Now, he would approach der Herr with all the hidden secrets he'd kept in the dark recesses of his soul. Hand them over to Him.

Hopefully, Gott would forgive the rest. Did der Herr fully accept general apologies along the lines of "I'm sorry for all my sins"? Or did He require an admission of every sin upon remembrance of it? Right now, it seemed Sam needed to confess them all, even though Daed said Gott had already forgiven him.

Gott, I'm in a mess of my own making.

Tears stung his eyes, and he closed them, then fell to his knees in the middle of the floor.

He heard the strike of a match. He could sense the added light as Daed lit the lantern on the middle of the table behind him. Its glow wasn't strong enough to reach the corners of the cabin, like the electric lights at PJ's haus, but at least it dispelled the grayness.

Sam heard the cabin door open and close. The room grew quiet, without the floor creaking beneath Daed's feet. Daed had probably gone outside to wait for the other men.

How did one begin to confess years' worth of hidden sins? This thing with PJ was just the head of an ugly boil that needed lanced. One that had been convicting Sam for, well, a while, if he were honest.

Gott, I don't know how to begin. I kum before You as the worst sort of sinner. I need You to search my heart, my thoughts, and find all the wickedness hidden within me. Even the things I've forgotten. Cleanse me of all my sins.

The next sound was that of a truck rumbling down the narrow lane leading to the cabin. It stopped, and there were faint, indistinguishable male voices, followed by the shutting of four vehicle doors. Viktor must've picked up the others.

Sam shifted, starting to feel uneasy. He went to stand, but an invisible force seemed to hold him down by his shoulders.

He forced his mind back to his prayer. Tears flowed as he listed every wrongdoing he could remember. Something inside him seemed to be bowing before the most Holy Gott, as well, taking over Sam's prayer. He yielded to it, and quieted his mind, just focusing on the *Lord, ach, Lord* that drew out and repeated as he completely surrendered himself.

A gentle hand came to rest on the back of his head. Another touched his left shoulder. A third, and fourth, flattened against his back. He hadn't noticed the door opening or closing. Hadn't heard the floor creaking.

Lord Gott, take my life, and make it completely Yours. Take my stubborn will, my passion, my self, and my pride. I want to be Yours alone. Lord, let Your will be done in me....

Sam didn't know how long he'd prayed when he resurfaced to consciousness. He was lying prostrate on the floor, and the hands touching his body were slowly lifting away. He pushed to his knees, swiped the moisture from his face with his shirtsleeve, and looked over his shoulder. Turned around.

Daed. Viktor. Reuben. Josh. David. All kneeling around him. Surrounding him with prayer, and joining him in it.

Where two or more are gathered in My name, there I am in the midst of them. Your prayers have been heard, Sam.

Fresh tears filled his eyes.

David started to rise, but Sam reached for his arm, stopping him. "I'm sorry for making your life miserable when you first came. For drugging you, for—"

David shook his head. "I forgave you a long time ago, Sam, when you came to Pennsylvania after the fire to apologize."

Sam had forgotten about that. So much had happened since then.

His newest cousin-in-law, Josh, leaned forward, still balanced on his knees. "What's going on with you, Sam? What's the emergency? And, most important, how can we help?"

Chapter 29

Orpah pursed her lips and furrowed her forehead, as if she were pondering how to begin the story.

Abigail tensed. She didn't want to know. She didn't. She didn't. She didn't.

Jah, she did.

Yenneke came into the room and laid a manila folder on the table. Then left again without a word.

Abigail sighed. "Maybe I don't need to know." It hurt her to say that, now that the big moment seemed to be at hand. But if it would make things easier to keep secrets as secrets....

She picked up the washrag and wiped the first plate, then rinsed the dish and set it in the slotted drainer. Followed suit with the second plate. The third.

Orpah said nothing. She lifted a towel and started drying the dishes.

Maybe she'd taken Abigail seriously.

Another minute or two of silence passed as Abigail started washing the silverware. "So—"

"Once upon a time," Orpah began again, "I met a man I loved very much. His name was Titus. But my parents didn't approve of him, mostly because they wanted me to marry Seth, one of my father's employees. He was quiet and...well, odd. He would follow me around, appearing unexpectedly when I was out with friends, or walking home. He scared me."

Abigail gawked at her. "You mean, he stalked you?"

"You could say that, jah. He watched me all the time. Stared. Never spoke to me. Just...." Orpah shuddered. "Titus lived in another Amish community. We saw each other at weddings, funerals, and frolics, and sometimes he made special trips to see me. That wasn't enough. I *had* to be with him. So, I told my daed I was going to visit one of my pen pals...Zelda."

Abigail smiled as she glanced into the other room. Zelda was settled in a rocking chair, a big ball of yarn—variegated with shades of white, gray, and black—by her feet. Her knitting needles clicked as she worked away.

"Daed permitted me to go, but when a month's visit stretched into three, he sent Seth to bring me home. Meanwhile. Titus and I had secretly gotten married by an Englisch justice of the peace, and I wanted to stay with Titus. Forever. But Titus didn't know how to tell his family and community that he'd married outside the church. So, I stayed with Zelda and her family, while Titus stayed with his parents. We would sneak out at nacht to be together as ehemann and frau. But during the time Seth was there to fetch me, Titus disappeared. Titus's brother tried to argue that he'd left to get away from me. That I was too forward, always seeking him out. That I made Titus uncomfortable. But Titus had willingly kum to me every nacht. And his parents seemed just as confused about his disappearance as I was."

Abigail stopped trying to scrub the last of the sticky syrup out of the dish Zelda had served it in.

"I agreed to go home with Seth. I didn't know what else to do." Orpah shook her head. "Then, on the way home, Seth...he dishonored me. And when I found myself pregnant, Daed tried to force me to marry Seth. He didn't believe me when I told him I was already married, because I didn't have proof. Titus had the marriage certificate." She released a long sigh. "Daed and Mamm started planning the wedding. They said I should be thankful Seth was willing to raise another man's boppli."

Abigail froze completely. The dishrag dangled limply from her fingers. Her heart pounded. Her lips parted, her breaths coming in spurts.

"When Titus's body was found, at the bottom of a well, the sheriff came investigating. Me. It was beyond awful, being considered as a suspect in the murder of the man I loved. Seth was questioned, too, since he was around when it happened. He was arrested the day before our wedding was supposed to take place, and later found guilty. I was so thankful to be free of him. So very thankful. But when Daed found out that Seth had violated me, he said I deserved it for being a loose woman."

"Ach, Orpah...Grossmammi." Abigail knew too well the pain of rejection. She reached out and touched her grossmammi's arm.

"I...I couldn't stay there. I left home again, and moved to Jamesport, where Titus's family lived. I wanted to be able to visit his final resting-place. I'll take you there sometime. His brother and I made peace with each other, and his sister and I became gut friends." Orpah managed a smile. "That's Yenneke. She's your gross-aenti."

Another relative. A strange warmth worked through Abigail.

"Your mamm and Darius are twins, you know. Darius looks just like Titus. Deborah, not so much. But nobody in the community believed me when I told them Titus and I had gotten married. Not until much later, when we found a copy of the marriage certificate. By then, Deborah had kum to believe the rumors that she and Darius were conceived out of wedlock. I presented proof to the bishop and the preachers, but they wanted to keep things quiet. A bad idea. When your daed started courting your mamm, I tried to explain that they were second cousins—Obadiah was the sohn of Titus's cousin. But Deborah didn't believe me. She was convinced I'd faked the marriage certificate."

"Is my daed's family still here?" Abigail held her breath.

"Besides Yenneke, a few distant cousins. Your daed's brother, Luke, and his family. His sohns are all married, except for Hen."

Abigail's stomach roiled.

Hen was her cousin?

It took Sam a couple of hours to track down PJ at her aunt's single-wide mobile home. Flanked by David, Josh, and Viktor, he marched up to the door and pounded it with his fist. The flimsy door gave under his hand.

Inside, the blaring television muted.

Sam bowed his head, remembering the passage from Isaiah 43 that Josh had read during the drive to town in Viktor's truck: "*When thou passest through the waters, I will be with thee; and through the rivers, they shall not overflow thee: when thou walkest through the fire, thou shalt not be burned; neither shall the flame kindle upon thee. For I am the* LORD *thy God, the Holy One of Israel, thy Saviour....*"

Lord Gott, let it be so.

Sam was jostled a bit as Josh and Viktor vied for position on the fiberglass steps. David stood a bit behind them, on the broken, uneven sidewalk, his fingers gripping the metal railing on one side of the stairs. It was nice to have backup. Daed and Reuben had insisted that Sam approach PJ with several witnesses, while they stayed behind to pray.

The woman who answered the door had salt-and-pepper hair. A cigarette dangled from her mouth. She peered warily at Sam and the other three men in turn. "Whatever you're selling, boys, I'm not interested."

Sam cleared his throat. "I'm here to see PJ. I...I'm Sammy Miller."

The woman puffed on her cigarette and stood aside to let them enter. "Go on back. End of the hall."

Sam started over the threshold, but a hand landed on his shoulder, pulling him to a stop. He glanced back and met Viktor's dark gaze. Viktor shook his head. "Nein."

Probably wise to keep this discussion up-front and public.

Sam looked at PJ's aunt. "Uh...could you send her outside, instead?"

"Whatever." The woman turned toward the hall. "Prudence James? Someone's here to see you."

Prudence James. Nein wonder she went by PJ.

Sam retreated down the steps and waited on the sidewalk with his friends.

A few minutes later, PJ emerged from the trailer, still dressed in the revealing outfit from earlier. David's face flamed red, and he looked away.

PJ stopped on the second step. Her upper lip curled in a sneer. "You know, when I asked you to meet me tonight, I meant alone."

Sam pulled in a breath and said a silent prayer. *Danki, Gott, for pardoning my part in the filth that still consumes PJ. Help me to be a witness for You.* Then he got straight to the point. "PJ, we both know the baby's not mine. What do you expect from me?" He lifted his arms in question.

PJ stared at him a moment. Then she looked to Josh, to Viktor, and finally to David, her face showing increasing disgust. "I want to talk to you, not the Future Farmers of America." Disdain dripped from her every word.

Josh gave a slight grin. "Current farmers of America, and fishers of men, at your service."

Meanwhile, nein-nonsense Viktor folded his arms across his chest.

Sam cleared his throat. "Anything you have to say to me, you can say in their presence." Hopefully, she wouldn't say anything that would make a sheep blush in shame.

"Fine." PJ looked down. "I want an abortion."

Sam swallowed a gasp. "Nein, PJ. You need to talk to the father."

"I did. He won't help. Refuses to admit the baby's his." She met his gaze again, her eyes pleading. "You're the only one who'll help me, Sammy. Please."

"I know Someone who can help," Josh said quietly. "Let me tell you about Jesus—"

She held up a hand. "I don't want to hear it."

Josh shoved his hands inside his pockets and bowed his head. Probably praying.

"I don't want to marry you, Peej." Sam forced the words past his aching throat.

PJ snorted. "I don't want to marry you, either, farm boy. I have plans for the future. Goals. A high-rise apartment in KC with my name on it. I have to get away from here." She gestured at her surroundings, then pointed to her belly. "Away from *this*."

"But abortion isn't the way." The practice disagreed with everything Sam believed. *Kinner are a blessing....* "There are plenty of couples, Peej, who are desperate for children and would gladly adopt the baby. Consider that. Shoot, I'd adopt the baby myself."

Daed had suggested he offer to do so. The idea had seemed ludicrous at first, but just as Sam spoke the words, a sudden willingness—eagerness, even—filled him. If he were to adopt the boppli, he or she would have a stable upbringing, centered around Gott, family, and the community. He or she would be surrounded by love.

Sure, Sam would be at the center of the gossip mill for a while. *Gelassenheit.* Being surrendered to Gott, to the point of sacrificing oneself to do the will of Gott, for the gut of others.

Just as Jesus had done for him.

Sam smiled. "I'll be glad to, PJ. Really."

PJ straightened and looked at him with her tear-filled eyes. Then she flung herself into his arms and held on tight. "I knew I could count on you, Sammy. If I don't...if I decide to keep the baby, I'll be in contact. And I'll name you as the father." She kissed his cheek and then stepped away. Before going back inside, she said, "Don't tell anyone my name. Ever. Got it?"

"Got it." Sam's smile widened. "See you around, Prudence Ja—"

She slugged him, then grinned. "You'll be an awesome dad, Sammy."

Chapter 30

Abigail finished the dishes in silence as she mulled over her grossmammi's heartbreaking story. If Abigail's grossdaedi hadn't been murdered—*murdered!*—she would have another relative to get to know.

Of course, if he were alive, her family dynamics would be completely different. Mamm would've known Obadiah as her second cousin.

And Abigail wouldn't exist.

She set down the final platter to be dried, then picked up the plastic pan of dirty dishwater. "Where should this be dumped?"

"In the lilac bushes, but I'll take it out. I'm not the one using crutches." Orpah held out her hands. "If you want to see the marriage certificate, it's in the folder on the table." She nodded in that direction, then took the pan from Abigail and went out the back door.

Abigail dried her hands, then sat at the table. Her fingers trembled as she lifted the folder and carefully opened it. There was a stack of papers inside, with the marriage certificate on top. She read it, then lifted the page. Just underneath was her grossdaedi's death certificate.

A hand touched her upper back and started slowly rubbing. "He was a gut man," Yenneke said. "I miss him every day, as Orpah does." Then the woman lowered herself into the chair beside Abigail. "Titus and I were born in this haus. We found the marriage certificate when we cleaned out Titus' room, after my parents passed."

Abigail blinked the tears from her eyes.

Outside, a horse nickered. Yenneke stood and glanced out the window. "Preacher Samuel is back, and Reuben Petersheim is with him."

Abigail held up the marriage certificate before returning it to the folder. "Preacher Samuel needs to see this."

Yenneke nodded. "I agree. Orpah says to let it go, but it's time the truth came out." She took the folder from Abigail.

Abigail took her crutches and followed Yenneke out the door, then slowly descended the porch stairs. Orpah stood by the wagon, talking to Preacher Samuel and Reuben. Yenneke hurried to join them. "You need to see this." She handed the folder to the preacher, even though Orpah violently shook her head.

Preacher Samuel glanced at Abigail as she approached the wagon. "Sam went to talk to PJ."

Abigail's heart stuttered. "Are they…back together? Again?"

Preacher Samuel frowned, the folder half-open, his finger between the flaps. He flexed his mouth. "I'm sure Sam will talk to you about it. We were praying until we felt peace."

Maybe he would. Or maybe he wouldn't, other than to give her a "Sorry it didn't work out." They might've scratched the surface of friendship. Moved beyond it, even. But they hadn't reached the tell-each-other-everything stage.

Although she'd pretty well had spilled her life story to him. And he was sure to hear Orpah's story, too. If not from Abigail, then from Preacher Samuel, judging by his facial expression as he scanned the contents of the folder.

But Sammy's story? Abigail didn't know much at all. Just the bare bones, really.

Didn't matter, though, if he'd gotten back together with PJ.

An engine rumbled, and a cloud of dust rose as a diesel pickup truck neared the driveway. It parked along the road by the mailbox. A second later, a door slammed shut.

Sammy jogged around the front of the vehicle, waved gut-bye to the driver, and started toward the haus.

When his gaze caught Abigail's, his expression was open. Friendly. More than friendly. Not the look of a man who'd just reconciled with his ex-girlfriend.

Why had he gone to see PJ? Abigail wasn't sure she wanted to know.

She would have folded her arms across her chest, but she still balanced on the crutches, making the posture impossible. So, she merely shifted her stance. She heard the rustling of the letter from Mamm that she'd shoved, unopened, into her pocket.

Sammy came straight toward her. "Hey, Abby. We need to talk."

⌒

Sam stopped three feet from Abigail, though he desperately yearned to move closer to her. To pull her into an embrace and hold her. To kiss her as he had earlier.

As he'd approached, he'd noticed her eyes take on a certain wariness. Maybe mixed with fear.

He hated to scare her, but maybe she should be afraid. It was time for him to kum clean about who and what he was. And, Gott willing, she would accept him for what he was—a man who'd made way too many mistakes.

A sinner, saved by grace.

"PJ," she squeaked.

Had Daed told her? Sam glanced over his shoulder. Daed shook his head.

Sam returned his attention to Abigail. "The fire today…it was at her haus." He moved another foot closer to her. "We need to talk." In case she didn't get the message the first time.

"If you want privacy, you can go back to Abigail's bedroom—just leave the door open," Yenneke said. "Zelda is napping in the living room. Or take the buggy for a drive."

A buggy ride would be the safest option. But he wanted to look into Abigail's eyes as he talked. Hold her hands in his.

Abigail cleared her throat. "I don't want to break up in my bedroom." She maneuvered herself backward several steps.

Break up? Sam blinked. But then, he probably should've expected that. If only because she was used to being tossed aside. He'd hated leaving Darius's haus with their relationship in such a state of uncertainty.

"Breaking up implies first being a couple." Orpah peered at them through narrowed eyes. "And you told me you were just friends, Abigail." With a wink, she added quietly, "Though that was some kiss in the kitchen at supper."

"Sam told me that he and Abigail are exploring the possibility of a relationship." Daed closed the folder and handed it back to Yenneke. "Orpah, you and I need to talk, too. Would tomorrow be a gut time for me to kum by with the other preachers?"

"Ach, so much time has passed." Orpah waved her hand dismissively.

"Better late than never. And with all the rumors floating around because of Abigail's arrival, the news will get out that she's your grossdochter, which will only generate more gossip."

Sam moved closer to Abigail, putting more distance between them and the others. "Right now, it doesn't matter how our relationship is defined." He wiped his sweaty hands on his pant legs. "We still need to talk."

"Go to Abigail's room and just leave the door open. You can rest assured, someone will peek in." Daed's voice was stern, but a twinkle flashed in his eyes. As if he knew there would be some kissing involved and wanted to give them a little privacy.

If Sam had his way, there would be some kissing, for sure. Okay, more than "some."

Abigail backed up another step, her gaze searching his. Then she turned. "Fine." She breathed out a sigh and started for the haus.

Sam trailed her inside. Zelda was snoring softly as Sam tiptoed past her. At her feet, a cat batted at a ball of yarn.

As Abigail entered her room, she pulled an envelope out of her pocket and tossed it on top of the dresser. She continued to the window, her back to him. Her shoulders shook.

Sam's entry caused a current of air that sent the envelope fluttering to the floor. He bent and picked it up, eyeing the return address. Abigail's mamm. "Um, Abby? You dropped your mail."

She shrugged. Then abruptly turned to face him.

Anger. Betrayal. Hurt. All three warred for dominance in her expression. Tears had pooled in her eyes. "PJ?" Her voice broke.

Sam scratched his head. Which emotion to address first? Probably should pray before anything else. He closed his eyes. *Gott, help me to know what to say. Guide my words.*

With a steady exhalation, Sam opened his eyes and gently laid the envelope on Abigail's pillow. Then he moved forward, trying to keep his stance relaxed. Nonthreatening. He extended his hands toward Abigail, palms up, in a show of submission. "I'm an open book. PJ was a mistake from the beginning. One I've regretted over and over. When I was helping fight the fire today at her haus, she came on to me. I told her I was seeing someone else. Then she made things worse—much worse—by announcing she was pregnant."

Abigail slapped a hand across her mouth. More pain clouded her beautiful green eyes.

Sam winced. Not the most tactful way of delivering unpleasant news.

"The boppli isn't mine," he clarified. "PJ and I haven't been together that way since August of last year. Before I was saved."

The rest of what he had to say would have to wait. Had to wait.

He moved closer, keeping his arms outstretched. "PJ and I are not back together. We won't be. Ever. Ich liebe dich, Abigail."

"But you're a rescuer." Her trembling fingers still covered her mouth. "You will feel like you need to rescue her, like you rescue everyone in trouble. It's what you do."

"But this isn't rescuing. This is committing. If you want me."

"You're an amazing man...."

He imagined he could hear an unspoken "but...."

He shook his head and moved on before she had a chance to say it. "Not so amazing, Abby. But before we get into that discussion...."

He picked up the letter. "Don't put this off. Sometimes, it's better to face things and get them over with."

∼

Sam was right, of course. Abigail's hands continued to shake as she shuffled the two steps to the bed and dropped onto the edge of the mattress.

Sammy crouched on the floor in front of her. She'd really rather have him seated by her side, his arms supporting her. His prayers calming her.

Sammy looked at her. "Maybe we should pray first."

"Please, do." At least part of her wish would be granted.

He nodded and bowed his head. "Lord, we don't know what's in this letter. You do. Let it be gut news and not bad. To heal and not harm. We ask these things in Jesus' name. Amen."

"Danki." Abigail took the letter from him, hesitated a moment, and then ripped it open. If only she could pray over it, as he did. She really should try to learn his tricks of getting Gott to listen.

Though maybe He had listened, at least to some of her prayers. This banishment to Jamesport hadn't been all bad. She'd met family she hadn't known existed. Discovered she was loved and wanted—by complete strangers, no less. And met an incredible man who'd proven himself to be a rescuer, in many different ways.

Maybe it wouldn't hurt for her to pray first, too. Before reading the letter.

She closed her eyes and bowed her head. But she didn't know what to say. It seemed petty to pray over a letter, though the contents might prove hurtful. And what she really wanted…. *Lord, I want to know You like Sammy does.*

She also wanted some kind of confirmation she was heard. Maybe she could offer a "Gideon's fleece" addition to her prayer. *Gott, if You hear me, I want an apology from Mamm. And an explanation.*

She doubted she'd get either one. More likely, she'd get a scolding for writing only once during the time she was gone. And that, a piddling two lines.

"Here goes nothing." She bit her lip as she pulled out the contents of the envelope. Two smaller envelopes were enclosed, one of them with a yellow Post-it Note attached.

Abigail,

I know you have questions. But I'm going to begin with an apology. I'm sorry. Read Mark's letter first.

Love,
Mamm

An apology? Really?

On the envelope just underneath the yellow sticky note, her name was scribbled—in Mark's handwriting.

Abigail's heart lurched. She handed the yellow note to Sammy. He read it, his expression turning concerned. Abigail slowly opened the envelope from Mark, afraid of what she would find. What if he disclosed that the whole thing was a lie, and said he wanted her to kum home?

She had been promised to him. But she'd since fallen in love with Sammy. At least, she thought she had.

Abby,

I don't know what to say. I don't even know how to tell you this, but Daed says you're really my sister. He told me this horrible story about your daed and my mamm...the stuff nightmares are made of, for sure. Your mamm verified it, though, and said I look exactly like Obadiah as a young man. She had other proof, too, such as letters your daed wrote to my parents, demanding the right to know his sohn. Me.

I don't know why my daed and your mamm didn't want to tell you, but I thought you should know. I'm sorry I didn't tell you as soon as they told me. I truly did plan to marry you...though, since we're really siblings, that isn't possible.

Kissing you the way I did, after I knew the truth…I guess it was my way of saying gut-bye, or maybe venting my frustration. I shouldn't have done it, though. It was wrong.

I've started taking Elizabeth King home from singings. Twice now.

I hope you'll find someone in Jamesport. Be careful, though—from what I'm told, you have lots of relatives there. Maybe you'll get to know them.

I'm praying for you.

> Best wishes,
> Mark

Abigail wasn't surprised to hear Mark was courting Elizabeth King. Elizabeth had always liked Mark. She had probably stepped in as soon as Abigail was out of the picture.

Abigail handed the letter to Sam to read. He scanned it quickly, then shook his head. "Too bad it took him this long to drum up the courage to tell you the truth."

"Mark isn't an impulsive person. He always has to weigh his options before acting."

Sammy's hand closed around hers. "A man knows when the woman he wants to marry appears. It makes him sit up and take notice."

Abigail felt a surge of…something. Hope? "What's all this talk about marriage?"

"I just want you to know that I…I notice you."

Not exactly a proposal. But then….

Sammy folded Mark's letter and stuck the sticky note on top of it. "Why don't you open the note from your mamm?"

Abigail pried open the other envelope and unfolded the letter.

Dear Abigail,

Mark showed me his letter before he sealed it. And he's right—you needed to know the truth. I just didn't want you to

think less of your daed. I know you loved him...and he loved
you. I know you think I married Leo quickly, since your daed has
been gone only six months, but there is nein love involved in this
match. Leo needs a frau and a mamm for his kinner. I need an
ehemann. I will always love your daed. Always.

Abigail wiped a tear away. Daed's death did leave a hole, even
though it was expected, since he had cancer. They'd had months to
say gut-bye and to grieve.

She swiped at another tear and glanced back at the letter.

I love you, too, and I'm sorry for the state of things right now.
Leo didn't tell me of his plans to send you away until we were
married. Mark was needed to do the farm work. And admit-
tedly, Leo wants to protect his reputation, as well as mine, in
this community. Nobody here but Leo, Mark, and myself knows
what your daed did. And if word were to get out that you and
Mark are brother and sister.... This seemed to be the best solu-
tion, though Leo was adamant you never find out. He trusted
Mark not to tell anyone.

I can't imagine the rejection you must feel, being sent,
unwarned and unprepared, to live with an onkel you didn't even
know existed. I don't blame you for being angry at me. I'm angry,
too, at how Leo is treating you. How he's forcing me to treat you.
You may be Obadiah's dochter, but you are my dochter, too. I
had a talk with Leo about it, and I think things will change. But
he still doesn't want you to kum home. Yet. Maybe after Mark
has married and moved on with his life. Or after you marry....

I hope that in time, you'll forgive me. Forgive us.

I allowed you to believe you had nein family other than us.
This isn't true. You've met my brother Darius already. There
are relatives on your daed's side. And your grossmammi—my
mamm—lives in Jamesport. Her name is Orpah Zook. I never
believed her stories about our family genealogy until years later,

when I did some investigating at the local public library. But by then, it seemed too late to apologize to her. I want you to get to know her. Listen to her. And don't make the same mistakes I did.

Someday, I hope all my wounded relationships will be made whole.

I'm starting with you.

Love,
Mamm

An apology. And an explanation.

Gott had heard Abigail's prayer.

Ineffable joy filled her. And a long-familiar verse Preacher David had read aloud on Sunday flashed through her mind with brand-new significance. *"For God so loved the world, that he gave his only begotten Son, that whosoever believeth in him should not perish, but have everlasting life."*

Whosoever believeth.

Whosoever....

And as Sammy took the letter from her hands, she bowed her head.

Chapter 31

Sam refolded the letter from Abigail's mamm and slid it back inside the big envelope, along with the note from Mark. It disgusted him that Mark had kissed Abigail passionately after discovering how they were related, but at least Mark realized he'd been wrong.

A tear dropped onto the back of Sam's hand—the one resting on Abigail's. He glanced at her bowed head. Her closed eyes. Her damp cheeks. Was she crying because of her mamm's letter? Or Mark's? Hopefully, she wasn't crying over PJ. He hadn't even told her the whole story yet. His stomach churned.

He put the envelope on the floor, scooted closer, and wiped the moisture from her face. "Was ist letz? If it's PJ, I'm sorry. I never should've...."

Her green eyes, made brighter by unshed tears, met his. "'*Whosoever*' means me."

Sam blinked. His brain scrambled to make the connection between PJ and "whosoever." Then he shook his head. "I don't understand."

"Preacher David's sermon on Sunday. Gott loves me. '*Whosoever believeth*,' he said. I believe." Her voice cracked, even as a broad grin broke through her tears.

"Ach." Sam smiled. He'd been there recently. A passage flashed through his mind. "*That if thou shalt confess with thy mouth the Lord Jesus, and shalt believe in thine heart that God hath raised him from the dead, thou shalt be saved. For with the heart man believeth unto righteousness; and with the mouth confession is made unto salvation.*" David had shared that passage with him in the loft of the cabin the day

Sam had been saved. That, and a lot of other verses from Romans. The Romans Road, he'd called the collection. Unfortunately, Sam couldn't remember all of them right now, but they were marked in his Bible.

Abigail gave him a wavering smile. "Coming to Jamesport was a gut thing, ain't so?"

"The best ever." He pulled in a breath. "Abby, there are some other things you need to know. Things I need to confess." He tightened his fingers around hers.

Her gaze searched his. Her lips parted.

Despite his best efforts to resist, he glanced at them. She leaned toward him.

His heart rate increased.

"Abigail? Sammy?" Zelda's voice broke into the ultra-charged silence. "I brought you some tea. I didn't know you were back here, until Yenneke mentioned you probably needed some refreshment. I offered to get you something and found a pitcher of sweet tea just sitting on the counter." She appeared in the doorway, holding two clear glasses of cloudy liquid.

Sam pulled back from Abigail, whose face flamed red as she looked away.

"Danki, Zelda." Sam accepted one of the glasses and took a huge gulp, just to give his mouth something to do. Then he spit the liquid back into the tumbler as he shot to his feet. "Ugh. That's bacon grease, not tea!"

Abigail grimaced.

Zelda frowned at the mug she still held, then gave it a sniff. "Really? It looked like tea."

Sam took the mug from Zelda and headed out the door to the kitchen. He needed something—anything—to wash the nasty taste from his mouth. He hesitated in the hall and glanced over his shoulder. "Please, kum on out to the kitchen, Abby. I have some things to say to you and to the ladies."

Might as well tell them all at the same time. Even though Daed had said the ladies already knew about the theft he'd committed, he still had to apologize to them, and let Abigail know he wasn't the amazing man she thought he was.

Though maybe she already knew. There was still the unspoken "but" he'd imagined that lingered in the air.

"I think we have lemonade." Zelda started after him. "It's on the counter, too."

Sam gave her a pointed look. "Let's be sure before we pour, jah?" He hated to think what else it might be.

~

Abigail picked up the envelope of letters off the floor and put it in the top drawer of the dresser, then dumped her unmentionables out of the plastic grocery bag and piled them on top. Getting the letters and her personal items out of view.

Sammy might not have realized what was in the bag, but she knew.

She pulled in a breath and hobbled out of the room.

Yenneke stood in the kitchen with Orpah, whose shaking hand clutched the manila folder. "I never gave you permission...." Her voice quavered. "It's water under the bridge."

"It's time." Yenneke's jaw firmed. "And Preacher Samuel agrees." She turned to Sammy with a smile that looked fake to Abigail. "Your daed took Reuben home, Sammy. He'll return shortly."

Sammy nodded. "I need to talk to everyone." Yenneke and Orpah stared at him as he set the two glasses of bacon grease beside the sink.

Zelda picked up the pitcher of yellow liquid. "Is this lemonade?"

"Pineapple juice," Yenneke said.

Zelda got out a clean glass. "Want some?"

Sammy nodded. "Please."

Zelda filled the glass with juice. "Abigail?"

"Uh, danki, but nein." She pulled out a chair and sat.

"What was it you needed to say, Sammy?" Orpah sat next to Abigail and reached for her hand.

Abigail grasped it, appreciating the warmth and protection it offered. Later, she would show her the letters from Mamm and Mark.

Sammy downed his juice in a single swig, then sat across from them. "First of all, I think Zelda's medication is off." He cringed as he looked at her. "Sorry, but you need to see a doctor. Mistaking bacon grease for tea…." He motioned toward the sink.

"What's wrong with me? I need some medicine, you say?" Zelda frowned. "I had a dose an hour ago. But I'll go take some more."

"Nein." Sammy held up his hand. "I mean—"

"I think you're right." Yenneke nodded. "We've been wondering. I'll call for an appointment."

"Second of all…." Sammy's gaze shot to Abigail. Then he looked at his feet. "Over a year ago, I stole medication from you ladies. Several times. It wasn't for me. I didn't take drugs. Never have. I lost my best friend because of them, when he was driving his car under the influence. But I wanted to chase someone out of town because I blamed him for my best friend's death."

"We know all that, Sammy." Yenneke frowned at him.

But Abigail sucked in a breath. The Sammy she knew and loved—the one she'd heard pray—would never do such a thing.

Sammy nodded, then lifted his eyes to Abigail's. "But Abby doesn't." He glanced back at Yenneke. Then at Orpah. And finally at Zelda. "And you don't know that I'm sorry. I am. I never should've done it."

"Ach, you should've asked." Zelda shook her head. "I would've given you whatever you needed."

"Nein, Zelda. I didn't need any of it. It was wrong, for many reasons." Sammy's voice shook. "I've since repented before Gott and made peace with the man I tried to run off with the drugs."

Abigail dipped her head. Her shock faded somewhat, diminished by her admiration of him for admitting what he'd done.

"We forgive you," Orpah said. "We forgave you a long time ago. None of us is perfect. We've all done things we shouldn't have."

Case in point, the story Orpah had shared earlier that evening. Abigail's mamm and daed…Mark…herself.…

"You're forgiven," Yenneke affirmed.

"Danki." Sammy knelt in front of Abigail. He grasped her left hand in both of his. "Can you forgive me for judging you when I had plenty of my own sins? Forgive me for not being the hero I wished I was."

She nodded, not trusting herself to speak. Instead, she reached out her right hand. With her thumb and forefinger, she lightly traced his cheeks, then moved down, on either side of his mouth.

Trembling, he grabbed her hand, pulling it to his lips. He lightly kissed each finger and then her palm. Her breath caught in her throat, and she heard the three maidals sigh.

"May I take you on a buggy ride to-nacht?" His gaze held hers. "I still have something I need to tell you."

"I…I guess. If I can leave the haus." She glanced at the three ladies.

Orpah nodded. "With Sammy, you can. Regardless of whatever he might've done in the past, we trust him completely."

As Sammy stood, the door opened.

Preacher Samuel came in. "Just passed by Luke Stutzman's haus."

Orpah and Yenneke exchanged glances.

"The fire chief's there. And some deputies from the sheriff's station."

Sammy jumped to his feet. "I need to go, then."

"We both do." Preacher Samuel held the door for him.

Abigail grabbed her crutches and stood. "I'm coming, too."

Chapter 32

Sam lifted Abigail into the farm wagon. She scooted to the middle of the seat as he climbed in beside her. His heart ached with regret over being interrupted yet again. At this rate, she'd never learn that she was going to inherit a boppli when and if she married him. Not that he was eager to tell her. He would rather forget the whole thing. Forget PJ.

He would rather have his innocence back.

He blew out a sigh of frustration as Daed drove the wagon down the road half a mile and pulled into the Stutzmans' driveway. Two county squad cars with flashing lights were parked in front of the haus. So was the fire chief's red Jeep.

Sam's rage boiled. He wanted to confront the arsonist for all the damage he'd done. For endangering Abigail. For destroying Sam's small-engine repair business and all the how-to books he'd saved from the haus fire over a year ago. But he didn't anticipate being allowed inside while the deputies and the fire chief were questioning someone.

He glanced over at Abigail. She had wadded up the fabric of her apron and now kneaded it with both hands.

If only he could tell her that everything would be okay. That it would all work out. He pulled in a breath. "Maybe the real arsonists will get caught, and you'll be officially cleared."

As Daed maneuvered the wagon alongside one of the squad cars, the front door of the haus opened. A loud wail came from inside. The sheriff and the fire chief emerged. Followed by a deputy leading Hen outside in handcuffs.

Sam's pulse pounded. Hopefully, Hen hadn't pointed a finger at Sam for the crimes he had yet to confess to the sheriff.

Crimes he planned on confessing, anyway, but in his own time.

"Whoa." Daed handed the reins to Abigail. "Hold these for me, please."

Sam vaulted out of the wagon as a deputy opened the back passenger door of the squad car. He wanted to position himself between Abigail and Hen—and near Hen, just in case the opportunity arose for him to confront Hen and demand answers.

Hen's glare ricocheted from Sam to Abigail and back again.

"What's going on?" Daed circled around the front of the wagon and approached the sheriff. "What'd he do?"

The fire chief nodded toward Sam, then glanced at Daed. "Arson. He admitted to starting all the fires. Claims he was just doing what he was told."

What he was told? Sam's heart lodged in his throat. The threat wasn't over, then.

Daed's attention shifted to Hen. "Who's had you burning barns, Hen?"

Hen bowed his head. "I had to obey. I had nein choice." His tone was resigned.

"Nein choice?"

Sam leaned forward, straining to hear. He needed answers, too, so he could understand how to help protect Abigail. Prevent other barns from getting burned.

Hen's shoulders slumped. "I don't want to say. His family is going through enough."

The sheriff grunted. "That's as far as we got. He refuses to say who, even though things might go a lot easier on him if he did."

Daed approached the squad car. "Hen…was it an Englisch person who told you to burn barns?"

"Nein—no." The answer was whispered. Regret filled Hen's face.

"Amish, then." Daed nodded. "And did this person say why?"

"He said Gott told him the barns needed to be burned because they had familiar spirits dwelling in them. And…and he quoted a Bible verse. Something about not allowing a witch to live." He looked up, his gaze almost apologetic as it rested on Abigail again. "Her."

Sam glanced at Abigail. She looked ready to cry or to throttle someone. Sam was ready to do the latter, to Hen. But not before he got the truth.

"Familiar spirits?" The sheriff spun around and whipped out his notebook and pen.

"Black cats. He said they are…evil." Hen frowned. "I mean, I thought they were just cats, but what do I know?"

The sheriff paused in scribbling on his pad. "God tells a guy to burn barns because of black cats? That's a first."

Sam never had paid much attention to the cats his family kept for catching mice. But now that he thought about it, they did have a black cat that had lived in the barn. Under the front porch now.

"He said she was a witch." Hen lifted his chin toward Abigail. "Told me she had to die."

Sam balled his fists and took a step nearer to Hen. "Who—"

"So, he contracted you for murder?" The sheriff jotted something else.

Hen shook his head. "I didn't sign any contract. I *have* to obey him. What he says, goes. He said to burn her in a barn, too."

Abigail made a tiny growling sound. "You intended to kill me."

"Were you blackmailed?" The sheriff ignored Abigail, his attention focused on Hen.

Hen shook his head again.

The sheriff put his pen back into his pocket. Sighed.

"But you *had* to obey him." It wasn't a question.

Daed crossed his arms across his chest.

Hen nodded.

Daed stepped nearer to the car. "Abigail is not a witch, Hen. She's your cousin."

Sam jerked his head up. "What? Nein way."

Daed ignored him. "Your onkel Obadiah's dochter. Her name is Abigail Stutzman. The letter from her mamm said she 'bewitched' someone. Not that she was a witch."

"My...*cousin?*" Hen's attention shot back to Abigail. Horror filled his gaze. He got into the squad car.

"Take him to the station." The sheriff closed the door on Hen and stepped back.

"I think I know who's behind all this." Daed spoke quietly. He unfolded his arms and tugged on his beard. "Hen's right—he has been taught, from the very beginning, to obey this man without question. He's also right about the family having been through enough. The man has a brain tumor. Inoperable at this point. They are giving him many different types of drugs to try to shrink the tumor enough to be able to operate. It's been causing a lot of problems. He sees things that aren't there. Hears things that weren't spoken. He's...." Daed looked away and sighed.

"Nein." Sam's stomach churned. "Bishop Joe? Seriously?"

Lines of sorrow etched Daed's face. "He could almost be classified as insane."

The sheriff raised his eyebrows. "We'll still need to take him in." He pulled out his pen again and frantically wrote something. "Amish bishop behind barn fires to eliminate black cats. Suspected of attempted murder. No one will believe this."

Daed's mouth thinned, then he nodded toward the squad car. "Is it okay if I pray with Hen before you go?"

The sheriff shrugged. "Go ahead, Preacher. Then we'll need to have a talk with the bishop."

Sam stepped forward. "I'll pray with him, Daed."

"Nein, Sohn. I'll do it. You take Abigail home. You two have things to talk about."

Jah. There was that.

Daed climbed into the backseat of the squad car next to Hen and shut the door.

Sam swallowed his fear and started toward the wagon, praying silently for strength.

Praying that Abigail would understand his need to offer to raise PJ's child. And that she would be willing to take the step with him.

Praying that they had a future together.

But what if Hen had told on Sam?

"Wait." Sam turned back around.

The fire chief raised his head. "What is it, Sam?"

"I have...things...I need to confess." Now probably wasn't a gut time, but it would save them from having to arrest him later. Save him from having to find someone to take the wagon back home. Save him from having a certain conversation involving a certain boppli....

The fire chief frowned. "Were you involved in the arsons?"

"Nein—no. But...a couple of years ago, I stole drugs from some Amish ladies and passed them on to someone else."

The fire chief glanced at the sheriff.

The sheriff studied Sam for what seemed an endless stretch of time. "A couple of years ago? Amish ladies. Anyone else? Anything recent?"

"No one else. Nothing recent." Sam didn't dare look at Abigail.

The sheriff frowned at him another long minute, then turned and walked to his Jeep. Opened the front passenger door. Reached inside the glove compartment and retrieved a black book. He thumbed through the pages as he sauntered back toward Sam.

"I knew you a couple of years ago, Sam, and I know you now. Last year, I witnessed you undergoing a major life change." With both hands, he extended the open book to Sam. "Read Romans nine, verse fifteen. Out loud, please."

Sam found the verse and marked it with his fingertip. "*I will have mercy on whom I will have mercy, and I will have compassion on whom I will have compassion.*"

Looking on, the fire chief worked his mouth but said nothing as the sheriff gripped Sam's shoulder. "In and of myself, I don't have the authority to say this. But I speak using the words of the One who does—the One who saved you and changed your life. *'Neither do I condemn thee: Go, and sin no more.'"*

Chapter 33

Abigail scooted over as Sammy climbed up beside her in the farm wagon, tears streaming down his cheeks. She wanted to open her arms to him and let him cry on her shoulder.

Her throat hurt from the effort required to keep her emotions under control the entire time she'd huddled in the wagon, a silent witness to the events unfolding before her: Hen's arrest. The undeserved mercy the sheriff and the fire chief had showed Sammy. And knowing the community would soon be knocked to its knees with the arrest of its bishop.

The bishop's family—including his dochter, Bethany—would be hurt. Confused.

Bethany had reached out to Abigail upon her arrival in town. Abigail needed to do the same for her.

"Abby." Sammy's voice cracked. "I still need to talk to you." He swiped his hands across his eyes. Cleared his throat as he reached for the reins. "I'm taking you to the cabin."

Abigail didn't know anything about a cabin. But Sammy had told her multiple times that he needed to talk to her. They kept getting interrupted. Maybe the cabin would provide some privacy. Prevent further intrusions.

Sammy clicked his tongue and flicked his wrists enough to shake the reins. The horse started pulling the wagon around the circular drive. At the end of the drive, Sammy stopped the wagon, then looked both ways before turning left onto the road.

"Can't you talk to me now?"

"I can, but...well, I'd like to look at you when I tell you what I have to say. Instead of being focused on the road."

A motorcycle roared past them.

He glanced at her and flashed a slight grin. "We'll be there in a few minutes."

Abigail nodded. "Whatever it is, it must be serious."

Sammy sighed. "It is."

Even more serious than learning Hen was her cousin and seeing him arrested for starting the fires? More serious than learning that Sammy had stolen drugs? Than knowing he'd been intimate with PJ in the past?

Sammy maneuvered the wagon down a two-lane dirt road. A few minutes later, they stopped in front of a small log cabin. "I'll lift you out. Just a second." He hopped down, took a key from his pocket, and jogged over to the porch. A second later, the door swung open, and he disappeared inside. Then a light flickered to life.

He came back outside and returned to the wagon. "This was a hunting cabin Daed got permission to use for the prayer meetings and Bible studies he organized. When the owner died, he willed the cabin to Daed." He helped her out, then reached for her crutches. "There are a couple of wood chairs in there, and a futon. It might be hard for you to sit on that, though, since it's low to the ground. But if you want to, I can help you."

Abigail made her way up the steps and into the cabin. She eyed the mismatched wood chairs.

"Those aren't very sturdy. Daed plans to replace them. As soon as our barn gets rebuilt, he wants me to help him make new furnishings for this place."

She nodded. "The futon looks comfortable." Her cheeks heated at the thought of snuggling with Sammy on the cushioned seat. Hopefully, in the dim light, he wouldn't notice her blushing.

He chuckled. "It's very comfortable, jah."

A shiver raced up her spine. She shuffled over to the low seat, trying to ignore the sense of longing that flooded her. She really needed to focus. Prepare herself to hear whatever it was Sammy needed to discuss with her.

She glanced back at the wobbly-looking chairs around the small square table. They really didn't seem safe. Though, if they could support the likes of Sammy and Preacher Samuel, they probably were stronger than they appeared.

"I'm going to help you sit. Trust me, okay?" Sammy's hands closed around her waist. She twisted in his arms and wrapped her arms around his neck.

He chuckled as he pulled her close against him and lifted her. The next thing she knew, he was on the futon. She was, too. Well, technically, she was on his lap.

She wanted to stay there, but she scooted off to sit beside him. He wanted to talk. She needed to let him.

Sammy's hand closed around one of hers, and he bowed his head. "Lord Gott, I'm trying to put You first in my life from here on out. I'm asking You to please go ahead of me. Clear my thoughts, and make my words plain. Above all, Your will be done. Amen."

Then he fell silent. His thumb slid over the back of her hand, leaving tingles where it touched. But he stared in the direction of his feet. If he were Mark, Abigail would assume he was thinking, planning out what he wanted to say. But this was Sammy. Speak-first-and-think-things-through-later Sammy.

Then again, he had prayed. Maybe he was waiting on Gott's direction.

She didn't want to rush der Herr. She bowed her head. *Give him the right words, Gott.*

What seemed an eternity later, Sammy cleared his throat. "I told you earlier that PJ is pregnant. I went to talk to her this evening. That's where I went after dinner at The Hen Haus. Took a few friends with me, so I wouldn't be alone with her. She wanted me to pay for an abortion, because the real father dumped her and told her it wasn't his. I told her nein."

Abigail's eyes widened. An abortion?

"I suggested she put the boppli up for adoption, instead. Then…." Sammy pulled in a deep breath. "Then I offered to adopt the baby myself. Because, the thing is, that boppli could've been mine. With the way I acted last summer, I could've fathered a child with her." He exhaled. Stared at his feet again. "But by the grace of Gott."

Abigail's breath lodged in her throat at the painful realization of how his past actions might have produced life-altering consequences. For both of them.

"Abby, she says she'll name me as father. Not exactly honest. But I am still committed to adopting…to raising the boppli." The words tumbled over each other in an apparent rush to be said.

Abigail's jaw dropped, her oxygen intake having been suspended. She forced herself to snap her mouth shut. It meant PJ would always be a part of Sammy's life, popping in and out to check on her child… maybe even coming on to Sammy. *It'll be all right. Breathe. Breathe. Breathe.*

"I'm…I'm…." A heavy sigh. His hand tightened around hers. "We are not alone in this," he whispered intensely. "Gott has a plan, and He is in control." Then he fell silent. Stilled. And shut his eyes.

Praying.

Abigail loved him for that. A man who prayed was beyond wunderbaar. She wanted him by her side for the rest of her life, praying for her. With her. Over her.

His eyes opened again. "Thing is, feuerzeug, I want to marry you." He raised his free hand and pressed a fingertip to her lips. "Shh. I think I know what you're going to say." A grin flickered on his mouth, then faded. "We hardly know each other. That's it, ain't so?" He pulled away before she could work up the nerve to kiss his fingers, the way he had hers.

She moistened her tingling lips with her tongue and nodded. "Sort of, jah." But what she did know about him, she loved.

His gaze flickered to her lips.

"The answer is jah." The words jumped out.

He chuckled. "Wait before you answer. Would you be willing to let me court you, with plans of eventual marriage, keeping in mind that if PJ decides to keep the boppli, we'll be raising a child that isn't ours?"

"It would be ours." Abigail pulled in a breath. "And jah, Sammy. It's still jah. Court me. Marry me. Love me. Forever."

"I know I don't deserve you—" His words died with a gasp. "Really?" He released her hand and turned to face her more fully her.

"I like—love—what I know of you, Sammy. You're a gut man, a praying man, and someone I want beside me, forever and ever."

Another smile flickered to life as he searched her eyes. His hands cradled her face and his lips brushed hers. "Abigail Stutzman, Gott willing, I'm going to marry you."

She leaned into him and breathed, "Ich liebe dich, Sammy Miller."

His hands slid from her face to her shoulders and down her back, and he tugged her nearer. Nearer. Nearer. "Soon, feuerzeug. But we have to go. I don't want to anticipate our wedding vows. But first...." His mouth lowered to hers again. "Ich." Kiss. "Liebe." Longer, deeper kiss. "Dich."

Epilogue

A wedding!" Aenti Ruth folded Abigail into a hug. "I knew Sammy was perfect for you. I knew it the moment I saw the two of you together. We'll have the wedding here, of course."

Abigail returned Aenti Ruth's embrace. "Danki. I really appreciate everything you've done for me."

"You're like a dochter to us, now that...." Aenti Ruth swallowed. "You never knew your cousins, of course, but your coming here has helped us heal. Giving us someone to love and care for...."

Onkel Darius patted Abigail's shoulder. "It's helped heal the whole family."

"The wedding won't be until November," Sammy stepped near to Abigail as she pulled away. "I need to go through the classes and join the church. And Abigail needs to transfer her membership. So we'll have some time."

"Plenty of time to prepare." Aenti Ruth stepped back. "We'll need blue fabric to make a dress. Plan where you're going to live...."

"Daed's gifting the cabin he inherited to us." Sammy reached for Abigail's hand. "As a wedding present."

"Really?" Abigail turned to him. "I love that place. It's so cute." And kind of special to her, since it was where Sammy had proposed.

"It'll be a gut starter home." Onkel Darius nodded. "But once the kinner start coming, it'll be time for Ruthie and me to move into a dawdi-haus. And then you can have this one, this farm."

"Right next door to me." Grossmammi wrapped an arm around Abigail's shoulder.

Aenti Ruth beamed. "Gott has given me another dochter to love, and now He's adding a sohn."

And He'd given Abigail a family. Unconditional love. Acceptance.

He'd answered her prayers before she even uttered them.

Danki, Lord Gott, for loving me so much.

About the Author

A member of the American Christian Fiction Writers, Laura V. Hilton is a professional book reviewer for the Christian market, with more than a thousand reviews published on the Web.

Laura's first series with Whitaker House, The Amish of Seymour, comprises *Patchwork Dreams, A Harvest of Hearts,* and *Promised to Another.* In 2012, *A Harvest of Hearts* received a Laurel Award, placing first in the Amish Genre Clash. Her second series, The Amish of Webster County, comprises *Healing Love, Surrendered Love,* and *Awakened Love.* A stand-alone title, *A White Christmas in Webster County,* was released in September 2014. Laura's latest series, The Amish of Jamesport, included *The Snow Globe, The Postcard,* and *The Birdhouse.*

Previously, Laura published two novels with Treble Heart Books, *Hot Chocolate* and *Shadows of the Past,* as well as several devotionals and a novella, *Christmas Mittens.* Laura and her husband, Steve, have five children, whom Laura homeschools. The family makes their home in Arkansas. To learn more about Laura, read her reviews, and find out about her upcoming releases, readers may visit her blog at http://lighthouse-academy.blogspot.com/.